A Fond Hope

VANESSA LIND

VANESSA LIND BOOKS

Follow the thrilling journey of Hattie Logan, a smart and resourceful spy for the Union during the American Civil War.

October 1864. As the conflict between the North and South escalates, Hattie is drawn into a dangerous web of intrigue when she learns of a plot to destroy US cities and kidnap President Abraham Lincoln. Embroiled in a tangled web of some of the South's most powerful figures, she sets out on a perilous mission to stop the enemy's plan at all costs.

As she races against time to stop the enemy's plans, Hattie must use all of her wits and bravery to navigate the treacherous world of desperate Confederates. Along the way, she encounters a cast of complex and intriguing characters, including a handsome Union officer with a troubled past, a cunning Confederate agent, and a group of powerful men who'll stop at nothing to achieve their goals.

Written in page-turning style, *A Fond Hope* is a thrilling tale of one woman's bravery and determination during the turbulent final months of America's Civil War. A fascinating historical novel of grit, valor, and resilience, this book is sure to be a hit with fans of historical fiction and spy stories alike.

*"Fondly do we hope—fervently do we pray—
that this mighty scourge of war may speedily pass away."*

President Abraham Lincoln
2nd Inaugural Address
March 4, 1865

Chapter One

OCTOBER 2, 1864

S trolling under a starry sky with Lieutenant John Elliott at her side, Union spy Hattie Logan could almost forget the country was at war. For October, the air felt close to balmy, and the easy rhythm of their steps on the boardwalk added to the comfort of having enjoyed a fine meal—fine for wartime, at least—with the man Hattie was coming to love.

"When do you think you'll recover your taste for port?" John asked. Illuminated by the gaslights along the street, his gentle smile added to her contentment.

"When the war ends," Hattie said. After a harrowing escape from a Rebel who'd tried to take over a Union gunship by serving the crew drugged alcohol, she'd lost her taste for wine.

John pressed his hand over hers. "So much will be different then," he said.

"So much will be better."

"Provided the outcome is as we hope."

"But General Sherman has taken Atlanta, and we've got control of the Shenandoah."

"For the moment."

She smiled up at him. "You do know how to ruin a lady's good mood, Lieutenant Elliott."

"Sorry. It's just that when everything seems to be going well, there's always a chance that disaster lies right around the corner."

"That's quite enough talk of disaster," she said. "I for one am putting my hopes in the future."

"And what, pray tell, will that entail?"

You, she almost said, but she checked the impulse. She'd known John Elliott for nearly two years. He'd supervised her work as a spy in Nashville, and together they'd survived an attack by the Rebel guerilla who'd killed John's wife. But until recently, she'd kept him at arm's length as she struggled with her feelings for her first love, a fellow spy who'd been captured and executed.

Now she felt as close as she might ever come to making peace with her memories, and she was glad to be here in Nashville, strolling beside the handsome and kind lieutenant. But John Elliott was a prudent man, steady in ways she was not, and he had his own memories to contend with. They would take things one step at a time.

"My future?" she said. "I suppose what I want most is a fresh start. A new beginning."

"No more spying? Somehow I can't imagine you not snooping around in things."

She swatted his arm. "You of all people should know it's not snooping. And I like to think my work will hasten our victory, even if only in some small way."

"I wouldn't call thwarting a Rebel plot to take over Lake Erie a small accomplishment."

"I had help, you know." But even as she said this, Hattie couldn't suppress the swell of pride she felt at having achieved something meaningful for the Union cause. Not that she intended to crow about it as some did. That would mean giving up spying, and she intended to do her part to make sure the war came to an end sooner rather than later.

"Having help diminishes nothing of what you did. Working with others is the nature of our enterprise. Which is why I'm glad you're staying on in Nashville to help with our Army Police work."

"Staying on for a while," she said. "If I'm needed elsewhere—"

"You are a restless one," he interjected.

"Not always. At the moment, I'm feeling quite content. Only..." Her voice trailed off.

"Only passing along rumors gleaned from Nashville's Rebel sympathizers isn't the sort of spying you signed up for," he said.

"I know it's important," she said. "Or at least it can be, every now and then, when something a woman whispers about at the market or in a shop or a hotel lobby turns out to have merit. It's just that I'm...impatient."

"You want more."

She squeezed his arm. "No more than what I've got right now."

Rounding the corner, they fell silent. Ahead, the street was ablaze with light. Hundreds of men—and some women and children too—came marching past them, a sea of black faces. Each marcher wore an oil-cloth cape, protection from the open flames of the torches they carried.

Hattie slowed her steps, taking in the spectacle. Beside her, John slowed, too. Side by side, they stood among a group of spectators, listening as a song erupted from the marchers.

We'll join in the struggle with hearts firm and true

We'll stand by our chief and the red, white, and blue

Hattie recognized the words to President Lincoln's campaign song. "It's a show of support for Mr. Lincoln in next month's election."

"Yes, and they're also petitioning Governor Johnson to proclaim their emancipation here in Tennessee just as President Lincoln did for Negroes in the Rebel states." John pointed into the night. "See how they're turning toward the Capitol?"

Indeed, the marchers at the front of the parade were veering off toward Capitol Hill, the highest point in Nashville. "I hope the governor grants their request," Hattie said. "Slavery is an abomination no matter where it's practiced. And we Northerners owe a debt to the Negro soldiers who've joined the Union cause."

A lump formed in her throat as she thought of Samuel, the Black soldier who'd given his life to save hers during the Rebel attack on Fort Pillow last spring. After all he'd done, she'd never even learned his last name. He'd had a wife and a baby girl, he'd told Hattie. She felt horrible knowing they'd never see him again.

The end of the parade neared, the marchers singing the final lines of the song:

We never will falter, our watchword will be

The Union, the hope of the brave and the free

As the last word reverberated, a dark object flew through the air in front of Hattie. One of the marchers ducked, narrowly missing being hit by the projectile, but his steps never faltered.

Another missile flew. Hattie whirled around to see one of the bystanders, a bearded man wearing dungarees and a straw hat, clutching a large rock in his raised hand.

She stepped toward him. "Drop that right now."

He leered at her, eyes narrowed. She smelled liquor on his breath. "You gonna make me, missy?"

"If I have to," she said.

John Elliott stepped between them. "Army Police," he said to the man. "You're under arrest."

The man looked him up and down. "You ain't no police," he said. "Got no uniform."

John gripped his arm. "You'll see my uniform in the morning. From your jail cell."

The man dropped the rock. It hit the ground with a thunk. "You can't throw me in jail. Just taking in the spectacle, same as you. Damned n—"

Hattie slapped his face. "You pelted rocks at those people. You could have killed someone."

"And what if I did?" The man spit on the ground, barely missing the hem of her skirt. "One less of 'em won't hurt nothing."

John tightened his grip on the man's arm. "We don't take kindly to murder in these parts. Or to assault. Come along now."

Hattie followed John as he dragged the man, cursing and stumbling, to Nashville's Army Police Headquarters two blocks away. The contentment she'd felt, her hopes for a bright future—these felt all but erased.

It was only one man, she reminded herself, and a drunken one at that. But her unease remained.

She waited outside John's office while he handcuffed the man and handed him off to the lieutenant working the evening shift. Only when she heard John returning, his footsteps firm and sure in the darkened corridor, did her spirits lift.

Reaching her, he touched her cheek. "You're all right?"

She nodded. "A bit shaken, that's all."

The corners of his lips turned in a smile. "Not too shaken to let that man know what you thought of him."

"I was thinking of Samuel," she said. "The Negro soldier who died while saving me during the Fort Pillow raid. He told me he was willing to do anything to elevate himself and his race. That's all those people are trying to do out there tonight. They shouldn't be attacked for it."

"They shouldn't." John took a set of keys from his pocket. "But I fear there are thousands more like that man I arrested, bent on punishing Negroes for pursuing the same liberties the rest of us enjoy."

"All the more reason for the Union to prevail in this war," she said.

"Victory is a good first step." He turned a key in the lock and swung open the door. "But even with the nation reunited, healing may be a long time coming."

She followed him into his office. He lit the gas sconce nearest the door, which spit and sputtered as he adjusted the wick.

"I've got to write up a report on that rascal," he said. "Don't want anyone turning him loose for lack of paperwork. It won't take long. Then I'll walk you back to your hotel."

"I can find my way, you know."

"And meet up with another like him? The next ruffian you slap might not back down."

"I suppose you're right." The streets of Nashville weren't as safe as they'd once been, and while she'd fended for herself in a good number of situations, she knew there were plenty of men about the city who'd prey on a woman if given the opportunity.

Smoothing her skirts, she sat in the chair beside John's desk. He settled into the larger chair behind it, then took up his pen. As he began to write, she looked about at office walls, which were nearly bare. Like most everything related to the war, Nashville's Army Police headquarters had been set up hastily, with everyone hoping for a swift end to the conflict. But the war had dragged on three and a half years now, and much as Hattie longed for it, the end was not yet in sight.

Her gaze returned to John. He sat square-shouldered, penning his words in careful, slanted script. She loved the way he looked when he was fully concentrating on a task, intent and engaged. It was the same concentration with which he listened when she had something to explain, as if she were the only person in the world that mattered.

He kept a tidy desk, its surface polished, the papers atop it stacked in neatly squared piles. She noticed an envelope at the far corner of his desktop. She couldn't read the address, but the stamp caught her eye.

"John, what's that letter?"

He looked up from his writing. "Sorry. Say again?"

"That letter at the corner of your desk. It has an odd postage stamp. Where's it from?"

"I have no idea. The clerk must have delivered it after I left for the day." He set down his pen and reached for the envelope. "No wonder it attracted your attention," he said, looking it over. "It's addressed to you. And the postmark is stamped Montreal."

"Canada!" Her heart leaped. She took the envelope from his outstretched hand.

"From your brother, you think?"

"I hope so. There's no return address."

He handed her a letter opener. "How would he know to write you here?"

"Murray Wilson." She slid the opener beneath the envelope's flap. "The gunner who helped ensure the Rebels didn't take over the *USS Michigan*. The captain sent him to Canada on the trail of the renegades. I gave him this address and asked him to give it to George if he happened upon him there."

John took up his pen again. "That seems unlikely," he said, ever logical. "Canada's a big country."

"But if I've been told correctly, George is a spy there."

"Ah, now I remember," John said. "With Lafayette Baker's National Detective Police, right?"

"That's what I was told." From the envelope, she pulled a sheet of paper folded in thirds. "If they're both hunting down rebels, Murray Wilson may well have crossed paths with him."

She unfolded the paper. Recognizing George's handwriting, rounder and looser than John's, she scanned the words:

My dearest sister,

You have no idea the joy I experienced when Mr. Murray Wilson stood before my desk and delivered news of you. After all these years apart, to think that you are engaged in an enterprise similar to mine!

We have much to catch up on, dear sister, far more than a letter can contain. I enclose here a ticket. Please come at your earliest convenience. Ask for me at the Bank of Ontario, Montreal.

Your loving brother,

George

She reached into the envelope and found the ticket. Printed in an arc near the top were the words *Grand Trunk Railroad*. At the bottom it said *Until October 31, 1864,* followed by an illegible signature and *Railroad President.* In the middle, next to the abbreviated *Pass.,* someone had penned her own name, *Hattie Logan.*

"Is it news from your brother?" John asked.

"Yes. It's been more than three years since I've heard from him." Scarcely able to believe her eyes, she scanned the page again. "He sent a ticket. He wants me to come to Montreal at my earliest convenience."

"Then you must go," John said.

She smiled. "You can't get rid of me so easily, you know."

"Nor would I want to." He reached for her hand, squeezing it. "Just promise to hurry back."

"I will," she said.

Close as they'd been during their difficult childhood, she could hardly wait to see George again. Images of a joyful reunion tumbled through her mind. However her future unfolded, she hoped he'd be a part of it too.

Chapter Two

OCTOBER 5, 1864

A nxious to see George, Hattie set out three days later, traveling from Nashville to Louisville and then on to Detroit and Montreal. All told, the trip took more than two days, and though she felt weary by the time her train approached Montreal, her excitement at seeing George buoyed her spirits. Growing up in a town where their family was shunned, he'd been her only companion, and she'd missed him deeply these past three years.

It wasn't only the war that had kept them apart. It was also their parents. Though they lived in Indiana, the older Logans supported the South, where Hattie's mother had grown up and where her father, Hattie discovered, was smuggling grain. They were unpleasant people, and George had been only too happy to enlist in the Union Army and leave home, causing his parents to disown him.

After George left, the Logans had shipped Hattie off to the Ladygrace School for Girls in Indianapolis, where they hoped she'd learn the refinements necessary to marry well. Instead, Hattie had run off with her friend Anne to Washington City to work for Allan Pinkerton's Detection Agency. She'd been spying for the Union ever since, and that was more than enough for the Logans to disown her too. The rejection stung, and without George, she'd felt untethered.

But that was all behind her now. Approaching Montreal, she imagined George as she'd last seen him, going off to join his regiment, tall and wiry, a sternness in his blue eyes until, spotting Hattie, he'd broken into a lop-sided grin and waved goodbye.

He'd have changed, she reminded herself. War did that to people. But he was alive, and she was eager to catch up on all that he'd been up to. *To think that you are engaged in an enterprise similar to mine,* he'd written. He sounded impressed. As the younger sister, she'd coveted George's esteem more than anyone else's, and it felt good to think she might have earned it.

Framed by the train's window, the Bonaventure Station loomed large, its stone walls, tall windows, ornate detailing, and steeply sloped slate roof giving it a distinctly European feel. The wheels screeched as the train slowed and then stopped. Hattie gathered her belongings and, filled with anticipation, joined the line to get off. A porter carried her satchel to the curb where an omnibus waited. She told the driver her destination, and he helped her inside, where she took a seat near a window. After other passengers filled the omnibus, the driver hoisted himself to his rooftop seat and set the horses in motion.

Like the train station, the city Hattie saw through the window made her think of pictures she'd seen of European cities. The homes and buildings she passed were mostly tall and narrow, casting long shadows in the late afternoon light. Most were made of stone, with steep roofs of slate or metal—for sloughing off snow, Hattie realized. The road they were traveling was paved with stones, too, as were many of the side streets. The boardwalks were bustling with people. Compared to American cities, where reminders of war were everywhere, the atmosphere seemed almost jovial.

As Hattie was taking it all in, the driver stopped in front of a three-story building with arched doorways and windows. Jumping down, he opened the omnibus door and called out, "Bank of Ontario."

The driver helped her down from the bus. At last, she would see George. Taking up her satchel, she had a moment's hesitation. What if he'd changed? What if something had transpired these past few days, and he wasn't here anymore?

Approaching the bank, she shook off her worries. She asked the doorman where she might find George Logan.

"You must be the sister he's said so much about," the man said. She'd expected a French accent, given Montreal's history, or perhaps British, since Canada was now a British colony. Instead, the doorman had the gentle, rolling speech of a Southerner. She'd been told the Confederates had a strong presence in this part of Canada, but she hadn't expected to encounter evidence of it so readily.

The doorman led her past the tellers' windows to a small office in the back of the bank. The man at the desk looked up as Hattie approached. A wide, familiar grin broke over his face. "Hattie! You came."

"Of course I came," she said, meeting his smile with her own. "When have I ever not done as my big brother asked?"

She let go of her satchel as he stood, crossed the office, and drew her into a hug. In his arms, she felt almost like a child again, safe and loved by the one person she'd always known she could count on.

He pulled back, hands on her shoulders, and looked her up and down. "This beautiful lady can't be my sister. What happened to the freckled, knock-kneed little tomboy I left behind in Indiana?"

"I never had knocked knees," she said. "It was only you who said so, to get my ire up."

"Well, you were a tomboy. You must admit that." Letting go of her shoulders, he leaned close. "And I believe I detect a few freckles beneath your face powder."

"A gentleman wouldn't look so closely," she teased. "But then you never passed for much of a gentleman."

"Ah, but that was years ago." He took up her bag. "Let's get you checked into a hotel." He waved a hand at his desk, which was cluttered with papers. "I've had enough of numbers for one day."

Following him into the bank's main lobby, she had a million questions, not the least of which was why her brother, like the doorman, spoke with a Southerner's drawl. She'd done the same, more than once, so she could mingle among Confederates and learn their secrets. So that must be what he was doing, too, here in Montreal.

The bank was hardly the place to speak openly of such things. She followed George across the lobby to a larger office. George's office door had been unmarked, but on this one, the words *Chief Teller* were written in gold letters across the glass. Inside, a balding man with a walrus mustache and long, curly muttonchops looked up from a stack of receipts.

"Mr. Campbell, my sister has arrived." George fairly beamed as he spoke. "With your permission, I'd like to clock out early and get her settled into her hotel."

The chief teller looked up from his work. "Arrived from where?"

A strange greeting, Hattie thought, but she answered, "From Tennessee, sir."

"And what news do you bring of the war?" Campbell asked.

The question took her aback. In Canada, she hadn't expected to be quizzed on the war, and with Campbell's accent distinctly British, she had no idea which side he favored.

"Only that people on both sides are eager for the war's end," she said.

"It won't do to hurry it along." Campbell made a shooing gesture with his hand. "Get going, Mr. Logan. I'm sure you and your sister have much to catch up on."

They left the teller's office. As they exited the bank, Hattie said to George, "Bit of an odd one, your boss."

"I suppose he is," George said. "But to his credit, he juggles quite a lot. You should see the money that comes through the bank."

"You were always good with numbers, even if you tried to pretend otherwise with Father. But I never thought you'd end up working in a bank, in Canada of all places. You must tell me how it is you came to be here."

"All in good time, Sis."

He started down the street, but Hattie stopped short, staring up at the most magnificent church she'd ever seen. Two massive towers stretched toward the sky, adorned all the way to the top with arched stained glass windows. Between them were three open archways that led to the cathedral's entrance.

Seeing she'd stopped, George circled back to her. "Notre Dame Basilica," he said. "Quite something, isn't it?"

"Spectacular."

"And wait till you see inside. But come along now. You stand there gaping, and everyone will know you're from out of town."

The hotel, St. Lawrence Hall, was only a stone's throw away. "Finest hotel in the city," George said as they entered the sumptuous lobby. "Only the best for my little sister."

He marched up to the registration desk She started to say she was perfectly capable of checking into a hotel on her own. But then she realized how long he'd been away. He wouldn't know how she'd grown up, wouldn't know to what extent the war was putting women in situations they'd not dreamed of before. Besides, this was his city. Why not let him exercise a little brotherly authority?

He requested a quiet room for her. "People come and go at all hours in this hotel," he said. She saw that this must be true as the lobby buzzed with the sounds of guests milling about. The Southern drawls she'd heard at the bank seemed even more prevalent here.

"I feel as if I'm back at Grandpa's plantation," she said as the clerk fetched her key.

"Grandpa would feel right at home," George said. "Southerners keep this place busy."

She was dying to ask what all the Southerners were doing here, but then the clerk returned with her key. She signed her name—her real name—in the guest registry. It was the first time in a long while that she hadn't signed as Hattie Thomas, the alias she'd used in much of her spy work. It felt good just to be herself, and even better to be here with George.

At George's suggestion, she left her satchel for the bellman to deliver to her room. "Let's get some dinner," George said. "There's a restaurant next door. Food's as good as any you'd get in Paris. Most folks staying at the Saint Lawrence dine there."

She'd skipped lunch on the train, and hunger now gnawed at her stomach. But if they dined among so many Confederates, she wouldn't be able to ask all the questions she had for George, nor could she speak frankly of her own activities these past few years.

"Before we eat, I'd love to see the inside of the basilica," she said.

George tipped his head, looking at her as if she represented a species of bird he hoped to identify. "As I recall, you hated going to mass with Mother."

"That's more about her than about her church. She found fault with everything I did."

"Understood." He pulled his watch from his pocket, checking the time. "We've got thirty minutes or so before the dining room fills up. Time for a quick look, anyhow."

~ ~ ~

Approaching the church, Hattie craned her neck to see the three large statues ensconced above the portico.

"Saint Joseph, the Virgin Mary, and Saint Jean-Baptiste," George said.

He pulled open a massive wooden door, and Hattie stepped inside. The pews were intricately carved, likely of mahogany. Massive paintings adorned the limestone walls. Overhead soared a ribbed vaulted ceiling, with three octagonal skylights illuminating a painted nave. But what took Hattie's breath away were the glowing blue hues that permeated the church. A gleaming blue floor led down the cathedral's center to a massive altar that was spired and carved in the gothic style. Light filtered through colorful stained glass windows, contributing to the overall blue effect.

"Stunning," she said in a hushed voice. "I've never seen anything like it."

"They say there's room for thousands to worship here," George said as they started up the center aisle. Nearing the front, they passed a handful of worshippers kneeling at their pews, eyes closed in prayer as they fingered the beads of their rosaries.

Here, Hattie saw more clearly the intricacies of the blue and gold artwork on the church's columns and arches. Towering over the altar was a painted statue of the Virgin Mary, serenely posed with a mass of roses clutched to her chest. Filled with reverence and awe, she could have gazed at the altar for hours. But not wanting to try George's patience, she circled around to the back with him.

"Let's sit a moment," she said as they neared the exit.

George nodded, and they slid into a pew. After a moment's silence, Hattie spoke, taking care to keep her voice quiet. "Tell me about your work."

He shrugged. "Not much to tell. I process checks, balance the books," he said, speaking as softly as she did.

"For Lafayette Baker?" she asked, naming the head of the Union's National Detective Police.

He straightened, his blue eyes taking on a new intensity. "Who told you about Baker?"

"A man from your regiment. Franklin Stone. He married my best friend."

"Stone. I remember him. Rather full of himself as I recall."

"That's Franklin." Hattie hesitated, wondering if she should try to explain her involvement in Franklin's having plunged into Lake Erie last month. But it was a long story, and for the moment, she wanted to keep the focus on George. "He told me Mr. Baker embedded himself with the troops and had you arrested as a traitor. I assured him that was impossible."

"I always could count on you to stick up for me."

"He also said there were rumors that some relative of Mr. Baker's—a cousin, as I recall—got you out of prison and set you up in Canada to spy on Mr. Baker's behalf."

"I don't know how that would've gotten spread around."

"Nor do I," she said. "But I'm glad it did, else I'd have remained sick with worry over you. I went straight away to see Mr. Baker in hopes of learning whether the rumor was true."

George frowned. "You shouldn't have done that, Hattie."

A familiar irritation rose in her. As much as she appreciated George looking out for her, he'd sometimes taken it too far, not trusting her as he should. But she curbed the impulse to point this out, not wanting to spoil their happy reunion.

"No harm came of it." Knowing it would only worry George more, she chose not to mention the advances Lafayette Baker had made when she was alone with him, grabbing at her breast under the pretense of showing her how he caught female spies. "But he refused to confirm that you were in his employ, much less tell me where I could find you."

"That was for the best, Hattie. Knowing too much could have put you in danger."

"I understand that," Hattie said. "As Murray Wilson told you, I've worked as a spy myself."

"As a courier, you mean, carrying messages in your skirts. That's what women do."

"I've carried a message or two, but what I've done mostly is spy. That's how I met Murray Wilson, intervening to stop the Rebels from taking over his gunship."

"To hear Wilson tell it, he rather singlehandedly saved the ship."

An old woman who'd been praying in a front pew shuffled by them. Hattie waited for her to pass before she replied. Murray

Wilson wasn't the first person to exaggerate his role in the work she'd done. Her friend and fellow spy Pauline Carlton was doing the same as she traveled the country giving lectures about her adventures.

"We can take that matter up with Murray Wilson another day, assuming he's still in Montreal. At present, I'm wondering what you're doing for Mr. Baker here. I assume your work at the bank involves gathering information. There certainly seem to be enough Confederates—"

He pressed his finger to his lips. "No explanations, Hattie. I mean it. The less you know about what I'm doing here, the better."

"But in your letter, you said we'd have much to discuss."

"Things have changed," he said. "No comparing notes. No discussions. A friendly visit. That's all you're here for. Nothing more"

The church bell began to clang, filling the sanctuary with sound. Hattie swallowed back her frustration. She should be happy just to be here with George. But she wished he would trust her, wished he'd realize she was more than just the little sister he needed to protect.

Abruptly, George stood. "Five o'clock. We'd best get to the restaurant, or we'll be waiting hours in line."

He turned to leave, and Hattie followed, a familiar pattern. George led, she followed. It would be hard to convince him it should be any other way.

Chapter Three

OCTOBER 6, 1864

With George's work at the bank, whatever it was, Hattie was on her own in Montreal until evening. He'd promised to give her a proper tour of the city on the weekend. In the meantime, she set out to explore.

The day was bright, the air cool, and she was glad for the light cape she wore. She started toward the river, a pleasant breeze tingling her skin. Reaching the harbor's edge, she stood on the walkway admiring the ships. Montreal's harbor seemed busier even than the harbor she'd seen in New York, tall masts crowding the sky. She wondered what sort of commerce was transacted here. She'd have to ask George. Maybe he'd at least be forthcoming about that.

She turned north, strolling along the harbor. Happy as she was to see George, she wished he'd take her more seriously. He seemed unable to imagine she'd done anything more than run letters for the Union. Murray Wilson hadn't helped, claiming he'd been the one to thwart the Rebels taking over the USS Michigan when in fact Hattie had been at the center of it.

No matter, she told herself. It was enough to be here with George in this beautiful city.

She came to a striking silver-domed building, its façade reminiscent of the United States Capitol in Washington. Proceeding inside, she discovered an indoor market space where vendors were selling meat, fish, and vegetables. Compared to markets in the war-torn US, this was a cornucopia of food. No wonder the meal she'd shared with George last night had been so delicious.

Leaving the market, she looped back in the direction she'd come. After passing through an expansive grassy park edged with cobblestones, she came to the Theatre Royal, another building in the classical style. Stepping up to the front portico, Hattie studied the playbills. From childhood, she'd loved the theatre. As she grew older, she'd even done some acting herself, reveling in the freedom she enjoyed onstage, becoming another person altogether.

Her acting skills had come in handy with her spy work too. Moving in Rebel circles, she'd played the role of a courier's wife, a Rebel sympathizer, and a seamstress. Most recently, she'd played the part of a sickly heiress, endearing herself to the Rebel captain who'd tried to take over the Lake Erie gunship.

Toward the top of the announcements was one for *The Hidden Hand*, billed as a drama of the Old South. Given how many Southerners there were in the city, an enactment featuring plantation life no doubt drew a crowd. But what got Hattie's attention was the mention of the show's stars, John McCullough and Alice Gray.

Alice. Hattie had met her years ago when she was performing at Grover's National Theatre in Washington City. Briefly in Mr. Grover's employ, Hattie had helped the actress through some temporary voice problems, and the two had become friends. Hattie had even toyed with the thought of trying to join her acting troupe.

What fun it would be to see Alice again! But across the announcement was a notice that tonight's show would be the final performance.

The box office was open. Hattie had barely enough cash in her purse—Canadian money George had insisted on giving her for any trifles she might wish to purchase—to buy two tickets for tonight's performance. She slipped the tickets into her purse, then hurried across the Place d'Armes to tell George.

Entering the bank, Hattie saw the doorman was absent, perhaps escorting someone to an office as he'd done with her yesterday. No matter. She knew where to find George.

But when she got to his office, she found his door closed. She knocked. Getting no answer, she tried the knob. Locked.

Turning to leave, she came face to face with Mr. Campbell, the chief teller George had introduced her to yesterday.

"Mr. Logan is indisposed." Campbell looked down at her over the top of his spectacles, his muttonchops waggling as he spoke,

"I see." She stepped aside, wondering whether his proximity was meant to intimidate her. "Where can I find him?"

"You may return in an hour. Perhaps he'll be back then."

"I suppose I could wait."

"You may return." Campbell gestured toward the exit.

Why did he insist on her leaving? It wasn't as if she intended to rob the place. But the chief teller's expression was stern, and rather than risk getting George in trouble with an impudent remark, she turned toward the exit. Still, sensing Campbell gazing at her as she retreated, she took her time crossing the lobby.

Nearing the door, she passed a veiled lady, dressed in black and standing at a teller's window. Beside her was a man Hattie instantly recognized. His physique was slender, and he dressed smartly in a dark coat and red ascot. His features were handsome, and atop his high forehead, his dark hair was thick and wavy. But what made her certain she knew him was the intensity of his eyes, which made him seem almost angry even as the teller counted out bills. It was a gaze she'd never forgotten. But clearly he'd forgotten her, for when he glanced in her direction, he showed no sign of recognition.

Just as well, she thought. Her last encounter with John Wilkes Booth, a fabled actor from a family of fabled actors, had been an unpleasant one. At the time, he'd been Alice Gray's sweetheart. Maybe he still was. That would explain his being in Montreal. But if he was with Alice, who was the veiled woman at his side?

Slowing her steps, Hattie fiddled with her purse as if looking for something she'd misplaced. Out of the corner of her eye, she saw the teller hand Booth what looked like a cheque, followed by a wad of bills. Booth folded the check and tucked it into the inner pocket of his coat. The cash he handed to the veiled lady, who slipped the bills discreetly into her purse.

Her curiosity roused, Hattie watched as the pair left the teller's window.

The doorman from yesterday came alongside her. "Help you, miss?"

"I came to speak with my brother," she said. "But I understand he's out."

The doorman glanced at the clock on the wall above the tellers. "Mr. Logan will be back soon, I expect. Any message you'd like me to convey?"

"Not at present," she said.

Reaching the exit, Booth held the door open as the veiled lady glided from the bank. Stepping out, he shut the door behind him.

The doorman shook his head as he and Hattie started for the door. "Folks start letting themselves in and out, I'll find myself without a post."

"Have you seen that man before?" Hattie said, keeping stride.

The doorman shrugged. "Once or twice."

"He's a well-known actor."

"Is he, now? Well, all sorts come and go from here." They reached the door, and he held it open for her. "Good day, miss."

She wished him a good day, then ventured out. Ahead on the boardwalk, Booth and the veiled lady approached a street corner.

Silly to go after them, she told herself. All she'd seen was an ordinary transaction with a bank teller. Still, she couldn't shake the feeling that something was amiss. If Booth was two-timing Alice in broad daylight, Alice had a right to know.

As Booth and the lady turned the corner, Hattie hurried toward them. Ahead was the basilica she'd marveled over yesterday. Maybe they were only sightseeing, she told herself. But then they turned into a squat stone building with signage that read *Martin & Carroll, Imports*.

Curious, Hattie thought. What business would a famous actor have with a Canadian import firm?

She turned back to the bank. After tonight's performance, she hoped to slip backstage and see Alice. When she did, she'd ask about Booth. Assuming he and Alice were still together, she was inclined to tell Alice about the veiled lady. Alice deserved better than a man who, however handsome, womanized at every opportunity.

As Hattie neared the bank, she saw her brother standing outside. With him was a red-bearded man Hattie recognized—Lafayette Baker, head of the National Detective Police in Washington City. George had more or less admitted to working for Baker, but it struck her as odd that a man of his importance, with so many responsibilities, would travel all the way to Montreal to check in on someone in his employ.

Mindful of her last unpleasant encounter with the detective, she veered toward the Place d'Armes, thinking she might cross over the plaza to her hotel before either of the men noticed her.

But she'd taken not three steps in that direction when George called out to her. "Hattie!" Turning, she saw him waving. "There's someone I'd like you to meet."

Puzzling. Yesterday George had expressed alarm at her having asked Mr. Baker about him. Now he wanted them to meet again?

As she neared the men, Baker reached a hand to touch her shoulder. "So this is the little sister who's come to visit."

Offering a polite smile, Hattie slipped past him to stand next to George. At least Baker didn't recognize her. Their previous encounter had been brief, and she had a feeling she wasn't the only woman he'd ever accosted.

"Mr. Baker, may I present my sister Hattie Logan," George said.

Dipping her head, she extended her hand, a proper lady. "A pleasure, Mr. Baker. I trust you're enjoying your time in this lovely city."

"Yes, yes," Baker said. "Rare for me to get this far north." He lifted an eyebrow. "I don't suppose George has said much about my work."

"My brother is reserved by nature." Glancing at George, she could see he was pleased with her response. "He says little about his own work, much less anyone else's."

"Good, good." Baker thumped George on the back. "Well, I must be going. Heading to Niagara tomorrow. Have you been, Miss Logan?"

"No," she said. "But I hear the Falls are spectacular."

"They are. George will vouch for that. You should visit at the first opportunity." He waved, then turned from them and walked briskly off.

"What is Mr. Baker doing in Montreal?" she asked George.

"Checking up on me," he said. "Someone has to, you know."

"I'm surprised you wanted us to meet," she said. "You seemed concerned I'd gone to him back in Washington."

"Better to put you in plain sight, my fair lady."

She wasn't sure what he meant by that, but she decided not to press the matter. "Speaking of fair ladies." She reached into her purse and took out the theatre tickets. "My friend Alice Gray is performing at the Theatre Royal tonight. I bought us tickets."

"You're friends with the leading actress? How did you manage that?"

"A little side venture I took in Washington, running the box office at Grover's National Theatre. Alice was with a traveling troupe that performed there, and we found we enjoyed one another's company."

Smiling, he shook his head. "My little sister. You truly are all grown up."

"I am," she said firmly. But she knew it would likely take more than a passing acquaintance with an actress to truly convince him.

~ ~ ~

That evening, the sun setting behind them, Hattie and George made their way up Saint Urbain Street toward Theatre Royal.

"This is a charming city," Hattie said. "I'd love to see more of it."

"And so you shall," George said, "when we make our tour this weekend."

"You seem at home here," she said. "Will you stay on after the war?"

"No," he said. "Comfortable as I am here, it's not the sort of place I envisioned settling down."

"Surely you won't return to Indiana," she said. "I visit my friend Anne there, but it's the last place I'd want to settle. Too many bad memories."

"I share your sentiment. Know where I'd actually like to go?" He leaned close, looking puckish as he had when they were young and he was proposing some outlandish adventure. "Oregon Territory."

"It's Washington Territory now," she said, proud to show she paid attention to such things. "Oregon has become a state."

"Either way." He flung his hand in a flourish. "You should hear what folks say about Oregon. Trees so big three men stretching hand to hand can't reach all around. Rivers choked with fish. "

"You always did like nature," she said.

"There's opportunity too. When the war ends, people will be streaming West. I'd like to be at the front of the pack."

"They'll be needing houses," she said. "And people to design them."

"Exactly. I'll just need to find someone looking for an architect's apprentice."

"Like you always wanted." She envied George. Even when they were young, he'd known what he wanted, had a plan. She'd been the impulsive one, as prone to follow her feelings as anything, something he'd often chided her for. "I don't suppose you'd want your little sister tagging along to Oregon."

He grinned. "Nothing I'd like better." He paused. "Well, maybe one thing I'd like better. A wife. Hearth and home and all that."

She shouldn't be surprised. Even before leaving home, George had shown a fondness for the ladies. "Have you met someone?"

He shrugged. "A few someones. But none who've stuck. Unlucky in love, I'm afraid. How about you, Sis?"

She couldn't suppress her smile. "Well, there's a certain lieutenant with the Army Police in Nashville. I'll confess to having thought of him now and again while I've been away."

"I knew it!" George said. "You've got a glow about you, the kind women get when they're in love." He shook his head. "Sadly, not something I know from personal experience."

"I don't believe that for a moment," Hattie said. "I was old enough when you left home to know you'd broken a few hearts in LaConner."

"Not the same as love," George said. "Not that glow."

"I suppose I should be flattered that you find me glowing, but frankly it makes me feel a bit like a firefly."

"The glow's about your face," George insisted. "Not your..." He gestured to the rear. "...posterior."

"Such manners you have. No wonder the ladies shun you," she teased. "In any event, I'm not ready to admit to being fully in love. Not yet, anyhow."

A carriage rattled by, leaving them momentarily silent. After it passed, George said, "I don't suppose you've been to see our parents."

"Only once," she said. "I went there hoping to find some news of you. I know you didn't part on the best of terms, but I figured you'd write to them. Mother wasn't exactly happy to see me."

"What about Father?"

"He wasn't home. But he sent a letter disowning me." She lowered her voice a notch. "Because of my spying."

"Not exactly die-hard supporters of the Union, those two. But, yes, I've written them, and they've written back."

"So I was right. Mother knew where you were all along."

"More or less. I suppose once I wasn't fighting for the Union any longer, she and Father were willing to entertain a word from me now and then, even if we weren't regular correspondents. In her last letter, Mother said Father has been unwell. Quite unwell, actually. I've been wondering if I should take a few days to go back and see him. He may be dying. That can't be easy."

Hattie tipped her head, gazing at him. "It's not as if Father has ever gone out of his way to consider your feelings. Or mine."

"He's an unhappy man," George said. "I see that more clearly now that I've been away. I'm not sure he had the capacity to give us any more attention than he did."

"Or to stand up to Mother?" Hattie said.

"That would require a good deal of fortitude, you must admit," George said. "Being younger, you might not remember, but there was a time when Father was more attentive. I suppose that's what makes me think I should at least make an effort to see him before he's gone."

"You know he's aiding the Rebels?"

"I wouldn't be surprised. But I don't see how you'd know that for certain."

"It was written in a coded letter," she said, keeping her voice low. "I intercepted it in Mr. Pinkerton's mailroom."

George shook his head. "You always were inclined toward the fantastical."

"I'm not being fantastical. I worked it through the code. It detailed a smuggling operation involving Logan grain."

He set his hand on her shoulder. "Look, Sis, I'm not saying it couldn't happen. It wouldn't be the first shady operation Father's been involved in. But this decoding business...I'm having a hard time picturing you working ciphers."

"And why is that?" Her question sounded more defensive than she'd intended.

He shrugged. "Logic was never your strong suit."

"I love a puzzle," she said, telling herself not to take offense. She didn't want an argument to spoil their evening. Her time here was short, more than might be required to convince George that she wasn't a witless child anymore. And it was true that he'd generally been the more careful and logical of the two of them, and she the one more inclined to act on impulse.

"Fair enough," he said. "You have been known to let curiosity get the best of you."

"Speaking of which," Hattie said, happy to shift subjects, "I saw something curious when I went looking for you at the bank today. There was a man I'd met before at a teller's window. In fact, he's the beau of Alice Gray, who'll we'll see onstage tonight."

"I don't see what's so curious about that," George said. "He must have come here with her."

"Maybe. But at the bank, he was with another woman. A veiled woman. The teller handed him a cheque and what looked like a large amount of money. He kept the cheque and gave the money to the woman. I found that rather strange."

George laughed. "There you go, proving my point about your fantastical inclinations. Cheques and large amounts of money are passed back and forth at the bank every day. It's what we do."

"But this man's an American," she said. "Why would he do his banking in Montreal?"

"Our customers include a number of Americans. Southerners in particular. And you shouldn't be nosing around in their transactions." He sounded almost cross.

"I wasn't nosing. It was just the..." She left her thought unfinished. There would be no convincing George that what Booth and the veiled lady were up to was anything out of the ordinary. And she had to admit her concern was based solely on supposition, not fact.

Still, it was hard to ignore her feeling that something wasn't right about what she'd seen today. John Wilkes Booth with a veiled lady and a large sum of money. Lafayette Baker in Montreal when he should be back in Washington running the National Detective

Police. And George wasn't helping, being so evasive. If she didn't know him as she did, she might suspect him of colluding with the enemy.

But that was ridiculous, more evidence of what George deemed her over-active imagination. Nearing the theatre, she let the thought go. As they went inside, she felt a familiar sense of anticipation. Once the show started, her cares and worries would melt away. The stage would become the only reality that mattered.

She'd splurged on seats near the front, and as she and George settled in, she was glad of it. From here, she could more easily slip backstage after the show and surprise Alice. Years had passed since they'd seen one another.

The lights dimmed, and Hattie relaxed into her seat. The curtain rose on a painted backdrop depicting the streets of New York and a forlorn newsboy—actually, a girl dressed as a boy, as the actor soon revealed. In the next scene, the backdrop changed to a Southern plantation, and Alice Gray came onstage. Dressed in a wide hooped skirt, her dark blonde hair falling in ringlets about her shoulders, she was every bit as lovely as Hattie remembered.

George leaned over. "That's your friend?" he whispered.

Hattie nodded.

"Stunning," George said. And from that moment on, whenever Alice was on stage, his gaze was fixed on her. She played the part of the newsboy child grown into a woman who, through a set of fortunate circumstances, had become a wealthy heiress. It was from those circumstances, and others that followed as the action unfolded, that the drama derived its name, the notion being that God's hidden hand was behind every twist in the plot.

As ever, Alice played her role with verve and determination, her character outwitting scoundrels and thwarted murderers at every turn. The show was riveting, and Hattie found herself lost in it, although she glanced at George now and then, confirming that his attention was entirely given to Alice.

The performance drew to a close, the evildoers brought to justice. Though reluctant to let go of the illusion, Hattie stood with George and the rest of the audience in an ovation that brought the cast back onstage for another round of applause. As the applause died down and the cast retreated, she took George by the arm. "Let's try going backstage. If I don't catch Alice now, I might miss her entirely."

He needed no convincing. Amid theatregoers streaming toward the exits, they pressed their way to the steps leading up to the stage. Staying as much as possible in the shadows, Hattie led George around the curtain to the theatre's inner sanctum. She felt the sort of after-show aura she remembered from her stint at Grover's National, a sense of collective accomplishment mixed with relief that the performance had gone off without a hitch.

Tonight, this being the final show, the mood was festive too. Someone uncorked a bottle of champagne, and there was a wave of laughter from the cast members gathered around. Hattie scanned their faces. She recognized John McCullough, the man who had the starring male role, but she didn't see Alice.

"She's probably in her dressing room." Hattie tugged George around the jovial clutch of actors toward a bank of doors off to one side. Most were open, the dressing rooms empty of people but strewn about with clothes.

Hattie rapped on the first closed door she came to. She recognized the man who answered as the theatrical's villain. This close, his makeup was jarring, with exaggerated lines and eyebrows drawn in for sinister effect.

"Sorry," Hattie said. "I was looking for Miss Gray."

"End of the hall," he said gruffly, then shut the door.

Hattie hurried to the door he'd indicated, George trailing behind. To her delight, it was Alice who responded.

"If that's you, McCullough, I'll be out in a minute," she called from inside.

"It's not McCullough," Hattie said. "It's an old friend."

There was the sound of footsteps, and then the door swung open. "Hattie Logan!" Looking ravishing as ever, Alice swept Hattie into a hug. "What a wonderful surprise." She ushered Hattie and George inside. "Don't mind the mess," she said with a grand sweep of her arm, indicating the costumes strewn about the closet-like space. "You know how it gets when a show closes down, all the mad rushing to gather things up. And this is the end of our season, so it's worse than usual."

Alice bustled to a settee alongside her dressing table and shoved aside an assortment of dresses and hats. "Have a seat amid the clutter and fill me in on what you've been up to. It's been..." Turning to face them, she stopped mid-sentence. "Ah, but first you

must introduce this handsome man you've got with you, Hattie."
Eyes sparkling, she leaned close and added in a stage whisper, "I
always suspected you'd land a fine one."

Color rising in her cheeks, Hattie laughed. "No landing with this
one. He's my brother. George, meet my friend Alice."

Alice cocked her head. "You mentioned a brother. But you said
nothing about his good looks." She extended her hand. "A pleasure
to meet you, Mr. Logan."

Grasping her fingers, George raised her hand to his lips, brushing her fingers with a kiss. With a winsome smile, he said, "The
pleasure is all mine. Your performance tonight was outstanding.
Entirely memorable."

"I suppose it's too much to ask that you would turn out to be
a drama critic as well. The friendly ones are few and far between
these days."

George laughed. "I fear no one would pay for my opinion. But I
stand by it all the same."

Claiming her spot on the settee, Hattie remembered Alice telling
her how badly the critics had treated her, especially when she'd first
started out. "The audience loved you tonight," she said. "That's all
that matters."

"I for one could scarcely take my eyes off you, so captivating was
your performance," George said.

"I'm so glad I came by the theatre today and saw the playbill,"
Hattie said. "Otherwise we'd have missed you entirely, this being
your final show. Where do you play next?"

"New York. But not for a few weeks." Alice sat at her dressing table. Only then did George occupy the space left to him on the settee. "And in the spring, Washington City. Besides a run in Buffalo, that's all I've got booked at present."

"Then you've got time to tarry a bit in Montreal," George said.

A look passed between them. "I suppose I do," she said. "The times I've performed here, I've never taken time to relax and see the sights. And I'd love to catch up with you, Hattie. How long will the two of you be in town?"

"George lives here," Hattie said. "I've come to visit him. I'd planned on a week." That was what she'd told John Elliott, and as much as she was enjoying her time here, first with her brother and now with her friend, she missed him already.

"I hope you took my advice and have joined up with an acting troupe," Alice said.

"Just a few bit parts," Hattie said. Alice didn't know about her spying, and while Hattie had every reason to trust her, her association with Booth gave her pause.

Swiveling in her chair, Alice pulled a comb from her hair, releasing a swath of curls. In her dressing table mirror, she eyed George. "And you, Mr. Logan? What occupies a charming gent like yourself in Montreal?"

"Nothing half as interesting as your work," he said. "Just a lackey's position at the bank down the street."

"George was always good with numbers," Hattie said. "But his true calling is architecture."

"Architecture!" Alice pulled a second comb from her hair, causing all her locks to swing gently about her shoulders. "Can you design a house? One of these days, I intend to quit wandering, and I want a house of my own."

"I'm afraid I have no professional training," George said.

"But you used to do all sorts of sketches," Hattie said. "They were quite good. Everyone said so."

"Everyone, meaning you."

"And Mr. Clift. He builds for a living. He knows a good design when he sees one."

"I've been keeping a list," Alice said. "Of the features I'd like. Nothing extravagant, really. Just a cozy little place to call my own. I shouldn't impose, having only just met you, but if you're willing, I could give you my list, and you could see what you come up with."

"I can't promise perfection," George said. "But I'd be happy to give it a try. It would be a nice distraction from tallying numbers."

A chorus of laughter sounded outside the dressing room. "Oh, but we're keeping you from your party," Hattie said.

Alice batted her hand in the air. "They don't care if I'm there or not. The attention all goes to McCullough."

"But you're clearly the star," George says. "He over-acted his part."

"Tell that to the critics." Alice stood. "In any case, I did a bit too much celebrating last night. Tonight I intend to go back to the hotel and get a good night's rest." She reached for her cloak. "But I'd love to see the two of you tomorrow."

George fairly bounded from the settee to assist Alice with her cloak. "Then we'll meet for dinner," he said. "Seven o'clock, Chez Antoine. I'll make reservations."

Standing, Hattie touched her brother's arm. "We mustn't presume. Alice may have other plans."

"Not at all," Alice said.

"But I saw John Wilkes Booth at the bank today," Hattie said. "I assumed he was here because of you."

"Wilkes?" Alice said. "Not a chance. After our last show together, I caught him in an amorous embrace with my understudy. I gave him one more chance, and then...well, let's just say I told him in no uncertain terms that I never wanted to see him again."

"Then I wonder what he's doing in Montreal," Hattie said.

Alice shrugged. "Came at John McCullough's behest, I suppose."

"Your unworthy leading man," George said.

Alice smiled. "That's kind of you to say. At any rate, all I care about Wilkes is that he keeps his distance."

George looked delighted at this assertion. "If you've got no one to escort you to your hotel, Miss Gray, it would be my pleasure."

Alice smiled. "I'm not sure what to do with such gentlemanly attentions after some of the cads I've been with. But yes, I'd like that, Mr. Logan."

"Then it's decided." George opened the door, holding it for the ladies. "We'll drop Hattie at her hotel, and then I'll take you round to yours. And tomorrow evening, we meet for dinner."

Hattie was beginning to see why George was unlucky in love. However careful he might be in other enterprises, he exercised little caution when it came to the ladies. But Alice was more than worthy of his attentions, and she didn't seem to mind that his flirtations skewed toward the obvious. Hattie only hoped that if anything developed between them, no one got hurt.

Chapter Four

OCTOBER 8, 1864

Saturday was the sort of glorious day that made autumn Hattie's favorite season—bluebird skies with a hint of crispness in the air, with abundant sunshine that made the autumn colors glow. George kept telling Hattie and Alice how lucky they were. During his years in Montreal, he'd found October a fickle month, as prone to freezing rain and sleet as it was to sunshine.

The interest George and Alice had shown one another the night they met seemed to grow with every encounter. At dinner last night, they'd smiled and laughed and tipped their heads together like old school chums. If they'd been anyone else, Hattie would have felt left out. As it was, she enjoyed seeing two people she cared about having such a good time together. She also felt a twinge of pride at having introduced them. She only hoped they had the sense to take things slowly. Her best friend, Anne, had rushed headlong into marriage, and now she was left raising her daughter by herself.

True to her word, Alice had given George her list of what she wanted in a house, and he'd told her he'd get to work on some drawings. With Hattie's ready consent, he'd also invited Alice to join them on today's sightseeing tour of Montreal, and Alice had been quick to accept. After a breakfast of delectable French pastries, they'd begun at Notre Dame Basilica. Alice had never before been inside, and she was as awed by the cathedral as Hattie was.

From there, George had toured them around Victoria Barracks, headquarters of the British military. Watching the red-coated soldiers doing drills on the lawn, Hattie was reminded of how she and Anne had sneaked away from Ladygrace School for Girls to watch Indiana's first regiment organized after Fort Sumter perform similar drills to an admiring crowd. Actual battle, she'd soon learned, was far more chaotic.

With Alice and George, Hattie also went back to Montreal Harbor. Many of the ships there were blockade runners, George said, going around the Union's blockades to deliver munitions, medicines, and food to the South. Registered in Canada, a theoretically neutral country, the ships had a huge advantage. If they managed to leave the South carrying an illegal load of cotton, a single round trip voyage might yield nearly a million dollars in profit, George said.

Hattie thought of the establishment Booth and the veiled lady had entered. According to the signage, it was an importation business. Was that a front for blockade running? If Booth was involved in such activities, that would explain both his presence in Montreal and the amount of cash he'd procured from the bank. But how did the veiled lady fit it?

Idle speculation, Hattie told herself. Booth wasn't with Alice any longer. That was all that mattered.

From the harbor, George took Hattie and Alice past the Customs House and then around to the jail and Gaoler's House. "All sorts of miscreants in there," he told them.

"I hope that includes John Beall," Hattie said, naming the Confederate rebel who'd escaped after she helped foil his plot to take over Lake Erie.

"John Beall?" Alice said. "Who's that?"

"Oh, a Rebel whose story I followed in the papers," Hattie said, for this was hardly the time or place to reveal her spying to Alice.

"He plotted to take over Lake Erie," George said, sparing Hattie further explanation. "Then he escaped to Canada, where he's likely planning more Rebel raids in the North."

"But the fighting is in the South," Alice said.

"The Confederates want to divert Union troops north," Hattie said. "Or so I've heard."

George set a hand on Hattie's shoulder. "My little sister knows things I never thought she would."

"She's a talented lady, your sister," Alice said.

"You're too kind," Hattie said. But the praise warmed her all the same.

Her feet started to ache from all the walking, and she was grateful when George hired a carriage to take them to McGill University.

As they wove their way through the campus, George pointed out the new buildings going up, the construction being funded by an American tobacco merchant whose operations had shifted to Montreal after the South left the Union. Judging from the size of the buildings, he was doing quite well for himself.

By the time they reached Mont Royal, the point from which the city derived its name, Hattie had gotten her second wind. Enthusiastically, she and Alice followed George up the winding paths to the top of the mountain, which despite its name was more an impressive hill.

Still, they enjoyed a commanding view of the city from the top. As they stood side by side, the sun sinking low in the sky, George pointed out various landmarks they'd passed. Hattie was impressed at how much of the city they'd seen in a single day.

They lingered as the western sky shifted in hues of orange and pink. Finally, the sun dipped below the horizon.

George turned to face Hattie and Alice. "I don't know about you ladies, but I'm finding myself rather ravenous for dinner."

"Me too," Alice said.

Hattie was hungry, too, she was also weary from all the walking. "You two go on to dinner," she said. "I'd just as soon go back to the hotel and put my feet up." Neither George nor Alice tried to persuade her otherwise, confirming her suspicion that they wanted some time alone.

At the bottom of Mont Royal, they caught an omnibus that returned them to the business district. Getting off in front of the St. Lawrence, Hattie bid George and Alice goodnight. Linking arms, they headed down the street. Watching as they disappeared around a corner, wistfulness came over Hattie, a longing to be with John Elliott again.

But she'd committed to staying the week, and that's what she'd do. There was much she still wanted to tell George, and much she hoped to learn from him. That might be more difficult with Alice in the picture, but opportunities would present themselves.

As Hattie turned to enter the hotel, two men emerged from the hotel's saloon. The larger of the two she didn't recognize, but even in the twilight, she was certain the smaller man was John Wilkes Booth.

She slowed her steps, lingering near the hotel's entrance as she listened to the banter between the men.

"You may be the champion at billiards," Booth said in the breezy manner of a man who was in his cups. "But next time you see me, I'll have made a double carom, bagging the biggest game this side of hell. Abe's goose is cooked."

The men continued down the street, and Hattie was unable to hear the stranger's reply. What was Booth bragging about? Probably just some pool talk about another opponent, she told herself. Nothing that should raise concerns.

The doorman held the door, and she went inside, vowing not to waste another thought on the actor. Alice was done with him. That was enough to satisfy Hattie.

Chapter Five

OCTOBER 11, 1864

Hattie's week in Montreal passed quickly. While George was at work, she spent her days with Alice. Together, they returned to many of the places George had taken them, stopping along the way to sample the wares of nearly every pastry shop in the city's central district. They spent evenings with George, who insisted on treating them to dinners in Montreal's best French restaurants.

Clearly he wanted to impress Alice, though where he got the money on his bank employee's salary was a mystery. For her part, Hattie could see that Alice was more taken by George's kindness and sincerity than on how much he spent on their meals. Hattie made sure to slip away each evening, allowing them time together.

For her last night in Montreal, Hattie asked if they could return to Chez Antoine, a request George was happy to accommodate. After an afternoon strolling the paths at Mont Royal, she and Alice went to the bank to meet George for dinner. As usual, he was in his office, poring over tabulations. Seeing them, he smiled brightly. "My two favorite ladies. How was your afternoon?"

"Splendid," Alice said. "Although I've decided your sister must be half mountain goat, the way she scampered up that mountain."

"It's George's fault. He had me climbing trees and racing up hills from the time I could walk."

"No mountains," George said. "Those are in short supply in Indiana."

"Plenty in Oregon, I hear," Alice said.

George must have shared his plans with her. Hattie supposed she should feel as if Alice was intruding, but in truth, it felt good to think of a future that might include both her friend and her brother.

Funny, she thought, how George had admonished Hattie's lack of logic, and now here he was, tumbling head over heels in love, or so it seemed. She'd cautioned Alice against a whirlwind courtship, citing Anne's troubles with the man she'd married on a whim. But Alice had laughed off Hattie's advice. Being with George, she felt younger and livelier than she had in years, Alice said. For once, she felt as if someone truly cared for her above all else.

As they stood at George's desk, Hattie leaned forward to brush a crumb from his chin. "Eating on the job, are you? You'll spoil your dinner."

"Guilty as charged." He raised his hands in mock surrender. Then he reached for a box on his desktop. "Ginger cakes," he said, lifting the lid. "Help yourself, ladies."

Alice reached for a cake. "Ginger. My favorite."

Hattie grabbed Alice's wrist. "George, where did these come from?"

"A customer. Grateful for services rendered. A difficult transaction, apparently."

"Which customer?" Hattie asked.

"A lady," George said. "That's all I know. She left them with the doorman."

"A veiled lady?" Hattie asked.

"Hattie, please," George said. "Enough with the veiled lady."

Alice looked quizzically from one to the other. "I feel as if I'm missing something."

Hattie let go of her wrist. "I spotted a veiled lady at the bank the other day. She struck me as suspicious."

"For no good reason," George said.

Hattie hesitated, wondering if she should mention Booth. No, that would be salt in Alice's wound, she decided. "I just don't think you should be eating cakes when you don't know who brought them. My friend Pauline did that, and she ended up poisoned."

"Pauline," Alice said. "Is that the actress you told us about? The one giving lectures for P.T. Barnum?"

"Bit of a huckster if you ask me," George said. "At any rate, these cakes are delicious. I'm inclined to have another."

As he reached toward the box, Hattie snatched it away. She dumped the cakes in the wastebasket, then set the empty box back on his desk.

George's eyes flashed. "That," he said, "was uncalled for."

"That," she said, "was prudence. Something you've lectured me on more times than I can count."

"You do seem a bit overwrought, Hattie," Alice said. "And all over a few sweets."

"If you'd seen how sick Pauline got, you wouldn't accuse me of being overwrought." Hattie drew a deep breath, knowing if she said more, she'd risk ridicule. "And she swears it was from cakes a veiled lady brought."

"But she hasn't any proof, has she?" Standing, George reached for his coat.

Hattie felt a sudden pang of regret, having overreacted as she knew she was prone to. Why couldn't she be steady like John Elliott? And logical like George?

"I suppose you're right," she said. "I just didn't want any harm to come to either of you."

The furrows in George's forehead relaxed. "I suppose I should thank you for tossing out the cakes before I ruined my supper."

Alice slipped her arm through his. "Chez Antoine does have a fine dessert menu."

"A wonderful way to end my time in Montreal," Hattie said, taking George's other arm. "Though I fear I'm going to have to let out the waist of every skirt I own when I get back to Nashville."

~ ~ ~

The food at Chez Antoine was as fabulous as before, made even more delightful by the camaraderie they shared.

"I'll miss you, Sis," George said, nudging aside his plate. "I wish I could convince you to stay a while longer."

"I tried," Alice said. "But she only blushes and mutters something about her Army lieutenant."

"He's not my lieutenant," Hattie said, hoping that the warmth she felt in her face wasn't proving Alice's point. "But I will admit to missing him."

"Next time you come north, you must bring him along."

"With any luck, the war will end soon, and we can visit you in Oregon instead," Hattie said.

"George, you only ate half your meal," Alice said. "Those cakes must have spoiled your supper after all."

He pressed his hand to his stomach. "I confess to feeling quite full."

"Me too," Alice said. "No dessert for me after all."

"Nor for me," Hattie said as the waiter slipped their plates from the table. "Alice, after your current bookings, might your acting bring you to Tennessee?" Hattie asked.

"I doubt it," Alice said. "But it might take me to Oregon." In the candlelight, her eyes sparkled.

George's lips turned up, but not in his usual winsome smile.

"George, are you all right?" Hattie asked.

"I'm perfectly fine," he said, sounding cross.

"You're certain?" she said.

"Absolutely. If anything, I've a bit of indigestion. All those rich cream sauces. I don't know how the French manage their waistlines."

"Corsets, no doubt," Alice said.

"I suppose I should get back to the hotel, given the early hour of my train tomorrow." Still eying George, Hattie set aside her napkin."

"Alice, if you're ready, we can walk Hattie back to her hotel," George said.

"That's not necessary," Hattie said. "We can say our goodbyes here."

"Nonsense," Alice said. "George is right. We'll walk you to your hotel and say a proper goodbye."

George paid their bill, and they left the restaurant. Stars twinkled in the clear night sky, and a brisk wind blew from the north, chilling Hattie's skin despite her cloak. Much as she had enjoyed Montreal, she was glad to be spending the winter farther to the south.

They started down the boardwalk. Halfway to St. Lawrence Hall, George stopped suddenly. His hand touched the base of his throat.

"What's wrong?" Alice asked.

"A bit of burning, that's all." He took another two steps, then dashed to an adjacent alley.

Standing on the boardwalk beside Alice, Hattie heard him retching.

"Those cakes," Alice said. "Do you truly think—?"

"Wait here." Hattie started for the alley.

"I'm coming too," Alice said, hurrying after her.

They found George leaning against a stone wall, doubled over, his hands on his stomach. As they approached, he straightened, wiping his face on his sleeve.

"Sorry," he said. "Something didn't agree with me."

Alarmed, Hattie took his elbow. "Can you make it into the hotel?"

"I – I think so."

Alice took his other elbow, and they guided him out of the alley and toward the St. Lawrence. As they reached the entrance, a bellman approached. "May I offer assistance?"

"Please," Hattie said. "I fear my brother has overindulged." She pressed the key in his hand and gave him her room number.

George leaned on the bellman as they started up the stairs. "It's those cakes, isn't it?" Alice whispered to Hattie. "But why would a bank customer want to harm him?"

It must be George's work with Lafayette Baker, Hattie thought. But she doubted George had told Alice about that.

"People do strange things." Hattie took Alice's arm, willing herself to remain calm. "Whatever the cause, George needs help. Go to the concierge, please. Ask him to send for a doctor. If he asks for specifics, say George is suffering from a severe attack of gout."

"But it's poi—"

Hattie pressed her finger to her lips. "We'll get into the specifics when the doctor gets here," she said in a low voice.

Alice nodded, then turned back down the steps. Hattie hurried to catch up with the bellman and George, arriving at her room as the bellman was unlocking the door. Eyes closed, face pale, George was leaning on him heavily.

The bellman guided George to the bed. He collapsed into it, his skin pale and clammy.

Hattie slipped the bellman a few coins. "You'll be all right with him, then?" the bellman said, eying George.

"He just needs to sleep it off," Hattie said.

The bellman left. Hattie poured fresh water into the wash basin. She wetted a washrag, then wrung it out. Going to George's side, she blotted his face with the rag.

George's eyes fluttered open. "Those cakes," he said weakly. "You were right, Sis."

"Hush," she said. "Save your strength. Alice is sending for a doctor."

He closed his eyes. "Don't want...her to see me like this."

"She's head over heels for you, George. You needn't worry about impressing her."

His face contorted, and he held his hand over his stomach.

"The pain—it's bad?"

He nodded, mouthing words she couldn't make out.

"The doctor will know what to do," Hattie said.

She hoped this was true. Pauline had had similar symptoms—queasiness, retching, sharp pains in her stomach—but they'd been milder. Watching her figure, she'd eaten only part of a cake, she told Hattie. George, on the other hand, could eat like a horse without gaining a pound. Thank heavens Hattie and Alice had arrived when they did, or he might have consumed the whole box of cakes.

She sat with him, murmuring comfort, wiping his face, bringing a basin when he retched. Where was Alice? Hattie hoped she hadn't run into trouble. The Confederates milling around the St. Lawrence lobby suddenly all seemed a threat.

Finally, there was a rap on the door. Alice entered, bringing with her a slight, white-haired man with stooped shoulders.

"The concierge was nowhere to be found, so I got the address and fetched the doctor myself," Alice said. "How is he?"

Rising from the bed, Hattie shook her head. Without waiting for an answer, Alice scurried past her. Kneeling at the side of the bed, she smoothed her hand over George's hair, whispering that everything would be all right.

Hattie approached the doctor. "I think he's been poisoned."

The doctor frowned. "By whom?"

"I'm not sure. A stranger had ginger cakes delivered to his office. Thinking it was an innocuous gift, he ate one."

The doctor's expression darkened. "Your friend said he has retched up some of his stomach contents already. Is that correct?"

"Yes," Hattie said. "A while ago."

He touched his hand to his chin. "Might be those cakes contained arsenic. Easy enough to procure, and its taste can be easily masked. He set down his medicine bag. "It's good I brought my pump."

Opening the bag, he took out a mahogany case, unlatched it, and removed a brass pump with three nozzles and two tubes protruding from it. "Gastric lavage can help in such cases," he said. "Cleans out whatever's left in the stomach."

Hattie wrung her hands. "Will that allow him to recover?"

The doctor began inserting tubes into the pump's nozzles. "Depends on how much he ingested. And on his fortitude." He eyed the washstand. "Is there fresh water in the pitcher?"

Hattie nodded. "It's about half full."

"That will do. Pour a glass, please." He took a pillbox from his bag, opened it, and handed her two white tablets. "Stir these into the water. Sodium chloride, to facilitate the cleansing."

Folding her fingers over the tablets, Hattie started for the washstand.

"You two ladies may want to retire to the hotel's lobby during the procedure," the doctor said, approaching George with his pump. "It won't cause undue harm, but I can't say that it's pleasant."

"I'm staying right here." Holding fast to George's hand, Alice now sat perched on the bed.

The doctor shrugged. "Don't say I didn't warn you."

The procedure was indeed unpleasant. The doctor set a wooden mouthpiece over George's mouth, then forced him to swallow the end of one of the tubes, which he accomplished with much sputtering and gagging. Once the tube was in place, the doctor used the brass pump to flush the saline solution Hattie had prepared through George's stomach, the contents emptying through the second tube into the washbasin.

Throughout the process, George thrashed and moaned. Alice stayed at his side, holding fast to his hand and whispering words of comfort.

Finally, the procedure ended. The doctor pulled the tube from George's throat, and he finally relaxed.

"His stomach should be empty now," the doctor said, wiping the pump with a rag. "That means no more poison will enter his system. But there's no way of knowing how much he has already absorbed. You'll have to watch and wait and see how he does. Keep him comfortable. Give as much water as he'll tolerate. That will help flush the poison from his blood. You say it came from a cake?"

"Yes," Hattie said. "Delivered by a stranger."

Alice rose from the bed. "Hattie had the good sense to throw the rest of them away. Perhaps we should try to retrieve them from the dustbin and go to the police?"

The doctor pulled the tubes from the pump, then fit the pieces back into the mahogany box. "I suppose you could. But it would take a chemist equipped with the proper equipment to confirm that the cakes contained arsenic. Even then, there would be no way of tracing the cakes back to an individual. Arsenic is easy to procure. Anyone can buy it."

Anyone, Hattie thought, including the veiled lady.

She paid the doctor, and he left.

For the rest of the night, she and Alice took turns sitting up with George. During her watch, Hattie filled her thoughts with prayers for George's recovery. She knew Alice did too.

Chapter Six

OCTOBER 12, 1864

The morning dawned with gray skies and a mist that wet the hotel room's single window. George had made it through the night, but his breathing remained shallow and his skin pale.

Alice worried her hands in her lap. "I wish there was more we could do."

"George has always been strong. He'll pull through." Hattie hoped this was true. "You should go back to your hotel and try to get some rest, Alice."

"I don't want to leave him. And you need rest too." Alice paused a moment. "How about I get us a room on this floor? I'll check out of the Ottawa Hotel and have my trunk moved here."

"Good idea," Hattie said.

Standing, Alice reached for her cloak. "And on my way there, I'll stop at the bank and let them know George is ill. They'll be wondering where he is."

"No," Hattie said. "Don't tell the bank."

"But he'll lose his position if he doesn't show up."

"The bank is where the cakes were delivered," Hattie said. "So the poisoning must be associated with his work."

"I don't see how his work at the bank would cause anyone to want to harm him," Alice said. "All he does is tally balances and process cheques."

Hattie glanced at George. He seemed to be sleeping peacefully, his breathing more regular than before.

"George doesn't just work with numbers." Better that Alice knew the truth, to the extent George had told Hattie. "Have you heard of the National Detective Police?"

"Vaguely," Alice said. "They're in Washington City, right?"

"Yes, but they have agents in other places. Including Montreal."

"Agents. You mean spies?"

On the bed, George shifted position. Hattie didn't think he could hear, but as a precaution, she lowered her voice. "Yes. Spies. George is one of them."

Alice tightened her grip on her cloak. "He told me nothing about that."

"I doubt he'd have told me either, but I knew it from other sources. Since I've been here, he's told me little of what he's doing. He wants to protect me, which I'm sure is why he kept you from knowing. But whatever the details, it seems clear he's gotten in over his head."

"A spy." Alice shook her head. "Do they know at the bank?"

"I'm not sure. But someone in Montreal knows, or he wouldn't have been poisoned. And they might not stop at one attempt. We need to get him out of here as soon as possible."

Alice's forehead tensed. "The condition he's in now, I don't see him being able to leave anytime soon."

"He'll get his strength back." Hattie hoped this was true. "In the meantime, it's best if we let people think he's gone missing, and we fear he's dead."

Alice shook her head. "I can't say he's dead when what I want most in the world is for him to live."

"Think of it as acting," Hattie said. "When you mourn someone's dying onstage, it doesn't make it so."

"I suppose you're right," Alice said, but she looked dubious.

"I know I'm right," Hattie said. It was time to come clean. "You remember me telling you I'd worked for the Pinkerton Agency?"

"Right. In the mailroom, opening letters."

"Yes, but I ended up doing more than that."

Her eyes widened. "You're a spy too? And that's what you're doing in Montreal?"

"I'm a spy for the Union, yes, but that's not what I'm doing here. Most recently, I've been working out of Nashville."

Alice glanced at George and then back at Hattie. "The two of you can certainly be tight-lipped when you want to be."

"We come by it honestly," Hattie said. "growing up in a home where the less said, the better."

Alice was quiet a moment, taking this in. "All right," she said. "We don't tell the bank about George."

"Not yet anyhow," Hattie said. "I'll go round there this afternoon, pretending to look for him without letting on that anything's amiss. I'll let them know he's gone missing, which they can confirm for themselves by checking his apartment upstairs. Perhaps word will get back to whoever poisoned him that their efforts succeeded. That way, they won't attempt any more harm, at least not to him. With their guard down, it will be easier for me to try to figure out who they are."

Alice jutted her chin. "I'm no spy, but I want to help."

"Good," Hattie glanced at her brother's prone form. "When George comes around, I'll need all the help I can get, convincing him we can only find the person who did this to him if he tells us exactly what sort of spying he's doing here."

~ ~ ~

As promised, Alice moved to the St. Lawrence, finagling the room that adjoined Hattie's. She had her trunk brought over, and Hattie moved her few belongings there so she'd have a place to rest.

Late that same afternoon, George woke momentarily from his sleep. Glancing about, he wondered aloud where he was.

"You're in good hands," Hattie said. "That's all that matters."

Alice cupped her hand behind his neck, raising his head as she held a glass of water to his lips. "Drink," she said.

George managed a few sips, then laid his head down. His lips formed barely audible words.

"Mind of their own," Hattie said. "If that's what he said, he's still our George."

Alice stroked his forehead. "Still our George," she repeated.

Hattie fastened her cloak about her shoulders. "I'm going out now." She glanced at George, unsure how deeply he was sleeping. "As we discussed earlier."

Alice nodded. "Bring some nourishment when you return," she said.

"I will," Hattie said. "But no ginger cakes."

~ ~ ~

At the bank, Hattie was glad to see the familiar doorman on duty. "I'll be leaving on the evening train," she told him. "I've come to say goodbye to George."

The doorman's smile clouded. "He's not in today, miss."

She widened her eyes in surprise. "But he has to be. He's expecting me. I can't imagine where else he'd be."

The doorman shook his head. "Nor can I. When Mr. Campbell saw he hadn't come in, he sent me up to Mr. Logan's apartment to check on him. The room was empty, and his bed was all made up. So either he didn't sleep there last night, or he rose early and left."

"But none of that makes sense." Hattie raised her voice, expressing alarm. "He took me to dinner last night, and I promised I'd come by this afternoon."

As she'd hoped, her loud protestations brought the chief teller, Robert Campbell, from his office. He strode toward them. "Miss Logan," he said upon reaching the entry. "I'm glad you've come round. We're trying to ascertain what's become of your brother."

Hattie studied his face, but it was difficult to read in his bland expression whether his concern was genuine or feigned. "I haven't the slightest idea, sir. This man tells me George failed to come in to work today. That's not like him. No matter what job he has held, I've always known him to be a faithful employee."

"Nor have we found fault with him up till now," the teller said.

Hattie drew herself up. "Then I must go to the police. They'll know what to do."

The teller held up his hand, palm out. "That won't be necessary, miss. The bank will make inquiries."

She shook her head, her curls bouncing at her shoulders. "But I was the last one to see him."

"She says they had dinner last night," the doorman offered.

"And all was well when you left him?" the teller asked.

"I wouldn't say well," Hattie said. "We dined at Chez Antoine's, myself and my friend and George. The meal was superb, but George said something didn't agree with him. Still, he walked my friend back to her hotel." She brought her hand to her mouth. "You don't suppose...I hope he didn't...you see, he'd had a bit of sherry with dinner, and the route took him along the river. What if he slipped and went in? He doesn't swim."

She swayed slightly as if she might swoon. The doorman caught her by the arm. "You mustn't jump to conclusions, Miss." He eased her into his chair.

"That's right," Mr. Campbell said. "I'm sure there's a logical explanation. Leave an address where we can reach you when you get home, Miss Logan. We'll send a telegram as soon as he's located."

"Oh, but I couldn't leave without knowing what's become of him," Hattie said. "I'll simply have to extend my stay till he's found."

The teller gave a little bow. "As you wish, Miss Logan. Though I don't see what that will accomplish."

His responses were polite and to the point, as one might expect of a man whose employee had gone missing. And yet he seemed to Hattie a bit too dismissive. Did he know about the cakes? Was he in on the plot?

"You're certain it wouldn't help to inform the police?"

Campbell set his hand on her shoulder. "Quite certain. I'm afraid the police here tend to make a mess of things. And frankly, their snooping around would be bad for the bank. George wouldn't want that. Many of our customers are, shall we say, averse to authorities poking around their accounts."

Taking a handkerchief from her purse, Hattie dabbed at her eyes. "If that's what George would say, I'll follow your advice. Thank heavens you're here to guide me at this difficult time."

Campbell acknowledged her gratitude, reiterating that the bank would do all it could to help find George. Then he returned to his office.

Hattie sat a few moments longer in the doorman's chair, long enough to convince him, she hoped, of her frailty and helplessness. Finally, she got up to leave, declaring she'd best return to her room before her nerves got the best of her.

Walking back to the St. Lawrence, she sorted through what she knew. Someone who knew of George's work wanted him dead or, at the very least, sidelined from whatever he was investigating for Lafayette Baker. George was going to have to come clean about what those investigations were.

Arriving at her hotel, Hattie stopped at the purser's office adjacent to the main lobby where there was a line from the telegraph office across the street set up to accommodate the hotel's American guests. Proceeding to the counter, she overhead three gentlemen sharing war news from the telegrams they'd received.

Hattie told the clerk she wanted to send a telegram to Mr. John Elliott in Nashville. Instead of naming the Army Police Headquarters, she gave the street address. With no guarantee anything she wrote would be private, she kept her message vague:

Delayed. Will advise as circumstances allow.

She paused a moment, wishing she could write something more personal. Then she signed it with her initials, *H.L.*

Chapter Seven

OCTOBER 13, 1864

George had a restless night, with lots of tossing and turning. But the next morning, he felt well enough to sit up in bed, propped up by pillows.

"You gave us quite a scare," Alice said, offering a glass of water.

He drank from it eagerly, then dabbed at his mouth with the edge of his bedsheet. "You must admit I know how to get a lady's attention." He attempted a smile, but his weak voice betrayed his condition. "I don't..." He ran his hand through his disheveled hair. "Don't know what hit me."

"You were poisoned," Hattie said. "Arsenic. The doctor confirmed it."

"Those ginger cakes," Alice said.

He glanced at Hattie. "Go ahead, Sis. Say you told me so."

"This time, I wish I hadn't been right. Apparently you've made some enemies in the work you've been so secretive about."

"Nothing secretive about my work," he said, latching onto Alice's gaze. "Ledgers and numbers."

"And spying," Alice said. "Hattie told me."

George eyed Hattie. "My little sister never could keep a secret."

"Not true," Hattie said. "When you're fully recovered, we'll compare notes. But first, we've got to find out who did this to you."

He shook his head. "Let sleeping dogs lie, Hattie."

She folded her arms at her chest. "We can't risk them trying to harm you again. Next time, they might succeed."

"And they could harm someone else," Alice said. "We have to get to the bottom of it."

"Don't tell me my sister has recruited you too," he said.

"I'm in this far," Alice said. "I might as well make myself useful."

George raised his head from the pile of pillows. "You've both admitted that whoever did this is dangerous. I'll not have either one of you taking that risk."

"I'm afraid that's not for you to decide," Hattie said.

"Especially not in your weakened condition." Alice nudged his chest with her finger.

He lay back on his pillows. "Neither one of you shows the least bit of shame in taking advantage of a man when he's down."

"Not if he intends to get in our way," Hattie said.

"At least let me help," George said. "When I'm stronger, that is."

"You can start by telling us what Lafayette Baker has you doing here," Hattie said.

George sighed. "As you readily observed, the bank is a beehive of Confederate activity. Baker posted me there to keep an eye on Confederate accounts. I was to take special note of any large transactions, funds coming in and funds dispersed."

"So someone must have found out you were doing that and gone after you before you reported their activities," Alice said.

He shook his head. "The Confederates don't care if their activities are reported. They're in Canada. Neutral, remember?

"But you're tracking a paper trail," Hattie said. "One that Baker's National Detective Police can use to thwart plans the Rebels would rather were kept secret."

"True," he said. "But the bank is discreet. Cheques are made out to trusted bank employees. The employees cash them, then turn the funds over to customers who are known Confederate loyalists. Unless you know the system, there's no way to trace the funds back to the source."

"Which is who?" Alice asked.

"The Confederate government," he said. "They've got commissioners here. Secret services agents too. Much of the money going in and out of the bank involves them."

"How much money are we talking about?" Hattie asked.

"Millions of dollars," he said.

The room fell silent a moment. "I understand Canada is neutral," Alice said.

"Theoretically," George said.

"Still, why go to the trouble of moving money around here?" Alice asked. "If the Confederates want to pay for something, why not just pay for it out of Richmond?"

"Depends on what that something is," Hattie said. "If it's a plot to cause trouble in the North—say, freeing Rebels from Union prisons—it makes sense to orchestrate the operations from here."

"Exactly," George said. "That's why Murray Wilson came here looking for John Beall. He planned to raid a big Union prison on Lake Erie."

"A raid that I helped thwart even if Murray Wilson is now taking credit for it," Hattie said.

George's eyes were watery, but his gaze was intense. "You really did more than courier work?"

"Quite a lot more," Hattie said. "I posed as a courier's wife in Richmond. I was arrested. The man with me was..." She still got emotional, thinking of what had happened to Thom Welton. "...Was killed. I escaped."

Alice's eyes widened. "You never told me that."

"Just as I didn't tell you I was a spy until circumstances warranted it. It's safer that way."

"Arrested. Escaped." George shook his head. "I had no idea."

There was more Hattie could tell him, about tracking down the man who'd betrayed her in Richmond, about befriending a Rebel spy who'd switched sides, about supplying information on a huge sale of illegal cotton. But that would have to wait.

Alice smoothed her fingers over George's forehead, brushing back a lock of hair. "You look tired," she said. "You should try to get some rest."

He closed his eyes briefly, then opened them. "At the bank, they must be wondering what's become of me."

"I took care of that," Hattie said. "They think you're dead."

"Dead? But I can't...I've got work to finish here."

"Your work here is compromised. Someone knows what you've been up to, and they don't approve. You've got to leave Montreal as soon as you're strong enough."

He clasped Alice's hand. "I don't want to go."

"If you stay, you'll end up actually dead," Alice said, her voice soft but firm. "I couldn't bear that."

"If Confederate spies are after me, I don't know how I can hide. Their network is extensive."

"Not so extensive as to reach into Oregon, I'll wager," Hattie said.

His lips turned in what was almost a smile. "That doesn't sound half bad. As long as you go with me, Alice."

"No one's going just yet," Hattie said. "Not till you're well enough."

"And I've got commitments in New York and Washington City." Alice smiled. "But when I'm finished with those, I'd love to meet up with you in Oregon.

His face relaxed. "I'd like that."

"Now close your eyes," Alice said. "From what I hear, it's a long journey to Oregon."

"Especially for a dead man," Hattie said.

~ ~ ~

By evening, much of George's color returned. He was even able to sit up on his own and eat a chunk torn from a baguette Hattie brought from the market. With Alice and Hattie seated at his bedside, the three of them shared stories from their childhood. None had been especially happy, and yet each recalled moments of joy amid the difficulties.

When that topic was spent, Hattie regaled them with stories of how she'd escaped a Richmond prison and gone on to spy in Tennessee.

"My little sister." This time, when George said this, there was an unmistakable note of pride in his voice. "You've done some remarkable things."

"And I intend to do at least one more," Hattie said. "Find whoever it was who tried to kill you."

"I don't care for that idea," George said.

"I'm afraid your opinion matters little," Alice said. "We've got you outnumbered."

"Lafayette Baker visited you this week," Hattie said. "Is there anyone who might have found out and felt threatened by that?"

"Baker's visit was no secret," George said. "You saw yourself that we conversed openly on the street."

"But you said he posted you here to gather information," Alice said. "So you must have told him something about Confederate transactions at the bank."

"It's more complicated than that."

Hattie's eyes narrowed. "Complicated how?"

"Complicated in that I'd rather not tell you."

"But you will," Alice said. "You must. We won't divulge a word of it, will we, Hattie?"

"We will not," Hattie said.

George looked from one to the other. "I believe I liked it better when I wasn't outnumbered. All right. But what I tell you must remain confidential. It involves people at the highest levels of government. You know how valuable cotton is now?"

"Quite valuable," Hattie said. "In Nashville, I was assigned to uncover details of a cotton sale worth nearly a million dollars."

George tipped his head, looking at her. "You continue to surprise me, Sis. So you know that the North with its blockades has been preventing the South from selling cotton."

"And the South hasn't wanted it sold either," Hattie said. "They're hoping pressure from the world market will eventually bring other nations to their side, forcing the North to lay down their arms."

"But I thought the South was running out of money," Alice said. "Not able to feed their soldiers. I'd think selling cotton would help."

"It would," George said. "And if handled through Union-authorized brokers, it would bring in tariffs that would help the Union too. As we speak, Confederate officials here in Montreal are arranging for the South to sell a billion dollars in cotton to the US government, to be paid for in greenbacks and meat."

"Trading with the enemy," Hattie said. "Mr. Lincoln would never allow that."

"He may have little choice," George said. "The US economy has its problems too. Without cotton, the balance of trade is skewed. Our supply of gold is depleted. There's insufficient confidence in greenbacks. According to Mr. Baker, the president has quietly authorized the US Treasury to issue cotton licenses to Southern growers who pledge loyalty to the Union."

"I shouldn't think there would be many of those," Alice said.

"There aren't," George said. "That's partly why this whole cotton-for-meat scheme is being handled in secret. If word got out that Mr. Lincoln is trading with the enemy, there's no way he'd win re-election next month."

"So what does all of this have to do with you, George?" Hattie asked.

"My instructions have been to facilitate the transactions in secret," he said. "Money in, money out. And that's what I've done."

"Did Mr. Baker come here to ensure you were being discreet?" Hattie asked.

George shook his head. "He knows I'm discreet. He was here because he's in on the cotton deals too."

"Because there's money to be made," Hattie said. "Our father did something similar, early in the war. Traded with the enemy. I decoded a letter about it."

"Decoded." Alice sound incredulous.

"Yet another talent I never dreamed my sister would have," George said. "As for Father, I'm sure he'd be in on this cotton scheme, too, if his health allowed it."

"So you don't think your monitoring these transactions has angered anyone?" Hattie asked.

"Only if I threatened to divulge the transactions to the wrong people," George said. "And I haven't."

Hattie eyed him closely. "But you must have done something. Something that made someone feel threatened."

George looked away.

"George," Alice said. "You must tell us."

He returned his gaze. "If I tell you and the wrong people find out, you could be in danger yourselves. I can't allow that."

"What if we're already in danger?" Alice said. "We've made no secret of associating with you."

"She's right," Hattie said. "The best way to ensure our safety is to tell us who might have us in their sights."

George looked down at his hands. He was silent a moment. Then he looked up at them. "I found some anomalies. In the ledgers. Funds channeled to places I hadn't seen before. In amounts that suggest the Confederates are plotting something substantial. I made copies of the entries. I tried to show them to Lafayette Baker, but he wasn't interested."

"I'm not surprised," Hattie said. "From what I observed at his office, his detective work seems slipshod at best."

"I haven't the utmost confidence in him either," George said.

"Would he try to harm you?" Alice asked.

"I don't think so. At least I hope not."

"The ledgers you copied," Hattie said. "That's where the answers lie, I'll wager. Tell me where they are, and I'll fetch them first thing tomorrow. Then we can go over them together and see if we can find any clues."

"They're in my apartment," George said. "I can get them myself when I'm stronger."

"You seem to have forgotten," Alice said. "You're dead."

"How quickly they write me off," George muttered.

"And for a dead man, you look quite exhausted," Hattie said. "Get some rest. We'll need your help tomorrow, going over those numbers."

Chapter Eight

OCTOBER 14, 1864

The next morning, Hattie left the hotel under the low cover of wooly gray clouds. A chill in the air warned that winter would soon set in. She walked briskly to the bank. Nearing the entrance, she was relieved to see the usual friendly doorman was on duty.

"Good day, Miss Logan," he said as she approached. "I don't suppose you've had any word from Mr. Logan?"

She withdrew the handkerchief she'd tucked in her sleeve and swiped the corners of her eyes. "I'm afraid not," she said in a tremulous voice. Then she drew herself up. "We must accept the inevitable, I'm afraid. My brother is lost to us. I've come to gather his things from his apartment. Would you be so kind as to let me in?"

"Certainly, Miss Logan." He ushered her inside. "Wait here, please, while I fetch the key."

He retreated to the chief teller's office. As Hattie waited for his return, she took note of the customers engaged in transactions. There was more activity than one might expect at such a small bank. Cotton deals, she thought.

Returning with the key, the doorman motioned for her to follow him up the stairs to the third floor. Continuing down the hallway, he stopped at the fourth door on the left. "Mr. Starnes has his quarters on the other side," the doorman said, turning the key in the lock.

"Mr. Starnes. Isn't that the bank's president," Hattie said, remembering what George had told her. "I'm heartened to know my brother was given a room on the same floor. Unless it was so Mr. Starnes could keep an eye on him."

"I doubt that, Miss. Your brother is...was a trusted employee." He swung open the door, and Hattie stepped inside. George's room was small but neat as a pin, the bed made and the clothes put away. His trunk sat on the floor at the end of the bed.

She wished the doorman would leave her to sort through George's things on her own. But he seemed inclined to linger, never mind his duties downstairs. Whatever trust the bank had in George seemed not to extend to her.

Mindful of her role as the grieving sister, she walked slowly to George's bed. Her fingers grazing his pillow, she sighed. Again she blotted her eyes with her handkerchief. Then she went to the end of the bed and opened George's trunk. Inside were copies of books by writers she knew he admired. Thoreau. Emerson. Rousseau. He couldn't possibly have lugged all these books with him back when he was with the infantry, she thought. He must have picked them up at bookstores here in Montreal.

She went to the dresser and began shuttling folded shirts to the trunk.

The doorman stepped toward her. "May I be of assistance?"

"No," she said quickly. "It's...it's selfish, I know, but it gives me comfort, holding in my hands every item George would have held in...in life. But I will need someone to transport the trunk to my hotel. Might I ask you to arrange for that?"

"Of course," he said. "I'll see to it as soon as you're finished."

She moved to the drawer containing George's trousers. It was here, he'd said, that she'd find the ledger he'd copied. But she didn't want to risk the doorman spotting a paper tucked in the drawer, nor did she want to move the paper to the trunk knowing it might be tampered with before delivery.

She looked up at the doorman. "If you please, I'd like to ride along with the trunk." She pressed her hand to her heart. "It's all I have left of my dear brother. But the strain of...of this has me feeling quite fatigued. Perhaps you could arrange for the transport now, so I won't have to wait?"

Uncertainty clouded the doorman's face, leading Hattie to suspect that the chief teller had advised him not to let her out of his sight. But his kindness prevailed over duty. "I'll see what I can arrange, Miss."

He turned from her, leaving the door ajar as he left the apartment. From the sound of his footsteps in the hallway, he was moving at a brisk pace.

Sensing she had little time, Hattie rifled through the stacks of neatly folded trousers. In the middle of the third stack, she found what she was after, a folded paper containing ledger entries copied in George's careful hand. She folded the paper in half again, then slipped it into her bodice.

She continued transferring George's clothes to his trunk. He'd need them in Oregon.

The doorman returned within minutes. With him was a small, wiry man in an Eton cap. "Here's your driver, Miss," the doorman said. "He and I will carry Mr. Logan's trunk downstairs when you're ready."

She set the last piece of George's clothing in his trunk, then shut the lid. "I can't tell you how much I appreciate your kindness."

"My pleasure," the doorman said. "Go on down to the lobby now, if you please. We'll come along behind with the trunk."

So you can go through it first, Hattie thought. No matter. She had the paper she needed.

Crossing the room, she stepped past the driver and the doorman. Then she stopped, turning back to them. "I nearly forgot," she said. "The last...the last night I saw my brother, he said a bank customer had delivered ginger cakes to him. He was quite taken by this act of kindness from a stranger. I'd like to know who that person is so I can thank them. Do you recall the delivery?"

"I do," the doorman said. "A messenger boy brought the box of cakes. But I have no idea who sent him."

Hattie might have asked for a description, but with all the business being conducted in Montreal, the city was crawling with messenger boys. Even if the doorman remembered what this one looked like, there were slim odds of her tracking him down. Besides, asking for details would only arouse the doorman's suspicions.

Better to leave well enough alone.

~ ~ ~

Back at the hotel, Hattie had the bellman bring the trunk up to the room she was sharing with Alice. After he left, she slipped next door. Alice and George sat perched on the edge of his bed.

"Our patient is getting restless," Alice said. "I feared I'd have to tie him down to keep him from wandering the halls."

"We'll have you out of here as soon as you're strong enough," Hattie said. "In the meantime, you can get to work explaining what all these names and numbers mean."

Pulling the paper from her bodice, she sat next to her brother. She unfolded the ledger he'd copied. Smoothing out the creases, she set it in her lap.

"This is money in," George said, pointing to a column of numbers. "And this is money out." He pointed to another column.

"And these names are the parties involved in the transactions?" Hattie said.

George nodded.

"What makes these out of the ordinary?" Alice asked. "Aren't they just more of those cotton-for-meat exchanges you told us about?"

"Some are," George said. "But some are different." He pointed to the second entry on the page. "See how this five thousand dollars comes from the Bank of Niagara?"

Scanning the page, Hattie pointed to another entry. "And here's the same amount, five thousand, going out to the Bank of New York."

"And here's another one," Alice said, pointing. "Three thousand coming in from the Bank of Niagara. The next day, three thousand goes out to the Bank of New York."

"Right," George said. "The amounts change, but the transactions are always in from Niagara, out to New York. And there are others besides what I've copied here."

"I still don't understand why these entries can't be for cotton sales," Hattie said. "Money coming in to pay for the cotton, money going out when it's sold."

George shook his head. "Cotton sales move in the opposite direction. Money comes in from a Union bank. Then it goes out to one in the South, passing to and from licensed brokers. But the names in the notations besides these transactions are always the same, and neither is a licensed cotton broker."

Alice ran her finger along the columns of names. "C.C. Clay and R.M. Martin. The money always comes in from Clay and goes out to Martin."

"It sounds as if we should have a chat with those two," Hattie said.

"No," George said. "I don't want you tangling with either of them. Clement Clay is a Confederate commissioner. Whatever funds he's moving must be authorized by Jefferson Davis himself."

Alice's eyes widened. "The Confederate president."

"That's right. Clement Clay is here to do his bidding. But Clay is known for his temper. Not someone you'd want to cross."

"What about R.M. Martin?" Hattie asked.

"He's fearless," George said. "Took a bullet in the chest saving the life of General Morgan."

"Leader of the Confederate guerillas," Hattie said.

"I can't get over you paying attention to such things," George said.

In spite of herself, Hattie felt a swell of pride, though she chose not to mention that much of her knowledge of Confederate guerillas came from firsthand experience.

"A bullet to the chest is a serious injury," Alice said. "Mr. Martin must be at least somewhat incapacitated."

"Not enough to prevent the Confederate Secret Service from taking him on," George said.

Hattie zigzagged her finger along the columns. "So there are substantial sums of money going from the Confederate Treasury to a secret service agent who conducts raids. And yet you said Mr. Baker had no interest in these transactions. Do you think he's involved?"

"I don't think so," George said. "Admittedly, he can be somewhat lacking in moral character. But I can't see him colluding with the enemy."

"You said he's profiting from the cotton deals," Alice said. "That sounds like siding with the enemy to me."

"In that, he's got the blessing of the Federal government," George said. "All the way up to Mr. Lincoln himself. That's different from protecting a Confederate spy who's receiving funds to pull off some big attack in the North."

"A plan big enough to convince someone that your suspecting it is a threat," Hattie said. "But who could have found out?"

"I'm sure there's a Confederate spy or two among the bank's employees," George said "I tried to be careful, making these copies, but maybe someone noticed."

"Which is why we're going to get you out of here as soon as we're able."

"I just wish you hadn't made a dead man out of me to do it."

Alice squeezed his hand. "All that matters is that you stay very much alive."

"And that no one comes after you," Hattie said.

"Or you. Best for all of us if we forget all of this." Taking the paper from Hattie's lap, he crumpled it into a ball.

She snatched the balled paper from his hand. "You're going to let Robert Martin carry out a well-funded raid that could harm civilians?"

"And give the South an edge in the war?" Alice said. "That's not something we can just ignore."

George lay back on his bed. "The two of you are quite possibly the stubbornest women in all of Canada."

"Determined," Hattie said. "That's the term I prefer."

Chapter Nine

OCTOBER 19, 1864

Four days later, Hattie and Alice entered Montreal's Bonaventure railway station with George in tow. Weak from his ordeal, he clung to Hattie's arm on one side and Alice's arm on the other.

Under the circumstances, making him look the part of an invalid had been easy. It was Hattie's idea, drawn from what she knew of how Kate Warne, her supervisor at the Pinkerton Agency, had disguised Mr. Lincoln to protect him from a threat on his life as he passed through Baltimore en route to his inauguration.

Glancing at George, Hattie thought Miss Warne could have done no better with his disguise. Rather naturally, owing to his weakened state, George shuffled along like the elderly man he was made out to be. Hattie had insisted on him dressing not in his usual dapper suit but in an old pair of trousers and a shirt that was frayed at the sleeves, items she'd purchased at a flea market stall.

She'd also bought the shawl that he now wore over his shoulders. Then, using skills she'd learned backstage, Alice had transformed George's appearance, graying his hair and adding wrinkles around his eyes and forehead.

They'd debated among themselves about whether it was too soon for George to leave. But with every passing day, he was growing more anxious for their safety, and they for his. But the journey west would be long, and the women worried he might not yet have the strength for it.

Alice had proposed going with him and then returning to New York for her next engagement. But George worried that if his identity were discovered, harm might come to her as well. He would send for her, he promised, after he got settled in Oregon and she'd completed her theatrical engagements.

Alice got George settled on a bench in the waiting area while Hattie went to the ticket window. Using the money George had given her, she purchased a ticket to Vancouver, British Columbia. From there, he planned to take a steamer to Astoria, Oregon. At the mouth of the Columbia, it was a small but thriving waterfront town where they hoped no one would think to look for him.

"My grandfather isn't well," Hattie said as the agent handed her the ticket. "My sister and I would be ever so grateful if you'd ask the conductor to look in on him now and then. We wish one of us could travel with him, but we're needed at home."

"I'll let him know," the agent said. "Don't give it another thought. There's no cause for worry."

If only you knew, Hattie thought.

Joining Alice and George on the bench, she handed him his ticket. Shoulders slumped, he took the ticket, then looked up at her slowly. She saw the alarm in his eyes.

"At the ticket window." Speaking in a hoarse whisper, he tilted his head, indicating the direction she'd come from. "With that big pile of luggage. Clement Clay. "

Taking care to show no reaction, Hattie patted his hand. "Don't worry, Grandfather. They're going to take good care of you on the train."

Head drooping, George closed his eyes. Exchanging glances, Hattie thought Alice must be hoping as she was that Clement Clay being here was merely a coincidence, not a sign that they'd been found out.

"Grandfather will want some water," Hattie said evenly. "There's a tin cup in his satchel. If you'll get it out, I'll see about filling it."

Alice did as Hattie asked, pulling the tin cup from George's travel bag. Taking the cup, Hattie stood. Eyes straight ahead, she started across the waiting area. As she passed the ticket window, she glanced at Clement Clay. He was a large man, not fat but broad at the shoulders, with a wide face, full beard, and steely blue eyes. Longer than was the fashion, his brown hair covered his ears.

As the porter transferred Clay's many trunks to a wheeled cart, the Confederate commissioner shifted his gaze to Hattie. Feeling the weight of his stare, she looked away, but as she did, she memorized Clay's features.

With steps steady and measured, as if all that mattered in the world was getting a cup of water for her ailing grandfather, she continued toward the exit. A porter directed her to the pump, where she filled the cup with water.

Water beading the tin cup, she returned to the waiting area. She handed the cup to George. As he drank greedily from it, she surveyed the room, looking for Clay. But he was gone.

"What became of the commissioner?" she asked in a low voice.

"While you were out, they announced the boarding of the 4:10 to Niagara," Alice said. "That's when he left."

Having drained the cup, George returned it to Hattie. "All those trunks," he mumbled. "As if he's leaving for good. Something's afoot."

They sat in silence, Alice clinging to George's hand as a granddaughter might. Hattie remained alert, perusing the station. If Clay had left town, they would have to try to find the other man whose name appeared in the ledger.

"Grandfather," she said, turning to George. "You haven't told us where we might find your friend Mr. Martin."

George lifted his head slightly. "Not sure."

"We must return his...his umbrella," Alice said.

"Remember?" Hattie said. "He left it in your room. Tell us what he looks like. Perhaps we'll run into him."

"Tall," George said. "A little stooped in the chest."

From being shot while saving his guerilla commander, Hattie thought.

"Blue eyes, mustache, goatee," George said.

"Sounds like a fine Southern gent for my sister," Hattie said.

Alice straightened. "You know I'm spoken for."

George tilted his head toward her. "Are you now?"

"I've eyes for none but you, Grandfather."

George's lips turned in the faint manner of a person for whom smiling had become yet another means of exertion. Hattie worried that the look was only half-feigned. Perhaps they should have kept him in Montreal a while longer. But every day at the hotel brought fresh worries that someone would spy him crossing the hall to the lavatory or catch her and Alice smuggling food into his room.

"I'm glad," he said. "Now you girls must promise me you'll leave within the week."

"Yes, Grandfather," they said, almost in unison. It was a promise he'd extracted already—that they were to be prudent in their investigations and bring them to a close within the week.

Hattie and Alice had assured him they would. But when he pressed the point, asking exactly how they intended to carry out their task, Hattie had demurred, saying he'd only nitpick her plans. In truth, she had no plan as yet. As George would be quick to point out, planning wasn't her strong suit.

She couldn't deny that in the past, she'd proceeded on whims and hunches. But no more. She was going to approach this matter logically, just as George would. The hard part was figuring out where to start. Alice was a wonderful companion, but she was looking to Hattie for direction.

Hattie wished John Elliott were here. Simply talking to him had helped her see her way clear on other matters. But he was too far away to be of any help, and she knew of no one in Montreal she could count on.

Unless...she grabbed George's hand. "Grandfather," Hattie said. "I forgot to ask where we might find Mr. Wilson."

He touched his finger to his chin. "Wilson, you say?"

"Murray Wilson," she said, speaking more softly. "Is he still in the city?"

The confusion left George's face. "Ah, yes. Wilson. Said he was renting a room near the Crystal Palace."

"The skating rink," Alice said. "We could rent skates and take to the ice."

George's brow furrowed along the lines Alice had drawn on his skin. "You'd best be gone from here before it's cold enough to skate."

Alice laughed. "From this morning's temperatures, I'm guessing that won't be long. I was wishing I'd brought my muff."

A conductor stepped into the waiting room, announcing that the westbound train was ready to board. Hattie glanced at the clock. "Right on time."

Alice helped George to his feet, and Hattie took his satchel. With George clinging to Alice's arm, they joined a queue of passengers on the platform. Moving forward a step at a time, they reached the conductor, standing near a plume of steam coming from the locomotive.

Hattie handed him George's ticket. "His health is fragile," she whispered. "Help him to his berth, and he should sleep most of the way."

"Certainly, Miss." Touching the brim of his hat, the conductor dipped his head slightly. He took the satchel from Hattie and handed it to a porter with instructions to see it safely to George's berth.

A lump forming in her throat, Hattie turned to George. Having just found him after these many years, she hated sending him off into the unknown. At least this time she had an idea where he was headed, and he had promised to write once he got settled in Oregon.

She leaned to kiss his cheek. "Goodbye," she whispered. "Take good care."

Alice leaned to kiss his other cheek. "Goodbye," she said. Her lips lingered on his cheek, and Hattie saw how they squeezed hands. Tears welled in Alice's eyes, and George's eyes glistened too. A whirlwind romance, Hattie thought, but it seemed strong and true.

George followed the porter onto the train. Hattie and Alice watched and waved as steam poured from the locomotive, the wheels slowly turning, the engine chugging along the tracks. Tears streamed down Alice's cheeks. Hattie circled her arm around her waist as the train shrank from sight. How odd, Hattie thought, that she was the one longing for the future while George was the one embarking on it now.

Taking a handkerchief from her skirt pocket, Alice wiped the tears from her face. "Never fell so hard for a man," she said.

"You'll be back together before you know it," Hattie said. She hoped this was true.

Chapter Ten

OCTOBER 20, 1864

No longer worried about George being discovered, Hattie and Alice felt free to come and go as they pleased. Few people, if any, would connect either of them with the Bank of Ontario employee presumed drowned in the St. Lawrence River.

The morning after saying goodbye, they found the hotel lobby buzzing with chatter, the words *raids* and *capture* seemingly on everyone's lips.

Hattie leaned to whisper in Alice's ear. "Raids. Do you think our Mr. Martin is involved?"

"I hope so," Alice whispered back. "If it means he's been captured."

Leaving the hotel, Hattie spotted a newsboy on the corner. "Extra, extra!" he called out. "St. Albans raiders captured!"

Fishing a coin from her purse, Hattie purchased a paper. She tucked it under her arm, and she and Alice proceeded around the corner to a café. Taking a small table near the back, well apart from other diners, they ordered coffee and croissants.

After the waiter left, Hattie unfolded the paper. Scanning the front page, she read aloud from it. "Twelve Confederates captured in Canada. $223,000 in US dollars recovered."

"That's a huge amount of money," Alice said. "Does it say where they got it?"

Hattie ran her finger down the column. "They raided a little town in Vermont. St. Albans. Set fires. Robbed banks. Killed people. One of the men who was apprehended admits to being a Confederate officer. He says the plot was commissioned to aid the South."

"Commissioned," Alice repeated. "In other words, paid for."

"Right. In retaliation for so-called outrages committed against the Confederacy." Hattie scanned farther down the page. "Since the raiders were captured on Canadian soil, they're demanding an investigation into what they say is a breach of Canadian neutrality. Vermont's governor has posted extra guards at the jail, fearing those sympathetic to their cause will try to break them free."

The waiter delivered their order. Genuine coffee, not the chicory stuff served back in Tennessee. Farther south, folks were lucky to get even that—they'd resorted to boiling acorns. And yet there seemed a general sense among Confederates here in Montreal that the tide would turn any day in the South's favor.

Alice forked a bite of croissant and lifted it to her mouth. "Heavenly," she said.

Sampling her fare, Hattie found the pastry warm and flaky, melting butter-like in her mouth. Swallowing, she said, "I wonder if Clement Clay's departure has anything to do with those arrests."

"Meaning he had to get out of town before he was arrested too," Alice said, forking another bite of croissant.

"Exactly," Hattie said. "It was no pleasure trip. Otherwise, why all that luggage? Those transfers of money from him to Martin—perhaps that funded the St. Albans raid."

Alice brushed a flaky crumb from her lips. "George was tracking an awful lot of money. Would one raid require that much?"

"I wouldn't think so," Hattie said. "There must be other plots in the works. It's curious that Clay would board a train to New York. If he were escaping to avoid capture, why not Richmond, where he'd be safe?"

"What about Robert Martin?" Alice asked. "Does the paper mention him?"

Hattie shook her head. "There are several names listed, but not his."

"Maybe he got away," Alice said. "Or he used an alias."

"Or he simply provided the money and is still here in Montreal."

"If he is, I don't know how we'll find him," Alice said. "All we've got is George's description."

Hattie nudged aside her empty plate. "We start by checking hotel guestbooks. Think you can get a look at the most recent pages of the St. Lawrence Hall registry?"

"Sure," Alice said. "I'll check at the Donegana Hotel too. They say it's crawling with Confederates."

"Good," Hattie said. "I'll work on the bank."

"I don't see how you'll find anything there," Alice said. "Not without George."

"There may be another way," Hattie said. "Although it could take some persuasion. And a bit of luck."

~ ~ ~

As Hattie stood in front of the Crystal Palace later that morning, cold nipped her fingers and toes. With its iron and glass façade, the former exhibition hall had been easy to find. South of Mont Royal, its barrel-vaulted roof soared above the surrounding homes.

What would George do? Hattie asked herself. *How would he apply his ever-sensible logic to finding Murray Wilson?*

She shook her head. With only the clue of Wilson's staying near the Crystal Palace to go on, George would say her quest was far-fetched at best, in keeping with her wild imaginings. But there was no harm in trying, she decided.

Canadian by birth, Wilson had returned to Montreal in an attempt to track down John Beall, who'd tried to take over Lake Erie. But from what George said, the trail had gone cold. By now, Wilson might have moved on.

You won't find him simply by standing here, Hattie thought. And so she set out along the north side of the Crystal Palace, strolling toward what seemed a promising cluster of slate-roofed houses.

From the opposite direction, a man in a topcoat approached. Hattie slowed her steps. "Pardon," she said, affecting the French accent common in the city. "I wish to find my cousin, Murray

Wilson. I'm told he lives in this neighborhood. I have an important message to deliver from my father."

"Sorry, ma'am." The man touched the brim of his hat. "Never heard of him." He picked up his pace, seeming eager to get away.

Hattie walked the length of one block and then another. At a house at the end of the second block, a middle-aged woman stepped from the front door, a basket of laundry balanced on her hip.

Hattie turned up the walkway. "Pardon," she said. "Might this be the Wilson residence?"

The woman shook her head. Without a word, she turned toward the backyard.

Discouraged, Hattie retraced her steps. She could knock on every door, she supposed, but she wasn't eager to attract that much attention.

She passed the Crystal Palace again. She would go two blocks to the south, she decided. Then she'd circle back. Beyond that, it made no sense to keep wandering. Wishful thinking, George would say.

On her southward trek, she was about to turn around when she spotted a boy who looked to be around ten years old playing inside a fenced yard with a spotted spaniel. Wrapped up as he was in tossing a ball for the dog to fetch, he didn't notice her approach. As she drew close and the lad looked round at her, she was heartened to see how closely he resembled Murray Wilson.

"Good day," she said. "Is your brother in?"

The boy laughed. "Which brother? There's Terrence, Harold, Paul, and Murray."

"Murray," she said, warm with satisfaction. "Is he home?"

"Not sure. Me and Buster, we've been out here a while." He eyed the house. "Lots of commotion in there."

"I expect so. Ten children, is it?" she said, remembering what Murray Wilson had told her.

"Eleven. New one born last month." He tossed the ball in the air and caught it. "S'pose I should get to my chores, or Ma will have my hide. You want to come in?"

"If I may," Hattie said. "So I can ask after your brother Murray."

"Follow me." The boy tossed the ball to the dog, then turned toward the house. The dog trotted behind, carrying the ball in his mouth. Hattie followed the dog.

The boy opened the door, and they stepped inside. "See what I mean about commotion?" the boy said. He darted past her, disappearing down the hallway.

From all around came the sounds of children laughing, crying, shouting. Hattie peeked through the nearest doorway, where two little girls were in a tug-of-war over a rag doll.

At the sound of approaching footsteps, she stepped away from the doorway to see Murray Wilson approaching, his head bowed over a tiny blanketed bundle at his shoulder. "Mr. Wilson," she said.

Looking up, he broke into a smile. "Why, Hattie Logan. Fancy seeing you here."

She returned the smile. "As I recall, you had a babe at your shoulder the last time we met."

He bounced the fussing baby. "The child your lady doctor friend delivered. I hope she's well."

"If you mean the child, I wouldn't know," Hattie said. "As for Edith, she'd gone East, last I heard."

Wilson leaned close. "I always meant to ask," he said quietly. "Is she a spy too?"

"Indeed she is," Hattie said.

Coming up behind him, a pigtailed girl tapped him on the back. "Not polite to whisper," she said.

With his free hand, Wilson yanked gently on one of her pigtails. "This one's aiming to author an etiquette book when she gets older."

The girl whirled out of reach. "And I'll use every one of my brothers as examples of what not to do."

He held the bundle of baby out to her. "Take him to your ma. Tell her he's hungry."

"Please." The girl took the bundle, hugging the newborn to her chest. The baby let out a wail.

"Please." Wilson made a shooing motion with his hands. "Now off with you."

The girl retreated toward the back of the house. "Let's step outside, shall we?" Wilson started for the door. "With all the noise around here, I find myself missing the gunboat."

"But you haven't gone back."

He shook his head. "I promised captain I'd hunt down Beall, and I aim to. But it's proving harder than I expected."

"Canada is a big country," she said.

"Indeed," he said. "Lots of places for a person to hide."

Taking a coat from the stand, he opened the door, and they slipped out into the cool air. Away from the hubbub, his face relaxed.

"Places to hide," Hattie said as they strolled down the walkway. "But at some point, Beall will need money."

"Right." Turning toward Mont Royal, Wilson took big strides as he walked, like a man unaccustomed to walking with a lady at his side. "That's how I came upon your brother. I saw Beall leaving the Bank of Ontario. I followed him up to the Customs House and over to the market. But I lost sight of him there. So I went back to the bank, pretending to have a question about a transaction. The teller referred me to your brother. I recognized his name from what you'd told me and decided it was safe to tell him my true business."

"He was impressed to learn how you rather singlehandedly saved the gunboat."

Wilson's face reddened to the tips of his ears. "I may have over-stated my role a little."

Knowing she'd made her point, Hattie chose not to press the matter. "For two people thrown together by circumstance, we worked rather well together on that effort. That's why I've come looking for you. I have another project to propose if you're willing. And I promise it involves no drugged liquor or diverted ferries. I shan't think your arm will suffer for it either."

Raising his left arm, which had been injured in the hubbub on the gunboat, he turned his hand front and back. "It has healed rather nicely, don't you think?"

"Remarkably," she said.

They strolled a moment in silence. Then Wilson said, "So, what is this proposal of yours?"

She tilted her head, looking up at him. "Are you interested?"

"If there's a chance it will lead me to John Beall," he said. "And if it gives me a reason to move on from here, so much the better. Mother needs all the help she can get, but some of the younger ones can step up."

It was clear the Wilsons couldn't afford hired help, and Hattie marveled at how Wilson, being a man, had felt any obligation to help at all.

"This would only take you away during working hours," she said. "But it might give you some insight into Beall's whereabouts. You'll recall that my brother, George, had a rather unusual placement at the bank."

"You told me as much," Wilson said. "Spying for some detective in Washington."

"Right," Hattie said. "But there has been, shall we say, an unfortunate incident. Someone tried to kill him."

Wilson stopped short. "I trust they didn't succeed."

"Not for lack of trying." Hattie paused a moment, then continued walking. "If I say more, you must vow to keep what I tell you in strictest confidence."

"Of course," Wilson said.

"The National Detective Police sent George to Montreal. They wanted him to monitor Confederate transactions at the bank. Then things got...complicated."

"An attempt on his life," Wilson said. "I'd say that's complicated. Who does George suspect?"

She cocked her head, looking at him. "You like this, don't you? Chasing down people who've done wrong."

He blushed again, though not so fiercely as before. "No more than you do, I'll reckon. But you're right. My pursuit of Beall has whetted my appetite for doing more."

"Good," she said. "To your question, George isn't sure who tried to harm him. He took up a matter to investigate on his own—several large transactions coming in from Niagara and going out to New York. He thinks someone found out he was watching and decided they needed him out of the picture."

Wilson's eyes narrowed. "One of the parties to the transactions?"

"That, or someone who's protecting them. One of the parties is a man named Robert M. Martin. The other is Confederate commissioner Clement Clay, who left Montreal yesterday with several large trunks in tow." She paused, wondering how much to tell. "It's just a supposition, but I'm guessing Clay's departure may be related to the Confederate raid in Vermont."

Wilson shook his head, his jaw set firm and a hard look in his usually friendly eyes. "Another raid. Why can't they just stick to the battlefield?"

"It's like it was with Beall," Hattie said. "Throw the Federals off-kilter in the North to gain advantage in the South."

He looked off at the wooded rise of Mont Royal, then returned his gaze to her. "And then there's the election. If they sufficiently frighten people, Lincoln won't stand a chance."

"I hadn't thought of that," Hattie said. "But you're right. Besides out-and-out victory, there's nothing the South wants more than for Lincoln to lose."

"Whatever they're planning, they need to be stopped," Wilson said. "How can I help?"

"We—my friend Alice and I—insisted George leave town. Whoever tried to kill him once could try again. I told people at the bank he'd fallen into the river after having too much to drink. So they think he's dead."

"And with your brother gone, there's no one at the bank watching what the Confederates are up to, right when they most need watching," he said.

She eyed him. "That's right. I thought bank work might suit you."

He straightened, grasping the lapels of his coat. "I've been told I'm good with numbers."

"And spying seems to suit you."

"But I don't see how I could convince the bank's manager to hire me," Wilson said.

"Leave that to me," Hattie said. "I've been known to be rather convincing when I put my mind to it."

Chapter Eleven

OCTOBER 26, 1864

Because of what George had explained about the cotton-for-contraband deals, Hattie knew that Lafayette Baker, head of the National Detective Police, had a keen interest in the goings on at the Bank of Ontario if only to line his own pockets.

So, after meeting with Murray Wilson, Hattie went to the telegraph office in St. Lawrence Hall and sent a telegram to Washington: *Indisposed. M. Wilson will be your man going forward. You can trust him.* She signed it simply *Logan.*

Two days later, when Wilson went to the bank to inquire about a position, the chief teller ushered him directly into George's former office, explaining there had been an unfortunate accident and the bank was in need of a comptroller. Some rudimentary explanations were given, and Wilson was left to his work. This Hattie learned from Wilson himself, who came round to St. Lawrence Hall to deliver the news at the end of his first day at the bank.

Going forward, he and Hattie agreed that meeting anywhere near the bank or the hotel was a bad idea. As the bereaved sister, Hattie couldn't afford to be seen with her brother's replacement. She asked Wilson to send a messenger boy with a note should he uncover anything useful.

After that, the waiting set in. As it turned out, this was something neither Hattie nor Alice did well. It didn't help that they were both anxious about George's journey.

Fortunately, the wait for word from Murray Wilson was short. Only days after he started at the bank, a messenger boy left a note for Hattie at the hotel desk. It said only *Tuesday, 8 am, Crystal Palace. M.W.*

Excited to learn what Wilson had uncovered, Hattie rose at sunrise the next morning. She dressed quietly, not wanting to wake Alice, who rarely fell asleep before midnight, a habit Hattie understood, knowing the late hours actors kept.

For the past few days, the skies had stayed mostly gray, the sun bursting through the clouds only for an hour or two at a stretch before retreating again. This morning, the air was cold enough to make Hattie shiver as she boarded the omnibus. When she'd come expecting to stay a week, she hadn't thought to bring a heavy cloak. But now it was nearly November, and she was wishing she had something warmer to wear.

She reached the Crystal Palace at ten minutes of eight. Owing to the cold, she walked a block around the exhibition hall to stay warm, envying the women she passed who were dressed more suitably for the weather. As she neared the end of her stroll, sleet began to fall, wetting her face with a mixture of rain and snow.

Turning to shield herself from the wind, she saw Murray Wilson approach. Happily, he'd thought to bring an umbrella. As he neared, he held it out to her, and she stepped beneath it, falling in stride as he turned east toward the town's center.

"Sorry to make you come out in this mess," he said. "But it seemed the safest way to speak with you."

"I hadn't realized Montreal would turn cold so quickly," she said. "If I'm forced to stay much longer, I may have to beg the use of a winter cloak and muff from one of your sisters."

"I've a sweetheart," he said, his face coloring a bit. "She'd gladly loan you some outerwear. But with what I've discovered, you might find your time here shorter than you think. Mr. Robert M. Martin made a withdrawal late yesterday. A substantial one. Cleaned out his account, as a matter of fact, including several thousand dollars that came in recently from the Bank of Niagara."

"A deposit by Clement Clay?" she asked.

He shook his head. "Jacob Thompson. Another Confederate commissioner here, I'm told. But I checked Mr. Clay's transactions too. The day before you spotted him at the train station with his trunks, he also cleaned out his account."

"So if the pattern holds, we may expect Mr. Martin to be leaving town soon," Hattie said.

"That was my thought," Wilson said.

They walked a moment in silence save for the sound of their boots on the wet boardwalk. As they neared McGill University,

Hattie spoke. "It seems my day would be well-spent at the railway station. The sooner I get there the better."

"Agreed." Murray looked over his shoulder, and his steps slowed. "The omnibus is headed this way. It will make a stop here. I'll wait with you, then continue on foot."

Much as Hattie hated to think of him battling the sleet while she rode comfortably under the omnibus's cover, she agreed this was a good plan. The closer they got to the center of town, the greater the risk of encountering someone whose suspicions might be aroused by the two of them conversing.

Horses clomped close, pulling the omnibus. Hattie turned to Wilson. "You still have the Nashville address I gave you, the one George used to contact me?"

He nodded.

"My situation may change quickly," she said. "If you can't reach me at the hotel, send a wire to Nashville."

He nodded. "I'll let you know. Your brother was onto something, tracking those unusual transactions."

"Just don't let anyone see you doing it," Hattie said. "And if a stranger sends ginger cakes, refuse them."

He looks at her quizzically.

"That's how they tried to kill George. Poisoned ginger cakes."

"Never much cared for ginger cakes myself," Wilson said.

"Good," she said as the omnibus came to a stop. "Take care of yourself, Mr. Wilson."

She started to climb aboard, but he reached for her arm. "One more thing. Yesterday, there was another unusual..." He looked up at the driver, who was waiting for Hattie to get on. "Another unusual entry. Involving a Mrs. Sarah Slater."

Hattie nodded. "I'll keep that in mind."

~ ~ ~

Within the hour, Hattie and Alice were at the railway station again, Alice still a bit bleary-eyed from having gotten up before noon. Satchels at their sides, they occupied an isolated bench in a corner of the station, situated so they could see people coming and going while attracting as little attention as possible.

"Remind me how we're supposed to recognize this Martin fellow," Alice said a bit crossly. She'd grown accustomed to her morning cup of French coffee, but Hattie had insisted they had no time to linger at a café.

"Blue eyes, mustache, goatee. A little stooped in the chest from where he was shot. That's what George said."

"And on the remote chance we spot him, you intend to follow after him, no matter where he's headed?" Alice asked.

Hattie patted her satchel. "That's why I brought a full bag and you brought an empty one."

Alice crossed her arms at her chest. "You go off on an adventure and leave me to the sleet and snow."

"I don't know how much adventure it would be. I only want to see where he's making off to with the funds he withdrew."

"If he's smart, the first thing he'll buy is a cup of coffee," Alice said.

Hattie took a coin from her purse and handed it to Alice. "Now that we're settled in, leave your satchel and go back to that little place we passed and get your coffee."

Alice's face brightened. "That sounds heavenly. But I can't take your money."

"George's money. He wouldn't want you going without your coffee." Playing the bereaved sister, Hattie had closed out George's account before he left. His savings over the years had been substantial, and after taking what he needed to get himself set up in Oregon, he'd insisted Hattie keep the rest for her and Alice's expenses.

Alice took the coin. "When this war ends, I intend to spend the entire day drinking coffee." She stood. "In Oregon, that is."

A satchel on either side of her, Hattie watched Alice leave the station. Even if she got cranky at times, Alice had been a great help and comfort, not to mention a good and reliable friend who was game for almost anything. Without her, Hattie couldn't imagine how she'd have managed after George fell ill. When she went off to her New York engagement, Hattie would miss her.

But they would see one another again, Hattie reminded herself. When George got settled in Oregon, he would send for Alice. Who knew? Maybe she and Hattie would even end up related by marriage.

As was often the case, Hattie's thoughts of romance turned to John Elliott. With only her cryptic telegram to advise him of her delay, she hoped he wasn't overly worried about her. One thing was certain—she definitely missed him.

Alice returned from the café looking considerably refreshed. While keeping an eye on the people coming and going, she and Hattie spoke of their past. Alice told of how she'd gotten her start in the theatre. Unable to read or write, she'd had to rely solely on her memory.

"That worked for the small parts," she said. "Then I started getting cast in bigger roles, and I knew I was in trouble."

"Did you go back to school?" Hattie asked.

Alice shook her head. "I couldn't stop what I was doing. My family depended on my income. A theatre manager found me crying one day, a script open in front of me. A nice elderly gentleman, he took pity on me. He taught me my letters, and I got so I could read most of a script. What I couldn't glean from the pages, I'd learn from prompting. Eventually, my career took off."

"When you performed with Edwin Booth?" Hattie asked.

"That's right. The more winsome of the Booth brothers." Alice gave a little shudder. "Besides his womanizing, there's an ugliness about Wilkes. He and Edwin sparred on many an occasion, owing in no small part to Wilkes's sympathies for the South."

"Not the first family to be torn apart over the war," Hattie said. "I wonder if he has left Montreal."

"I certainly hope so," Alice said. "I'd rather not run into him."

"I don't blame you." Hattie hesitated. She didn't want to pour salt in what was clearly a deep wound. But she and Alice were close now, and she didn't think she should be keeping secrets either. "I had a bit of a run-in with Wilkes myself."

"How's that?" Alice said.

"It was back when you and I first met, while I was filling in for the box office manager at Grover's National Theatre. I went looking for you after the show, and he cornered me backstage." After the years that had passed, Hattie still felt her stomach clench. "A friend—my supervisor at the Pinkerton Agency—came upon us, and he backed off."

"Thank goodness," Alice said. "I must say, he frightened me more than once, especially when he'd been into the whiskey."

"I'm glad you left him," Hattie said. "You deserve better."

"And I've found it." Alice reached to pat Hattie's hand. "Thanks to you."

Just then, the stationmaster approached. "I noticed you ladies have been waiting quite some time," he said. "May I be of assistance?"

"My sister here is an actress," Hattie said, picking up the first thread that came to mind. "We're waiting for her wardrobe to be brought so she can go on to her next engagement."

"An actress, you say?" The stationmaster squinted at Alice.

"That's right," Alice said.

"Sorry not to recognize you," he said. "The wife's a bit religious, you see. So I don't get to the theatre. Would you like me to check on your wardrobe?"

Alice glanced at the clock. "That would be wonderful. I've already missed one train, and I'd hate to miss the next. It was to be transported by carriage from the Theatre Royal."

The stationmaster took a pen and notepad from his vest pocket. "The Royal," he said. "And under what name should I inquire?"

"Laura Keene," Hattie said, naming a popular actress of the day.

The stationmaster scribbled a note. "Very well," he said. "I'll send one of our messenger boys at once."

As he hurried off, Alice leaned close to Hattie. "That should keep them puzzling for a while. By the time he finds out Miss Keene hasn't been in Montreal this year, we should be long gone from here."

"With any luck. Especially since that gentleman over there looks a lot like Robert Martin." Hattie nodded at a man approaching the ticket window. He wore a mustache and goatee, and his shoulders hunching inward.

Glancing that direction, Alice straightened. "Indeed."

A man and woman came up behind Martin. Drawing a sharp breath, Hattie turned away.

"What's wrong?" Alice said. "You look as if you've seen a ghost."

"Those two behind Martin. The man is Dr. Luke Blackstone. He had me arrested in Richmond. My friend..." Even now, having acknowledged her feelings for John Elliott, Hattie struggled with remembering how Thom Welton had died. "My friend was executed."

Alice squeezed her hand. "How awful."

"That's not all," Hattie said, keeping her voice low. "Blackstone tried to introduce yellow fever into American cities, using the cast-off clothing and blankets from patients he'd treated. He also developed an incendiary method called Greek fire. It burns even on water. And that woman..." Her voice trailed off.

Alice glanced past Hattie at the woman, veiled and dressed in black. "What about her?"

"I'll explain in a minute," Hattie said. "But first, can you go up there and see if you can find out where they're headed? Get in line as if to inquire about your wardrobe. I'd go myself, but Blackstone might recognize me."

"Sure." Alice stood. "Wait here."

As Alice strode across the station, Hattie turned, trying to will away the thumping of her heart. Deciding that revenge shouldn't be the driving force of her life, she'd tried to put Luke Blackstone out of her mind. She supposed she shouldn't be surprised to see him in Montreal, a hub for Confederate sympathizers. And yet the effect of seeing him was visceral. Deep inside, she equated him with danger.

And then there was the veiled woman. Plenty of widows in the city, as George had pointed out. Maybe she wasn't the person Hattie had seen coming out of the bank with John Wilkes Booth. Then again, maybe she was.

Beneath her skirts, Hattie's leg jittered nervously. She glanced at the clock. What was taking Alice so long? Maybe Hattie shouldn't have sent her up there alone. One wrong word and suspicions would be aroused.

After what seemed like an eternity, Hattie heard the sound of Alice's spritely footsteps. Arranging her skirts, Alice reclaimed her place on the bench.

"I thought you were never coming back," Hattie said.

"I struck up a conversation with the widow," Alice said. "About the dreadful sleet and the approach of winter. She's glad to be heading south. The ticket agent interrupted our conversation to get her name for the ticket. Sarah Slater. She's going with those two men to New York."

"Sarah Slater," Hattie repeated. "Murray Wilson told me she made a large withdrawal from the bank yesterday, along with Robert Martin."

"And now they're here together." Alice patted Hattie's satchel. "Looks as if you're headed to New York."

Hattie shook her head. "Not on that train. Luke Blackstone would recognize me."

"Then I'll go." Alice reached for her satchel.

Hattie had to smile at her enthusiasm. "Carrying an empty bag?"

"All right." Letting go of the handle, Alice reached for Hattie's bag. "I'll take yours."

"No," Hattie said firmly. "I don't want you coming up against the likes of Blackstone. And I don't trust that woman."

"She seems friendly enough," Alice said. "Plus she's in mourning. How dangerous could she be?"

"I've seen her before," Hattie said. "She was with John Wilkes Booth. Or at least I think it was her. It's hard to say with the veil."

"So she has poor judgment when it comes to men," Alice said. "Not the first to fit that bill."

"I know it doesn't make sense," Hattie said. "But there was something off about the two of them."

Alice let go of Hattie's bag. "You have a point. Wilkes isn't exactly the sympathetic type. I don't know why he'd go about with a widow."

"And remember what I said about my friend Pauline?"

"That she got poisoned by ginger cakes?"

"Delivered by a veiled lady," Hattie said.

Alice glanced back at the ticket window. "They've moved away from the window. Heading toward the platform." She glanced at the clock. "The eastbound line leaves in ten minutes."

"Don't go, Alice," Hattie said. "We'll leave together tomorrow. You have to go to New York for your engagement anyhow. No one will question your arriving there early."

Alice's face clouded. "You do realize how populated New York is, don't you? I don't see how we'll ever find them there."

"We'll put our heads together," Hattie said. "We'll find a way."

Chapter Twelve

OCTOBER 30, 1864

After two days of wandering New York City, Hattie feared Alice was right. They'd seen no sign of Blackburn, Martin, or the veiled lady.

"Maybe they're no longer in New York." Hattie sank onto her bed in their room at the LaFarge Hotel, next to the Winter Garden Theatre on Broadway. "Maybe they've gone south."

Alice pushed off her slippers. "One thing's for certain. My feet can't take much more aimless walking."

"If only Miss Warne was still here," Hattie said. Arriving in the city, she'd tried to find her former Pinkerton supervisor at the address she'd used last spring. But the flat had been let to someone else, and the person who came to the door said she knew nothing about the previous tenant's whereabouts. After the uninspiring tasks she'd taken on for Mr. Pinkerton in New York, perhaps Miss Warne had moved on to more exciting work.

That had left Hattie with only her determination to rely on, and as she was quickly discovering, determination didn't count for much when searching for three people in a city the size of New York.

"There must be someone who can point us in the right direction," Alice said.

Hattie rubbed the back of her neck, easing out the tension. "I can't think of anyone," she said. "Unless...well, there's John Elliott."

"Your lieutenant," Alice said. "But I don't see what help he'd be from Nashville."

"He might know someone here. Someone with Confederate connections."

Alice smiled. "You don't need an excuse to send him a wire, you know. It's enough to say that you miss him. Heaven knows I'd reach out to George if I knew where he was."

She was right. First thing in the morning, Hattie decided, she'd wire John Elliott.

~ ~ ~

Under gray skies, Hattie set out the next morning for the Western Union building. After a good night's rest, her feet protested only a little, and the thought of connecting with John, even if only through the telegraph wires, lightened her step.

There was something alive about New York, she decided as she proceeded down Broadway. Wagons, carts, carriages, and omnibuses crowded the street, with traffic running rather haphazardly in both directions.

Ahead, she spotted the Western Union building, tall and elegant with a spire at its peak. Crossing the street to reach it was no small feat. She had to dart between horses and drivers that seemed intent only on their destinations.

Like so much else in the city, the telegraph office felt oversized, and yet even at this early hour, it was jammed with people going to and fro from desks where they penned their messages to the windows where they paid for their transmissions.

Hattie stood in line for a desk. In a top hat, the man ahead of her took his time, crossing out and rewriting his words. Satisfied at last, he left, and Hattie took her turn at the desk. In her mind, she'd gone over and over the words she might pen. But now that she stood with the blank form in front of her, she was unsure what to write. She settled on a short, simple message. *In New York City. Need contact here. Send word via W. Union. H.L.*

There was much more she wanted to say, but aside from the expense of each word, there was the problem of telegrams passing through the Army Police Headquarters in Nashville, where John might not appreciate the ribbing he'd get from his colleagues if she wrote from her heart.

Rather than torture their feet again with another fruitless search, Hattie and Alice spent a pleasant afternoon touring the city, traveling from point to point by omnibus. They climbed up the Trinity Church spire, taller even than the Western Union building, where they took in a spectacular view of New York and its harbor. As it turned out, Alice had an affinity for graveyards, and so they strolled through the one beside the church, where they found the markers of such notable figures as Alexander Hamilton.

Returning to Broadway, they stopped in several shops. Alice bought a new bonnet adorned with green ribbons, and Hattie admired a red silk dress but refrained from buying it. Nearing the hotel, Alice wanted to stop at the Winter Garden Theatre, where she'd be performing.

Inside, Hattie saw the theatre was aptly named. Strategically placed tropical plants lent a garden-like illusion despite the pre-winter chill outdoors. Alice took her through the empty auditorium, which in a theatre always hinted at promise and possibility. They crossed the massive arched stage, then proceeded to the manager's office.

"I want to let Edwin know I'm here," Alice said.

The Edwin in question was Edwin Booth. Hattie knew Alice's big break in theatre had come when she'd played alongside Edwin Booth in Baltimore, but she hadn't known he was managing this theatre.

Meeting Edwin, Hattie decided his younger brother John Wilkes was the more handsome of the two. But Edwin struck her as more approachable, perhaps because he was less taken by his own charms.

"My dearest Alice," he said in the clipped voice of an actor who favored the classics. "How good of you to have agreed to perform in our little burlesque." He shook his head. "I've been moving our productions to the Shakespearean, but every now and then, one must give the audience what they want."

"I look forward to the part," Alice said.

"And you've arrived early," Booth said. "A rare behavior in an actor. How was the Montreal season?"

"Splendid," Alice said. "I became reacquainted with an old friend there." Turning to Hattie, she made her introductions. "Hattie Logan, Edwin Booth."

Booth clasped her hand warmly. "A pleasure to meet you, Miss Logan."

"Likewise, Mr. Booth. I look forward to attending the show."

"Come early, and I'll see you have a pass to get in," Booth said. "Any friend of Alice is a friend of mine."

Alice and he exchanged some theatre gossip. Then they said their goodbyes. Booth retreated to his office, and Hattie and Alice left the theatre.

"You didn't tell me Edwin Booth was the manager here," Hattie said.

Alice shrugged. "Didn't think of it. There are Booths everywhere you look among theatre folks. Father, sons, sons-in-law."

"Edwin seems more pleasant than his brother," Hattie said.

"Night and day," Alice said. "Though Wilkes is dashing. I'll give him that."

"Are they close?"

"They have their differences, as brothers do. But they perform together on occasion." Alice stopped to indicate a placard mounted outside the theatre. BOOTH BENEFIT FOR THE SHAKESPEARE STATUE FUND, it read. FRIDAY

EVENING, NOV. 25. JUNIUS BRUTUS, EDWIN, AND
JOHN WILKES BOOTH.

"That's right after your burlesque ends, isn't it?" Hattie asked.

"Yes. It pains Edwin to have to stage burlesques at all. He's a
tragedian at heart. But as he said, the crowd wants what it wants."

They stopped in front of the LaFarge. "Do you suppose it's too
soon to expect a response to my wire?" Hattie asked.

"Not if your lieutenant is as madly in love as I expect he is," Alice
said. "Go on to the telegraph office and check. I'll head upstairs
and freshen up for dinner."

Trying not to get her hopes up, Hattie set off down Broadway
again. John was a busy man. He couldn't drop everything just to
answer her wire. And he might not even have any contacts in New
York.

The street was every bit as crowded as it had been in the morning,
but the energy in the air was subdued, weighed down by the collective weariness of a day's work done. George would be miserable
in a city this big, Hattie thought. She didn't mind the crowds, but
George's talk of forests and seas captivated her. She hoped it would
have the same effect on John Elliott.

She shook her head. No more daydreaming about life after the
war ended. The task at hand was to track down the people who'd
tried to kill George and make sure they harmed no one else.

By the time she reached the Western Union building, the traffic
had thinned considerably, and she was able to cross the street without feeling as if a carriage might run her over at any moment. The
telegraph office was likewise quieter than it had been that morning,

and she had to wait only a few minutes in line to inquire about a telegram.

The clerk shuffled through his alphabetized box. "Logan, Logan," he said aloud. "Ah, here it is. To H. Logan, New York. From J. Elliott, Nashville. That's what you're after?"

She nodded, taking the yellow envelope from his outstretched hand. She stepped away from the counter and opened the flap, doing her best to ignore the trembling of her fingers.

Frederick Curtis is your man. 221 Water St. Headed S. Tenn. Col. Truesdail to assist in my absence.

Seeing how John had signed his message, her heart thrummed.

Fondly, J.E.

She returned the half-sheet to the envelope and slipped it into her purse. She was glad for the information about Mr. Curtis. But she didn't like the idea of John heading to South Tennessee. She knew from the papers that Confederate guerillas led by General Bedford Forrest were running raids in that part of the state. Even if certain townspeople were less than friendly toward Union officials, John would be far safer in Nashville.

~ ~ ~

The next morning, Hattie and Alice set out for the Water Street address John had provided. They rode the omnibus, the address being across the bridge on the Brooklyn side of the river. It took them to a four-story brick building. The sign beneath the arched entryway read *Curtis and Company, Export and Import.* Another trading business, Hattie thought, remembering the building she'd seen the veiled lady enter with John Wilkes Booth back in Montreal.

Inside, Hattie inquired with the clerk about Mr. Curtis. At first, the man tried to put them off, but Alice turned on her charms. She told him they were shirttail relations visiting New York, and their trip would be incomplete without at least saying hello to their cousin.

Finally, the clerk relented, taking their names and leading them into a first-floor office. "Mr. Curtis," he said. "Your cousins are here. Miss Hattie Logan and Miss Alice Gray."

The man behind the desk looked up. His face was long and thin, and he looked to be in his thirties, his hairline receding and his chin clean-shaven. "Cousins, you say?"

"On your mother's side," Alice said.

"From Tennessee," Hattie said. "Our brother sent us. John Elliott, recently of Nashville."

His face relaxed. "Ah, John Elliott. Now I see the connection. Although I must say, you two are the fairer of the family."

Curtis dismissed the clerk, then rose to greet them. "You've brought a message from Nashville?" he said.

"No message," Hattie said. "We're trying to locate three Confederates who left Montreal for New York earlier in the week. Robert Martin. Luke Blackstone. Sarah Slater. Lieutenant Elliott suggested you might be of help."

He eyed them sharply as if assessing again what sort of business they were about. "I didn't think Elliott's work extended to Montreal."

"It doesn't," Hattie said. "I was visiting my brother there."

"He was nearly poisoned to death," Alice said.

Curtis's eyes widened. "And these three you're after had some part in that?"

"We have reason to think so," Hattie said. "And it's possible they intend to harm others."

"Maybe even here in New York," Alice said.

Curtis looked from one to the other of the women. "Step outside with me, ladies," he said.

They followed him not just out of the office but onto the street. He walked them briskly to the corner, which they had to themselves.

"Halfway down the next block," he said, tipping his head slightly. "You'll find 178 ½ Water Street. A trading company, or so the signage says, but every Confederate who comes through New York makes a stop there." He offered what seemed a rueful smile. "Not that my business is entirely legitimate either. I carry contraband to the South. Returning north, I carry information the Confederates would rather I not divulge."

Alice folded her arms at her chest. "You're a spy," she said. "I thought as much."

"I like to think of it as trading in secrets. But, yes, despite my dealings with the South, my allegiance lies with the Union. I daresay that the folks who own that building down the street are rather firmly in the other camp."

"Would they let us inside?" Hattie asked.

"Not without some convincing bona fides," Curtis said. "They've always got a man on watch."

"There must be some way in," Alice said.

"I'm afraid not," Curtis said. Then his expression brightened. "But I've another idea. I propose we dine together tonight, ladies. We are cousins, are we not? Seven o'clock. Delmonico's. You know it?"

"Everyone knows Delmonico's," Alice said. "Best place to eat in New York."

"And a special favorite of the Confederates," Curtis said. "With any luck, we'll find your trio there."

Hattie hoped he was right.

Chapter Thirteen

NOVEMBER 1, 1864

D elmonico's took up three floors of an elegant triangular building on a street corner in the city's financial district. With a whispered request to the maître d', Mr. Curtis secured a table on the second floor. Nearby, a Reserved sign was prominently displayed on a large round table.

"This is where our sort of people congregate," Curtis said as they took their seats, speaking in a stronger drawl than he'd used earlier in the day.

"Cloth-covered tables. Printed menus. It's as if we'd been whisked away to Paris." Dressed to the hilt, her face powdered and her hair swept up beneath her new bonnet, the glint in Alice's eyes suggested she was enjoying herself.

"You do have good taste, Cousin Fred." Like Alice, Hattie spoke with a lilt suggesting she'd just stepped off a plantation.

She studied the menu, hoping her eyes didn't betray her shock. Fifteen cents for a baked potato. That would pay for an entire meal back in Nashville. But she supposed such prices were to be expected in a restaurant where the waiters were gloved and the lights from the glass chandeliers glowed with a brilliance that seemed to rival the sun.

"Chicken a la Keene," Alice exclaimed. "Named after the famous actress, I presume. That's what I'll have."

"An excellent choice," Curtis said. "Though Delmonico's is also known for their steak. Would you care to try it, Hattie?"

"I hate to seem the country bumpkin," she said. "But the prices are rather astounding."

Curtis laughed. "My treat, remember. It's not often I get to dine with two lovely women." His tone was light and upbeat. He was enjoying this charade.

"And you've saved us from the dreadful tedium of the ladies' dining room," Alice said. "I'm ever so grateful for that."

The waiter came for their order, which Curtis insisted must include a bottle of wine. "Delmonico's has the best wine selection in all of New York," he said as the waiter departed. "It would be criminal to dine here without sampling a bottle."

Curtis's business must be booming, Hattie thought, like so many other businesses in New York. The profiteers would probably just as soon the war went on forever. But Curtis wasn't in this entirely for the money. From what he'd said, every transaction he conducted in Richmond was fraught with peril. Military men could legitimately traffic in secrets. For civilians on both sides, it was a crime punishable by death.

The waiter returned with their wine. Curtis poured them each a glass. They talked of the upcoming elections, a subject of much interest throughout the city. With Union forces finally taking control of the Shenandoah Valley, Mr. Lincoln's prospects had improved considerably. But from the chatter Hattie was able to overhear from surrounding tables, Southern sympathizers were still holding out hope for the president's defeat.

Much as Hattie wanted Lincoln to prevail, the setting required she speak as a Southerner would. "An incumbent hasn't been elected president in more than thirty years," she said, citing a fact John Elliott, who tended toward pessimism, had shared with her.

"And under that butcher Grant, the Union has suffered far more casualties than earlier in the war," Curtis said. "Voters can't possibly like that."

"I sense a feeling of general unrest here in the North," Alice said. "I hope it won't extend beyond the ballot box."

"It's peace we all want," Hattie said. "We've suffered enough."

"I wonder, cousins, how the votes of Tennessee can be counted, with so much unsettled there," Curtis said.

At that moment, the maitre d' brought a group of five men to the reserved table. Hattie immediately recognized the tall man with the goatee and slumped chest. Robert Martin.

She glanced at Alice, who nodded slightly, indicating she'd noticed him, too.

Curtis slapped his hand, palm down, on the table. "By Jove, there's my friend John Potts Brown. If you'll excuse me, ladies, I'd like to say hello."

Hattie and Alice assured him this was fine.

Rising, he strode to the reserved table. "Why, if it isn't Fred Curtis," said the stoutest of the men seated there.

Hattie listened intently as the stout man introduced his dinner companions to Mr. Curtis. In addition to Robert Martin, there was another young man with dark, deep-set eyes, introduced as an officer named John Headley. Beside him sat Robert Kennedy, a stocky man, young and bearded. Between Kennedy and John Potts Brown sat a thin, older man with wild gray hair and a scraggly beard. Learning his name, James McMaster, Mr. Curtis remarked on his editorial work at the *Freeman's Journal*, a widely read newspaper with Southern leanings.

After chatting briefly with John Potts Brown about the state of shipping and the transport of cotton, Mr. Curtis left the men to their menus and returned to his seat.

"Mr. Brown runs a stellar trading business only a few blocks from here," he told the women. At the other table, Brown's lips turned in a smile, indicating he'd heard.

Hattie fell silent. Sipping from her glass of wine, she could hear quite a lot of the discussion at the next table. No doubt reassured by the presence of Curtis, the men spoke freely.

"I reckon we can muster 25,000 New Yorkers who hate Lincoln as much as we do," said the newspaperman, McMaster.

"The National Flag of the Confederacy is going to look right pretty waving over City Hall," said the stout man, Kennedy.

"A warning of what will befall every Northern city if the present system of war continues," McMaster said. "New York is worth twenty Richmonds"

Martin held out both hands, palms out. "Gentlemen, gentlemen. Let's not get ahead of ourselves. We've got only a week to finalize our plans. Headley, the chemicals are ready?"

Chemicals. Hattie thought of Luke Blackstone and his Greek fire, leaving Montreal with Robert Martin and Sarah Slater.

"To be retrieved Monday night," Headley said. "One hundred forty-four vials."

Kennedy chuckled. "Enough to get half the town burning, I'll wager."

"Just leave the docks alone," Curtis's friend Brown said. "We can't have commerce interrupted."

McMaster slapped his back. "We know, we know. Money to be made. But I hope you realize when this thing is done and the Confederacy finally gets the recognition it deserves, your business may not be quite as lucrative as it is now."

"Commerce adjusts," Brown said, his tone testy. "What about the men? Are they ready?"

"Six of the most trusted in our local temple, standing by," Mc-Master said.

Temples, Hattie knew, were how the Sons of Liberty were organized. Formerly known as the Knights of the Golden Circle and the American Knights, the Sons of Liberty wanted to expand slavery. They'd been behind John Beall's plot to seize a Federal gunboat and free thousands of Confederate prisoners. Now it seemed they were up to no good in New York. The question was what to do about it.

~ ~ ~

Only after they'd finished their meal and left Delmonico's did Hattie and her companions have a chance to compare notes on what they'd overheard. The details had been scant, the conspirators having moved on to other topics. But Hattie, Alice, and Fred Curtis agreed they'd heard enough to be alarmed.

"It sounds as if McMaster is high up in the Sons of Liberty's organization," Hattie said as they approached the omnibus stop. "And that means violence, even against civilians, to achieve his aims."

"Like the St. Albans raid," Alice said darkly.

"With a week to get ready," Curtis said.

"Which puts their plot, whatever it is, right on Election Day. One-hundred forty-four vials of Greek fire, 144 buildings burned."

"The incendiary method your friend perfected," Alice said.

"Luke Blackstone is hardly my friend," Hattie said. "But yes, he's the one behind Greek fire. I saw a demonstration of it once, burning on a river back in Indiana. Water has no effect on it."

"Manhattan has burned before," Curtis said. "Three times, as a matter of fact. If they start 144 fires simultaneously, there's no way the fire department can keep up. Especially if they target the camphene and turpentine distilleries. Or the lumberyards. Or the gas works."

"I expect the police will be interested in learning about this," Alice said.

"Don't be so sure," Curtis said. "The commissioner is quick to discount anything he attributes to rumors."

"But we heard them ourselves," Alice said. "And we can name names." She paused. "One of them struck me as familiar. But I can't think from where."

"Two of the men at that table—Brown and McMaster—have a lot of influence in this city," Curtis said. "Good luck getting them hauled in for questioning."

"The police could question the others," Alice said.

"Where would they find them in a city this size?" Hattie shook her head. "If they succeed, they'll create chaos. Even if Lincoln prevails in the election, his victory could be called into question. We need to go straight to the Federal authorities."

"That doesn't sound any easier than convincing the local police," Alice said.

"It isn't," Hattie said. "Unless you know the right person."

Chapter Fourteen

NOVEMBER 3, 1864

Returning to the town where she'd first worked as a spy, Hattie found herself in the last place she'd ever have expected to be—at the doorstep of Lucy Hamilton's house in a high-toned Washington neighborhood. On this unseasonably cold November day, the sound of the knocker was loud and foreboding against the solid oak door. But it produced the desired result. The door swung open, revealing a gray-haired, dark-skinned servant.

"I've come to see Miss Hamilton," Hattie said. "Miss Lucy Hamilton," she added, uncertain whether Lucy had sisters. "I'm a..." She searched for the best descriptor. Not friend. Lucy would laugh out loud at that. "An acquaintance."

"She expecting you?" the servant asked,

"No, but if you'll advise her that Miss Hattie Logan is at the door, I'm sure she'll want to see me."

This Hattie said with more confidence than she felt. In all likeli-
hood, Lucy would turn her away. There was more than bad blood
between them. But Lucy's family was better connected with Secretary of War Edwin Stanton than anyone Hattie knew, and Hattie
believed Mr. Stanton was the person best positioned to act on the
information she was delivering.

"Step inside," the servant said. "Before you catch a chill. You can
wait in the foyer while I check with Miss Hamilton."

Hattie gladly came in from the cold. The Hamilton's foyer was
all gilt and crystal, attesting to the family's wealth and status.
Lucy's father was a prominent New Hampshire politician who'd
brought his family to Washington City at the start of the war,
positioning himself for any wartime advantages that might come
his way.

Lucy had worked with Hattie in Allen Pinkerton's War Department mailroom. There, she was forever reminding the other girls
of how important her father was and how she was working not for
money but for the Union cause.

The grandfather clock at the end of the hall ticked away the
minutes as Hattie waited. Weary from the day's train ride from
New York, she shifted foot to foot, wondering how it was that in
the home of someone as influential as Lucy's father, a guest was
not invited into the parlor to sit. An uninvited guest, she reminded
herself. She was lucky to have gotten past the door at all.

The figure who finally came down the stairs was not the servant
but Lucy herself, resplendent in a blue gown that looked as if it
had come straight from Godey's Lady's Book. In her drab plaid

skirt, Hattie felt dowdy. But then Lucy always had a way of making herself the center of attention, whether in dress, speech, or action.

"Dearest Hattie," Lucy said. Reaching the bottom of the stairs, she came toward Hattie with open arms. She smelled of jasmine, a scent she'd favored back when they'd been cooped up in Mr. Pinkerton's tiny mailroom together.

Setting her manicured fingers lightly on Hattie's shoulders, Lucy brushed her cheek with a kiss. "What a pleasant surprise. I was just about to have tea. You must join me."

Without waiting for a response, Lucy turned and ascended the stairs, sashaying in a way that Hattie suspected had drawn the eye of many a young man. Hattie followed, treading softly. She thought she'd been ready to face Lucy again. Nearly three years had passed since she'd betrayed Hattie and Thom Welton. Hattie had told herself it wasn't fair to blame Lucy, who'd crumpled easily after being arrested herself. But now, seeing how readily Lucy had slipped back into a life of ease, her ire rose.

Anger was not conducive to her purpose, Hattie reminded herself as she trailed Lucy into an upstairs sitting room. They each took a chair. On the round table between them, the service was already set out, including a plate of frosted petit fours. With graceful elegance, Lucy poured the tea. *She has matured,* Hattie thought. *I should concede that point at least.*

"It's good of you to see me," Hattie said. "I rarely go calling unannounced. But I'm only in Washington for a short while."

"How could I not see you, after all we've been through together." Lucy sipped from her delicate porcelain cup. "Dreadful, how things ended for Mr. Welton."

"Yes." It took all Hattie's restraint not to point out that things might have taken an altogether turn had Lucy kept her mouth shut about their spy work. But Thom was gone now, and there was no rewriting the past.

"I know how you felt about him," Lucy said. "It must have been difficult for you to move on."

This was Lucy's idea of sympathy, Hattie supposed, but it came off as criticism. She chose to ignore it.

"You've moved on quite nicely, it seems." Picking up her teacup, Hattie sipped her tea. She thought of reaching for one of the pretty little cakes, but Lucy hadn't touched them.

Lucy sighed in the dramatic manner Hattie remembered. "Dull as dirt here in Washington," she said. "Mother drags me along on her social calls, and I must endure the interminable chattering of her lady friends. If not for my suitors, I should go stark raving mad." Her eyes sparkled, begging Hattie to ask for details.

Hattie complied, knowing that Lucy's favorite topic was herself. "Have you several at one time, then?"

Lucy laughed. "But of course. It's the only way. Keep them vying for your attention. It's quite a pleasant diversion." She lowered her voice in a conspiratorial manner. "I do have my favorites though. I just don't let on." She nodded at a large bouquet of white roses atop a side table. "Only yesterday, Robert Lincoln sent me flowers."

"The president's son," Hattie said.

"The very same," Lucy said. "He's a bit awkward, to tell the truth. Like his father. But I do him the favor of a dance now and again." She eyed Hattie the way she used to in the mailroom when she had a bit of juicy gossip to share. "Can I trust you with a secret?"

"I've kept quite a few," Hattie said. "Including yours."

If Lucy took offense at this, she didn't show it. "One of my suitors has been hinting at marriage. I expect by spring we'll be engaged."

"Who would that be?" Hattie asked.

Lucy looked shocked. "Why, that's the part that's a secret." Her eyes narrowed, and she leaned close. "But I'll tell you this. He's quite handsome. And famous."

"How exciting," Hattie said. "I shall have to watch the papers for your wedding announcement. Unless you plan to keep that secret too."

Lucy smiled primly. "Mother would never allow that. But look at me, talking only of myself. What of you? Have you resettled back in—was it Illinois?"

"Indiana," Hattie said. "I've returned now and again. And I've traveled a bit. Most recently, I was in New York. Before that, Montreal."

"My, my," Lucy said. "You do get around. Don't tell me you're still with the Pinkerton Agency."

Hattie shook her head. "But I do pick up the occasional bit of intelligence. That's the reason I'm here. I have some information that needs to reach someone at the highest levels of government. I thought you and your father might help."

Reaching in her purse, Hattie took out a slip of folded paper and handed it to Lucy.

Lucy unfolded the paper. Her lips moved as she read silently what Hattie had written. Looking up, she said, "A Confederate plot to set New York City afire. How did you come by that information?"

"Through a series of events," Hattie said vaguely. "I'm quite confident it's accurate. Can you persuade your father to deliver that paper to Mr. Stanton?"

"But of course." Lucy refolded the paper. "He'll put a stop to that nonsense."

"I surely hope so," Hattie said. Lucy's self-importance aside, she was the surest conduit Hattie had for reaching the Secretary of War. She prayed that would be sufficient to save New York.

Chapter Fifteen

NOVEMBER 7, 1864

S tanding on a balcony of the Lafarge Hotel, Hattie pulled her cloak tight. The night was clear and cold, yet the stars overhead were no match for the lights that filled the street below. Acrid smoke rose from the scene, stinging Hattie's nose.

"Can you believe all those people?" Alice said, standing beside Hattie.

"There was a similar parade in Nashville last month," Hattie said, recalling how warm and safe she'd felt standing beside John Elliott. "Only that was a parade of Negroes seeking their emancipation."

The faces of those now marching down Broadway, bedecked in oilcloth capes and carrying torches, were white. Some carried banners announcing their purpose, to encourage voters to choose Mr. Lincoln at the ballot box tomorrow.

On a balcony to the right of where Hattie and Alice stood, an older man scowled at the procession. "What those folks need is a bullet in the belly," he said to the woman standing beside him.

Judging by the crutches and limping of some of the marching men, they'd already taken bullets for their country. Hattie was tempted to point this out, but there was no sense arguing with someone so firmly in the Confederate camp.

From the balcony to her left came a friendlier comment, spoken by a man in a wide-brimmed hat. "Brings to mind a prairie fire," he announced to no one in particular. Doffing his hat, he swept it in the air. "The prairies are on fire for Lincoln."

"I'm just glad the town's not on fire," Alice said in a low voice.

"As am I," Hattie said softly.

Much as she disliked Lucy Hamilton, she'd come through. Yesterday, detachments of Union soldiers, rumored to number in the thousands, had descended on New York. Under the command of General Butler, known as "Beast Butler" for the stronghold he'd put on New Orleans earlier in the war, the troops had cordoned off Manhattan. Guards surrounded Central Park's water reservoir, and infantrymen on ferryboats were monitoring marine traffic on the Hudson and East Rivers.

"There could still be trouble tomorrow," Alice said. "Since it's the voting they aim to disrupt. I'd feel safer if the men we saw at Delmonico's were arrested."

"Robert Martin especially," Hattie said. "More than ever, I suspect him of trying to kill George."

"What about your veiled lady?" Alice said. "Sarah Slater. I thought you suspected her."

"I do. But who knows where she is now."

"We could still go to the police about Martin and the others," Alice said.

Hattie shook her head. "It appears Mr. Curtis was right. The papers quoted the police commissioner as saying there's no reason for General Butler and his troops to be here. He says the threat is only the product of someone's wild imaginings."

"Then we set him straight," Alice said.

"Not him," Hattie said. "General Butler. I intend to see him tomorrow, whatever it takes"

~ ~ ~

Going out the next morning, Hattie sensed the election day tension in the air. The course of the nation—and quite possibly the outcome of the war—hung in the balance.

She prayed the presence of the soldiers on the city's street corners would be enough to discourage the conspirators from disrupting the election. But she was determined to stop them entirely, and that meant somehow gaining an audience with General Butler.

She began by approaching the soldiers standing watch, asking where she might find the general. But none took her seriously. She was glad she'd discouraged Alice from coming along. Rehearsals for the burlesque had begun, and this barrage of rejections would not have been worth her rising early.

Lacking information, Hattie had little choice but to guess where she might find the general. She caught an omnibus headed south, passing through the financial district to the southern tip of Manhattan. Getting off near the harbor, she proceeded to the slip for the Governor's Island ferry. Only last spring, on a dreary gray day, she'd met with Kate Warne here

Today the air was crisp, the sun shining and the sky a brilliant shade of blue. The harbor looked as busy as ever, vessels coming and going from the docks. Some, she now knew, might be carrying cotton, owing to the secret arrangement George had described.

How complicated war could be, she thought. And yet at the personal level, it was simple. Devotion to a cause. Sacrifice. Loves lost and, on the rarest of occasions, loves found.

Her wait for the ferry was short. As it pulled from the dock, she watched Manhattan's skyline recede. Ahead, Governor's Island came into view. The ferry landed near Castle Williams, a circular fortress at the island's tip. Built of red sandstone, Castle Williams was part of a system of fortifications designed to protect New York. Its curved walls featured only the smallest of windows, allowing soldiers to fire on enemies approaching from the water.

These days, Hattie knew, Castle Williams housed prisoners. It also seemed a likely spot for General Butler to keep watch over the city.

Getting off the ferry, she strode confidently toward a guard who looked older than the rest. Her choice was intentional. Younger guards, she'd found, tended to be the most zealous in their duties.

But as she approached, she feared she'd misjudged this one. Eyes narrowing, he looked her up and down. "State your business," he said.

"I've a message for General Butler," she said. "Relevant to his assignment in New York."

"The general takes his marching orders from General Grant," the guard said. "And last I heard, Grant don't wear a skirt."

"But I know who's behind the plot to set New York on fire," she said.

"Course you do. Your husband, was it? Caught him cheating, did you?"

Hattie refrained from stamping her foot, a show of annoyance that would only affirm his belief that she was some irrational female with a personal grievance.

"I know none of the men personally," she said. "I overheard them making their plans. How is it, do you think, that the orders were given for Butler to bring soldiers here?"

The guard straightened. "Orders came direct from Mr. Stanton. Not from some little filly like yourself."

Two little fillies, actually. But it was clear Hattie could say nothing would get through to this guard.

"It seems my journey has been in vain," she said. "Good day, sir."

Not quickly enough to miss the guard's satisfied *harumph,* she started back toward the dock. Glancing over her shoulder, she saw the guard engaged in conversation with a younger soldier. *Gloating over how he turned away a pesky female,* she thought.

Seizing the opportunity, she veered back toward the path that encircled Castle Williams. Halfway around the structure, she came to an unguarded door. Pressing herself against it, she jiggled the door's handle.

To her surprise, it opened easily. She slipped inside. No prisoners would be kept behind an unlocked door. That meant there was a good chance one of the hallways before her led to the officers' quarters.

"You there!" a voice cried out. "Stop!"

The younger guard she'd seen talking to the older one came hurrying her direction. Reasoning that officers would be housed on the Castle's top floor, allowing them a view, she took the stairs as quickly as her skirts allowed. The stairs went up in a spiral, and within moments, she was out of view of the guard.

Pressed against the stairwell, she paused, listening for the guard's footsteps. She heard them not on the stairs but on the stone floor below. *He thinks I'm headed for the prison,* she thought. *To aid a prisoner.*

Treading softly, she continued up the stairs to a landing. Ahead was an open doorway, guarded by a sentry.

Taking a deep breath, Hattie approached the sentry. "I've come to see General Butler. On behalf of the Army Police. The Army Police of Nashville." She thought John Elliott would forgive her for this exaggeration. "I know the Army of the Cumberland is not General Butler's concern," she added quickly. "But I've brought a message for him."

The sentry frowned, looking her over. "A courier, are you?"

"That's right," she said. Even her own brother could fathom a female courier easier than he could a female spy.

The sentry held out his open hand. "Give me the message. I'll see that he gets it."

Hattie straightened. "I'm to deliver it in person. Directly to General Butler."

The sentry shook his head. "Insistent," he said under his breath. "Wait here."

He disappeared through the doorway. Waiting for his return, Hattie rehearsed what she planned to say. Direct. Logical. That was the best approach.

Moments later, the sentry returned. "The General will see you," he said brusquely. "For a moment only. He's a busy man."

"Of course. Thank you."

She slipped past him. The room she entered was spare, furnished only with a desk and chair. A fire burned in the grate, giving the air a modicum of warmth. Hands clasped behind his back, the general stood at the room's single small window, looking out toward the city.

"General Butler," she said, for he seemed not to have noticed her.

He turned. If he bore any resemblance to a beast, Hattie thought it must be a trussed hog. His barrel chest extended through his belly, and his coat fit so snugly that his brass buttons looked ready to pop. His eyes, small and deep-set, added to the effect.

He stared at her blankly, and she felt obliged to continue speaking. "I've come about the conspiracy, sir. The plans to set fire to New York. I have information about the men who planned the attack."

"I was told you had a message from Nashville."

"I came from Nashville, yes. But my message is about New York. The names of five men involved in planning the attack that brought you here."

Butler waved his hand toward the window. "I see no attack. Do you?"

"No, sir. But that was the point of your coming, wasn't it? To ensure that the Confederates' plans to ignite fires throughout the city were interrupted?"

He sighed. "I'm inclined to side with the Superintendent of Police. The whole thing appears to be a hoax."

"I assure you it isn't," Hattie said. "I overheard the men planning it. They spoke of 25,000 men setting off 144 firebombs. The plotters include two men of prominence here in New York. There's John Potts—"

"The police have pursued all leads," he said, cutting her off.

"They haven't pursued this one," she said. "It would be in all the papers if they had. These men need to be brought to justice, sir. Look at how they've diverted your troops from battle, just by the mere threat of what they were plotting."

"I appreciate your concern, ma'am," the general said. "I'm sure you're an asset to the Army Police back in Nashville. But you're wasting your time here."

Hattie glanced at his desk, strewn with papers. "Perhaps if I wrote down the names, you might find cause to look into them."

"Suit yourself." He turned back to the window, resuming the position she'd found him in.

Crossing the room, she took a scrap of paper and a pen from the desk. On the paper, she wrote in a firm, clear hand the names of the five men from Delmonico's. She drew a set of double lines under *Robert Martin*. Beside his name, she wrote *Confederate funds funneled through Bank of Ontario.*

She set down the pen and the note. She hoped the general would act on what she'd written. But he didn't seem much inclined to.

She mustn't feel discouraged, she told herself as she slipped from the room. She'd done all she could. But her unease lingered. So many men with evil intentions. And at least one woman too.

Chapter Sixteen

NOVEMBER 11, 1864

Hattie found Delmonico's every bit as elegant the second time around, even if this time she and Alice had to foot the bill.

But the warm satisfaction of a good meal did little to offset her discouragement. Coming here had been a last-ditch effort. General Butler had pulled out his troops the day after she'd talked with him. No arrests had been made.

After that, Hattie had gone to see Frederick Curtis's office, hoping he might suggest how the conspirators might be brought to justice. But the clerk there said Mr. Curtis was in Richmond and not due back until the end of the month.

So, Hattie had proposed to Alice that they go one more time to Delmonico's, hoping at least one of the men they'd seen there before would be there again. Alice had readily agreed. As before, they'd played the part of Southern ladies. But without Mr. Curtis, they were forced to eat in the ladies' dining room, limiting their view of other diners.

From conversations all around, Hattie heard mostly complaints about the election results. In the end, Mr. Lincoln had won in a landslide, defeating his opponent with a strong percentage of both the popular and electoral votes.

"The tyrant prevails," a lady at the next table said.

"The South simply must preserve its independence," her companion said. "Else we'll lose every civil right our men have died to protect."

Hattie couldn't have been happier about the election's outcome. She couldn't pretend to know all the ins and outs of the political landscape, but she appreciated Mr. Lincoln's having emancipated the slaves, even if only in the South. And she had fond memories of the president having spoken to her and her friend Anne along Pennsylvania Avenue during their time at Pinkerton's.

As they rose to leave, Alice said, "There's no place like Delmonico's in Nashville, I'll wager."

"True," Hattie said.

"I don't know why you're in such a rush to leave here with your lieutenant off doing who knows what at some fort," Alice said. "You could stay another two weeks here, keep me company during my engagement. By then your lieutenant will likely have returned."

"I hope so." Hattie had lain awake nights, worrying about John out in the field. Only yesterday, she'd read in the papers that Confederate General Hood's troops had crossed the Alabama-Ten-

nessee border and were advancing north, aided by Bedford Forrest's guerillas. She didn't want John caught up in the fighting.

Exiting the ladies' dining room, Hattie and Alice slowed their
steps, studying the diners at the tables they passed.

"A lost cause, I fear," Hattie said under her breath.

She turned to Alice. But Alice had left her. As quickly and
resolutely as her skirts allowed, she was weaving among the tables.

Her heart thumping in her chest, Hattie followed. A waiter
glanced at her curiously, but he did nothing to stop her, perhaps
assuming she was meeting a gentleman here.

Alice neared a table where three people were seated. One was
a slim, clean-shaven, pale-eyed young man. Another was a pretty,
dark-eyed woman—a stranger, it seemed, and yet there was something familiar in the way she carried herself.

The third, his hand entwined with the woman's, was no
stranger. He was John Wilkes Booth. Wilkes, as Alice called him.

Looking up, Wilkes let go of the woman's hand. He smiled sar-
donically as Alice barreled toward them. "Ah, here's an old friend
come to say hello."

Alice set a fisted hand on her hip. "I have nothing to say to you."
She turned to the woman. "Don't be swayed by his charms. He'll
leave you as sure as he left me."

Coming alongside Alice, Hattie took hold of her arm. "Alice, this
isn't the time or place to air your grievances."

"One should not presume," the woman at the table said. With a
manner that was both direct and haughty, she spoke in an accent
that sounded vaguely French.

"I'll presume as I please," Alice said. "It's for your own good."

The other man at the table shifted in his chair. "You do seem to leave a trail of sorrowful women in your wake, Wilkes."

"Don't mistake me for sorrowful." Alice turned her gaze on Wilkes, her eyes venomous. "You turned me out like a dog. I regret every tear I wasted on you."

At nearby tables, conversations ceased. Heads turned, the other diners getting up in the drama.

Hattie tugged Alice's arm. "You've made your point. Leave them to dine in peace."

"You think he gave me a moment's peace, the scoundrel," Alice said, her voice trembling.

Wilkes stood, his chair scraping the floor. "I'll not have my honor besmirched."

Hattie met his gaze. "Whatever honor is besmirched has been your own doing."

His eyes flashed. "I don't recall asking your opinion."

"No more than I asked for your advances the last time we met," Hattie said.

"How dare you make such an accusation," Wilkes said. "I've never met you before in my life."

His words stung. "You most surely have," she said as evenly as she could manage. "Come along, Alice. He's not worth your breath."

Alice returned her attention to the woman. Following her gaze, Hattie realized she had in fact seen the woman before. Twice, as a matter of fact. But on each of those occasions, a veil had obscured Sarah Slater's high cheekbones and dark eyes. The woman who'd withdrawn substantial sums from the Bank of Ontario. The woman they'd seen with Luke Blackstone and Robert Martin.

"When he leaves you for a sixteen-year-old, don't say I didn't warn you," Alice said to Sarah Slater.

Wilkes leaned forward, his gaze shifting from Alice to Hattie and back to Alice. "Another word out of either one of you, and I'll have you thrown out of this establishment."

Looking up, Hattie saw that the maitre d' was already striding toward them, his attention no doubt roused by their raised voices. "Come along, Alice," she said. "You've said your piece."

Alice stood a moment, eyes locked with her former lover. Then she turned and followed Hattie out of the restaurant.

After the heated scene, Hattie welcomed the cool, stiff breeze they encountered as they started down the sidewalk.

"Sorry," Alice said. "I had no intention of making a scene. I knew Wilkes would be in New York soon. But I'd hoped to avoid him. When I saw him hand in hand with that woman, I couldn't contain my anger."

"He wronged you," Hattie said. "You have every right to be angry."

"If he'd left me civilly, it wouldn't have been so bad," Alice said. "But I caught him writing love letters to a girl who was only sixteen. Then I discovered he'd bought her a gold ring, set with pearls and inscribed with their initials. This for a girl he scarcely knew, and all the while he was carrying on with me. What a fool I was. It rankles me, how women fawn over him."

"He was none too happy about you pointing out his flaws just now," Hattie said.

Alice offered a weak smile. "The same goes for you. You touched a nerve with him."

"He's a man who needs to be put in his place," Hattie said.

"I just hope you haven't made an enemy on my behalf," Alice said.

Hattie linked arms with her. "Men like him are all bluster," she said. "What intrigues me is the woman. Did you recognize her?"

"No," Alice said. "Should I have?"

"It's hard to know for certain," Hattie said. "But I think she's Sarah Slater."

A look of recognition came over Alice. "From the train station in Montreal. I was so focused on Wilkes I didn't notice. But now that you mention it—with those dark eyes and high cheekbones, she does look like the woman I spoke with in Montreal. What a ninny I am! She could've led us to Martin."

"You mustn't fault yourself. If it hadn't been for you giving Wilkes a piece of your mind, we'd never have recognized her."

They neared the omnibus stop, the gas lamps hissing overhead. In the distant sky, a bank of clouds closed over a nearly full moon.

"You said you saw them together before," Alice said. "Wilkes and Sarah Slater."

Hattie nodded. "When I first came to Montreal, I saw them at the bank together. They left with a cheque and a large sum of money. I was curious, so I followed them."

"Wilkes didn't recognize you?"

Hattie shook her head. "I stayed back from them. Plus it's been more than three years since he happened upon me backstage. The lighting was dim."

"Where did they go?" Alice said. "Him and Sarah Slater, I mean?"

"Into some sort of shipping establishment."

"George told us about all the trade the South conducts through Montreal," Alice said. "Maybe Wilkes is involved. He fancies himself an investor. Last I knew, he'd put a good deal of money into Pennsylvania oil." Alice clapped her hand over her mouth.

"What is it?" Hattie said.

"Last summer," Alice said, uncovering her mouth. "Wilkes and I were in Boston. He introduced me to some of his associates. They were all in Boston for some sort of meeting. I figured it was about the oil. But I just realized—remember me saying I recognized one of the men from our last time at Delmonico's?"

"Right. But you couldn't place him."

"John Headley. He was at that Boston meeting with Wilkes."

Turning thoughts over in her mind, Hattie was silent a moment. "It could be Headley has an interest in both oil and plots against New York. Or it could be that Boston meeting wasn't about oil at all."

"That's what I'm thinking now," Alice said. "I wish I'd asked more questions. But things were already so rocky between Wilkes and me." She glanced over at Hattie. "But I know one thing for certain. Unlike his brother Edwin, Wilkes despises everything about the North. He should be watched."

"We shouldn't jump to conclusions," Hattie said. "He's entitled to his opinions."

Alice raised an eyebrow. "And his associations with a known conspirator?"

"A conspirator whose activities have been curtailed."

This was good logic, Hattie knew. Better than chasing after wisps of suspicion. And if she still felt unsettled, well, this was war, after all.

Chapter Seventeen

NOVEMBER 25, 1864

After their encounter with John Wilkes Booth, Alice was even more insistent that Hattie stay on in New York. It wasn't so much that she feared running into her former lover, she said, but for moral support. Having confronted him, she feared her fellow actors would turn against her. The Booths were revered in certain circles, and if Wilkes was known as something of a womanizer, many took it as a display of his prowess.

"You could stay till the burlesque is over," Alice told Hattie. "Then I won't feel so alone. And with your lieutenant off in the hinterlands, you've no reason to hurry back to Nashville."

"For all I know, he's back in Nashville already," Hattie said.

"Then send a wire," Alice urged. "If he's back, you can leave on the first train. If not, you can stay here with me."

Happy to have an excuse to inquire about John, Hattie wired Colonel Truesdail of Nashville's Army Police.

Year's end. That was all Truesdail said in his reply.

Hattie counted off the days on the calendar. Five weeks. She'd waited this long. She could wait a while longer. Some women had been waiting years for their men to come home from battle.

She told Alice she'd stay through her show. After that, Alice would go on to Buffalo to visit her mother, and Hattie would go—where?

To Indianapolis, she decided. If she couldn't be in John Elliott's arms, she could at least surround herself with the love of her friend Anne Duncan and her family.

In the meantime, she needed to distract herself from her longing for his return. When the burlesque opened, Hattie went every night. The burlesque, called Fra Diavolo, was quite droll. Sitting in the balcony section, she watched the theatregoers watching the show. She whispered lines to herself, learning some of the smaller parts just for fun.

There had been a time when she'd thought she'd like to live as Alice did, performing night after night before an adoring crowd. But Hattie had seen enough of the drawbacks of that way of living to give her pause. And these days, even Alice seemed to have tired of it. When this run was over, she'd committed to one more show, a benefit for John McCullough, who'd starred with her in Montreal. After that, she intended to go West and settle down with George.

Fra Diavola ended the night before Thanksgiving. At the curtain call, Alice bowed again and again, along with the rest of the cast. Having bought their separate train tickets to leave on Saturday, Hattie and Alice spent the next day packing.

The day after that, they did a final round of sightseeing. They climbed back to the top of the Trinity Church steeple, admiring the view of the city one last time. From there, they took a stage up Fifth Avenue to the recently constructed Central Park. Much as there was to see the city, Hattie enjoyed strolling through the woods. Though the trees had long dropped their leaves, the air was pleasantly cool, the sky streaked with only a few wispy clouds.

How lovely it must be here in the summer, Hattie thought. But the park would be crowded then. Today, they had the pedestrian paths almost to themselves. There were still finishing touches to be added to the park, but the lakes and stone archways created an altogether pleasant effect, and Hattie felt herself relaxing. George would enjoy this, she thought. So would John Elliott.

Having walked an invigorating loop through the park's southern end, Hattie and Alice started back to catch the stage. All at once, a man called out from a wooded area to the left of where they were walking.

Hattie froze. "Did you hear that?" she said in a low voice.

"Yes." Alice stopped beside her. "But I couldn't make out the words."

"He said *toss it.*" Beyond a clump of trees, Hattie saw the outline of a shack, one of several the city was tearing down to make room for the park. Then came the sound of a glass bottle breaking, followed by a loud bang. A flash of fire, and black smoke puffed up from among the trees.

"What in the world?" Alice said.

From the vicinity of the shack came another man's voice, saying something about sand. Then the flames died back, and the smoke dwindled to a thin stream.

"Perhaps we should investigate," Hattie said.

"The ground's soggy," Alice said. "A swamp between here and there."

From the direction of the shanty came more voices, their words were indistinct. As Hattie and Alice stood listening, the voices faded, and there was only silence.

"Probably just idle youths having a bit of fun," Hattie said.

She and Alice continued on their way. On their way out of the park, Alice spotted a policeman. She flagged him down, and they told him what they'd observed.

The officer shook his head. "Those shanties attract all sorts of ne'er-do-wells," he said. "Sounds like the hooligans have run off. But I'll have a look all the same."

He tipped his hat, then headed in the direction they'd indicated.

"I hope he catches up with them," Alice said as they began walking again.

"Me too," Hattie said.

Alice turned to her. "Something's bothering you. I can see it in your face."

"It's that man mentioning sand," Hattie said. "Why use sand to put out a fire when you could use water?"

Alice cocked her head. "Unless it's the type of fire you told me about. The kind water can't extinguish. You think those men from Delmonico's are going to try again to burn down the city?"

Hattie eyed the direction they'd come from. "I'd like to think not. But I suppose anything's possible."

Alice looped her arm through Hattie's. "Don't be all doom and gloom. It's our last night in the city."

Hattie offered a smile. "I do tend to imagine the worst."

Still, as they boarded the stage, Hattie found it hard to shake the feeling that something was amiss.

~ ~ ~

After treating themselves to an early dinner at the Astor Hotel, Hattie and Alice proceeded to P.T. Barnum's Museum. Hattie had been there last spring with Pauline Carlton, who was now part of Barnum's traveling show, giving lectures on her adventures as a spy.

Alice had never been inside the museum, and she was keen to see it before leaving tomorrow. As they strolled past the exhibits, Hattie was pleased to see that Alice's interests, like her own, lay more in the wonders of the natural world than in exhibits featuring his human curiosities, as Barnum called them.

They spent a good deal of time admiring the living hippopotamus, brought to America from the River Nile, and the living whale brought from the coast of Labrador, now swimming in a tank filled with water from the East River. They marveled, too, at Barnum's Aquarial Garden, exhibiting a wide variety of colorful fishes.

"Oh, I do wish George could see this," Alice said. "He told me marine life fascinates him."

"He's always loved nature," Hattie said. "It makes me happy to think of him living in a part of the country known for its natural beauty."

"What I wouldn't give for word from him," Alice said.

"There will be a letter waiting in Nashville," Hattie said. "We just have to wait for John to get back."

"The end of the year," Alice said glumly.

"Not so long now," Hattie said. "The time will pass quickly." She hoped this was true.

As they neared the exhibit's exit, she spotted Phineas Barnum, the museum's proprietor. Pauline had introduced them, and Hattie recognized him easily by his wide nose and slightly disheveled hair.

"I'll be right back," she told Alice.

Mesmerized by a tank of sea horses, Alice nodded. "I'll be here."

Hattie hurried after Barnum as he left the exhibit. Catching up with him in an empty hallway, she plucked his sleeve. "Mr. Barnum," she said.

He turned to gaze at her, his expression stern. "Are we acquainted, ma'am?"

"Hattie Logan," she said. "I'm a friend of Pauline Carlton. We were traveling together before she signed on with your show."

His face relaxed. "Ah, yes. I remember you now."

"I haven't heard from Pauline in a while. Is she well?"

"Quite," Barnum said. "Folks in the western states love her. Next week, her show opens in San Francisco."

"I'm glad to hear it," Hattie said. "When you see her next, please let her know I asked after her."

"I shall." He dipped his head slightly. "A pleasure to see you again, Miss Logan. I hope you'll be staying on for tonight's lecture. It promises to be truly spectacular. A renowned man of science."

"I intend to be there," Hattie said.

They said their goodbyes. Returning to the sea horses, Hattie found Alice just as she'd left her. With some prodding, she got her to come along to the lecture hall. Tonight's speaker was renowned Harvard professor Louis Agassiz, who according to the advertisements would enlighten them on the wonders of the natural world.

But just as they settled into their seats, an alarm was raised. "Fire!" yelled one of Barnum's employees.

Taking Alice by the hand, Hattie leaped to her feet. Smoke poured from a lower corner of the auditorium. Heart pounding, she pointed to a nearby exit. "That way," she said.

Stepping toward the aisle, they found their way blocked by a screaming woman. The man beside her was urging her forward, but she seemed frozen in place.

"Move along!" a man yelled, but the woman screamed louder still.

From behind, someone shoved Alice. She stumbled but caught herself.

"Order! Order!" one of Barnum's ushers called out.

Letting go of Alice, Hattie gripped the screaming woman firmly by the arm.

The screaming ceased. "Let me go!" The woman tried to pull herself from Hattie's grasp. "I won't be accosted by a stranger."

"You must vacate the premises," Hattie said. "In a calm and orderly fashion. Mr. Barnum insists."

The woman's expression softened. "Mr. Barnum sent you?"

"In a fashion. Come along now."

Alice took the woman's other arm, and she and Hattie escorted her toward the aisle, releasing the bottleneck behind them. In the acrid air, Hattie's eyes burned.

"The flames!" The woman coughed. "And the smoke! We shall all die."

"We shall not." Hattie nodded toward a line of ushers moving up the aisle toward the blaze. "Mr. Barnum's men are carrying water."

"Thank heavens," the woman said.

But Hattie knew the water would have little effect. Not if this was Greek fire. She plucked a man from the bucket brigade by the sleeve as he passed.

"Sand," she said. "Not water. Smother it."

He looked at her curiously, then continued on. She could only hope he and the others would act on her advice

"What did you say to that man?" the woman demanded.

"I told him his efforts are appreciated," Hattie said.

They reached the stairwell. In the narrow confines, the sense of panic was palpable.

"Watch your step," Alice said.

Squeezed between her and Hattie, the woman looked for a moment as if she might resume her screaming. But in her gown, negotiating the stairs did require concentration, and she only muttered her discontent as they descended.

Outside, the clanging of fire alarms disrupted what would otherwise have been a calm, clear evening. A growing crowd milled about in front of the museum, passersby joining with those who'd escaped the fire.

Releasing the woman to her companion, Hattie looked up and down Broadway. "It's not just Barnum's," she said. "Flames are coming out of the hotel across the street."

"And Wallack's Theatre," Alice said, her forehead creased with worry "It's on fire too."

"The conspirators didn't give up after all," Hattie said, a hollow feeling spreading through her chest. "They were only waiting for an opportunity to strike."

"What we saw this afternoon," Alice said. "At Central Park. Was it them, do you think?"

"Quite possibly," Hattie said. "We should have tried to catch them instead of leaving it to the police."

"There's no sense second-guessing ourselves," Alice said. "Let's get back to the hotel.

The omnibuses were full, so Hattie and Alice set off on foot, heading up Broadway toward the LaFarge Hotel. Block after block, they passed knots of people standing outside burning buildings, flames shooting into the night.

As they passed Lovejoy's Hotel, Hattie overheard a man say, "This is the work of Rebel emissaries. I'd bet my eyeteeth on it."

"You can't know that for certain," said the woman beside him.

"The Richmond papers called for the burning of New York City," the man said. "In retaliation for what Union armies have done in Rebel territory."

Retaliation. That was what the men at Delmonico's had been after. Now it looked as if they'd got it.

As they neared the LaFarge, Alice gasped. "The Winter Garden. It's been struck too."

Across the street, Hattie saw theatregoers in all their finery clustered outside the Winter Garden, gazing back at the building they'd vacated. "Right in the middle of the Booths' benefit performance," she said.

Alice shook her head. "The Confederates going after one of their most ardent supporters."

But on closer inspection, the opulent Winter Garden wasn't on fire after all. Apparently, it was the blaze at the LaFarge that had caused the alarm. Flames shot from the window of a corner room on the hotel's second floor, where Hattie and Alice were also staying.

Hattie counted the windows. "Not our room," she said. "But close."

Alice pressed her hands to her heart. "My wardrobe. Costumes, playbills, scripts. All that I've accumulated from years of acting. Gone in an instant."

"It can be stopped," Hattie said, hoping this wasn't just wishful thinking.

Squinting up at the flames, she edged toward the firefighters pumping water at the blaze. Reaching them, she spoke to the man nearest her. "It's Greek fire!" Over the noise of the steam pumper, she had to shout. "Water has no effect!"

"Move aside." The firefighter stepped in front of her. "This ain't no place for a lady."

"But you need to understand," she said. "This is no ordinary fire."

He shook his head, his gaze fixed on the flames. "Looks ordinary enough to me."

"Trust me," she said. "I've seen it burn on a river."

"Sure, lady. If you say so. But by my book, water's the thing."

She looked up at the blaze. Sure enough, the flames were sputtering out.

"Curious," she said. But the man had moved away from her, still aiming his hose.

She returned to Alice. "I don't know what you did," Alice said. "But it worked."

"I didn't do anything. The water made no difference. Somehow, it went out on its own."

"I don't care how it got put out. I'm just glad the threat has passed."

"Agreed," Hattie said. But she couldn't shake the feeling that she'd failed somehow, that if she'd put the pieces together properly, the attack on New York might never have happened at all.

Chapter Eighteen

NOVEMBER 26, 1864

After a night of tossing and turning in a hotel room that reeked of smoke, Hattie and Alice went the next morning to the New York City Police.

"We have information about the fires set last night," Hattie told the officer at the desk.

Immediately, they were ushered into a back room, where they were advised to wait for the sergeant in charge of the investigation.

"Mr. Curtis was wrong," Alice said, settling into one of the room's straight-backed chairs. "The police do have an interest in Confederate plots."

"They do now," Hattie said, taking a seat beside her. "Since half of Broadway was burning last night."

The door opened, and an officer entered. Tall and mustached, his eyes shone with a sincerity that reminded Hattie of Murray Wilson back in Montreal.

With a nod, he sat behind the desk. "Sergeant Jenkins," he said by way of introduction. "I understand you ladies have information about last night's incendiary incidents."

Hattie straightened. "We do indeed." After weeks of doing what she could on her own, with only Alice to help, it felt good to have his attention.

Jenkins took a small stack of paper from a desk drawer, then took a pen from the inkwell. "Names," he said.

"Alice Gray," Alice said.

Jenkins tilted his chin. "The actress?"

Alice dipped her head, a coy look that never failed to get attention. "That's right."

"I saw you perform at the Winter Garden last week," Jenkins said. "*Fra Diavolo*. Lovely show." He turned his attention to Hattie. "Were you also part of the cast?"

"No," Hattie said. "My name is Hattie Logan. I'm a..." She paused, wanting to choose her words carefully. "An associate of Nashville's Army Police."

His eyes narrowed ever so slightly, suggesting skepticism. He jotted her name beneath Alice's. Beside it, he wrote *Nashville,* and next to that, *Army Police,* followed by a question mark.

"You can verify my association with Lieutenant John Elliott," she said. "When he returns from the field."

He did not write this down. "The two of you traveled to New York together?"

"Yes," Alice said. "We came from Montreal. There was a poisoning, you see. Of Hattie's brother."

Jenkins frowned. "A poisoning, you say?"

"That's right. We came here hoping to get to the bottom of it, so to speak." Alice's hands flew as she spoke, as was often the case when she got animated. "We went to the Montreal train station, you see. The Bonaventure. We had reason to believe certain Confederates there were up to no good. They'd withdrawn large amounts of money from the bank. Hattie's brother worked there, and—"

"Circumstances led us to New York," Hattie interrupted, fearing Alice's longwinded storytelling might cause Jenkins to lose attention altogether. "While dining at Delmonico's recently, we were privy to the conversations of men who were plotting against the city."

"They spoke of mustering 25,000 men who hated Lincoln as much as they did," Alice said. "And they said how nice the Confederate flag would look, waving over City Hall."

At this, Jenkins perked up. *25,000 men,* he wrote on his paper.

"They also mentioned chemicals," Hattie said. "One hundred forty-four vials of a substance that would set the town afire."

This, too, Jenkins wrote down. "Very helpful," he said. "Firefighters have gone into the hotel rooms where the fires were set. Beds and other furniture were drenched with a substance containing phosphorus."

"Greek fire," Hattie said. "I know of a chemist who concocts it. A man engaged in traitorous activities. Dr. Luke Blackstone."

To her delight, Jenkins wrote down Blackstone's name too. At last, there was a chance that he would be brought to justice. What

Blackstone had done to her and Thom Welton could not be un-
done, but at least he might be kept from doing more harm.

"Did these men give any indication of when and where they
might strike?" Jenkins asked.

"I recall them mentioning Monday night," Alice said. "Isn't that
right, Hattie?"

Noting the confusion on Jenkins' face, Hattie rushed to clarify.
"The conversation we overhead was the week before the election.
Via an..." What to call Lucy? "An emissary, I was able to get word
of their plans to Secretary Stanton in Washington."

Jenkins' grip on his pen tightened. "You're responsible for General Butler having brought his troops to New York earlier in the
month?"

"Indirectly, yes," she said, but from the look on his face, it was
clear he found this farfetched. "But what matters at this point
is that we know the names of the men at Delmonico's. Robert
Kennedy. James McMaster. John Potts Brown. John Headley.
Robert Martin."

"Hold on, hold on," Jenkins said. "McMaster, you say? The
newspaper editor?"

"Yes. He was at the table at Delmonico's."

"And John Potts Brown—he owns a shipping company down
along East River, doesn't he?" Jenkins set down his pen. "Sorry,
Miss Logan, but I'm having a hard time believing that men of such
stature would lower themselves to pouring a phosphorus solution
over hotel furnishings and lighting them on fire."

"Some underlings likely carried out the plan," Hattie said. "But the men I named were behind it, I assure you."

"Tell him what we saw at Central Park yesterday," Alice said.

"It might be nothing," Hattie said, unsure whether the incident was worth mentioning given the sergeant's overall skepticism. "But while strolling through Central Park yesterday afternoon, we heard what sounded like glass breaking, followed by the sound of an explosion and a burst of flames."

"And we heard men's voices," Alice said, "though we couldn't make out what they were saying. The trees obscured our view, but this was all happening in the vicinity of some sort of shack. Leaving the park, we found a policeman and told him about it."

Nodding, Jenkins made a note. "The city needs to get rid of those shanties. They draw all sorts of ne'er-do-wells. Were you able to give a description of the men involved?"

"I'm afraid not," Hattie said. "They fled before we could get a good look."

"The superintendent is keen on rounding up suspects in last night's fires," Jenkins says. "He's made clear he'll bring them before a military tribunal, to be hanged with dispatch if found guilty. He has issued an order requiring all persons arriving from insurgent states to register with the military here. Otherwise, they'll be treated as spies."

"You'd best be checking persons arriving from Canada too," Alice said.

"As well as members of secret organizations," Hattie said. "The Sons of Liberty, the Order of American Knights."

Jenkins wrote none of this down. "I'll say one thing for you ladies. You're full of ideas."

Fanciful ideas, Hattie thought. *That's what he's thinking.* "I can tell you that the Army Police in Nashville take seriously the threat of men involved in such groups. I hope you and your fellow officers will remain vigilant. You may well find the plot is more extensive than you think."

"I should think all those hotels set afire would convince you of their capabilities," Alice said. "We saw at least six fires burning between Barnum's and the LaFarge last night."

"Fourteen fires in all," Jenkins said. "A strain on the firefighters. It's a wonder they managed to put them out."

"I've no formal training in chemistry," Hattie said. "But I observed a demonstration of Greek fire in Indianapolis last summer. It was conducted on the river."

Jenkins' brow knitted. "On the water?"

"Yes. Water won't put out Greek fire. For all their heroic efforts last night, I doubt the firefighters put out the fires with their hoses. The flames were mostly contained in hotel rooms, yes?"

"Right."

"With the doors shut?"

"So I'm told."

"Then I believe the fires burned themselves out. Because of the chemicals involved, oxygen would be necessary to keep them burning."

Jenkins pushed his notes aside. "Possibly. I'm told a box of inflammatory material, found in a vacant room at the Metropolitan

Hotel, was brought to the station a few hours ago. In the open air, it burst into flames."

"There you go." Alice patted Hattie's knee. "She knows what she's talking about."

Pushing back his chair, Jenkins stood. "I appreciate you ladies coming in," he said. "But I've got to move along to other interviews. The city is understandably on edge, and it behooves us to make arrests as soon as possible."

"You've considered, I hope, that the instigators may be headed for Canada," Hattie said.

He chuckled. "I'm afraid Canada is a bit beyond our jurisdiction."

"But don't you see," Hattie said. "If Confederate plotters continue to escape over the border, these acts of sabotage will continue. They'll drag this war on forever."

"We'd best leave concerns about the war to General Grant, don't you think?" Jenkins' tone was that of a father speaking to a clueless child.

Hattie stood, and Alice beside her. "Robert Kennedy. James McMaster. John Potts Brown. John Headley. Robert Martin," Hattie said, repeating the names she'd given.

"Yes, yes." Jenkins strode toward the door, which he opened and held for them.

"What about Wilkes?" Alice said, speaking in a low voice to Hattie. "And Sarah Slater?"

Hattie shook her head. They'd already stretched the limits of what Jenkins considered relevant. There was no sense going out on a limb over nothing but bad feelings and hunches.

They left the police headquarters through the same door they'd come in. Outside, stray snowflakes drifted from wooly clouds hanging low over the city.

"We should have told them about Wilkes," Alice said.

"What would we have said? That he accosted me and treated you unfairly?"

"There's the money you saw him get. And his association with John Headley."

"Neither of which constitutes a crime," Hattie said. "Or links him in any way with last night's fires."

"But he was here in the city," Alice said.

"Onstage at the Winter Garden," Hattie said. "In a drama that the fires disrupted."

"What about Sarah Slater?" Alice said. "Wilkes gave her that wad of cash. Then she made another large withdrawal and left Montreal in the company of Robert Martin, who very likely had something to do with George's being poisoned."

"Guilt by association," Hattie said. "And tenuous guilt, at that. We've done what we can, Alice. Now we just have to hope it makes a difference."

"You sound like you're giving up," Alice said.

"Sometimes it's best to acknowledge when you've reached a dead end," Hattie said. It was a lesson George had tried to instill in her on more than one occasion. "And Jenkins has a point. General

Grant and his men are the ones who'll bring the war to an end, not us."

"Can't come soon enough for me," Alice said.

"Or for me." The snowflakes were falling with more determination now. Hattie glanced up at the sky. "Especially with another long winter setting in."

"Don't be discouraged," Alice linked arms with her. "Come with me to Buffalo. I'd love for my mother to meet you. You can regale her with stories of your spying."

"It's kind of you to invite me," Hattie said. "But I want to check in on my friend Anne. Her husband has disappeared, and in some ways, it's my fault."

Alice squeezed her arm. "Oooh, another story. Do tell."

"There's not so much to tell," Hattie said. "Anne's husband was wrapped up in the Sons of Liberty. Aboard the Lake Erie gunboat, I confronted him with his wrongs. He leaped from the boat and hasn't been heard from since. So the matter is unsettled. Rather like where we are with the current situation."

This dour outlook seemed to subdue Alice. But moments later, the bounce returned to her step, and her face brightened. "The holidays are upon us," she said. "Come to Buffalo, and we'll celebrate in style."

"I haven't let myself think of the holidays. We're so close to the end of the year, when John is due back, and yet it feels so far away."

"All the more reason to make your celebration special," Alice said. "So you're feeling fresh and exuberant when he returns."

"Exuberant. That does sound appealing."

"Your lieutenant won't want to return to an old sourpuss," Alice said. "If you're bent on frowning all the way to New Year's, those lines at the corners of your mouth will become permanent."

Hattie's free hand went to her face, feeling for creases. "It's that obvious?" she said.

"It is," Alice said.

"Well, then," she said. "How about this? You go see your mother in Buffalo. I'll go to Indiana to see my friend Anne. Then you come spend Christmas with us in Indianapolis. Anne's family couldn't be more welcoming. They'd love to meet you. I can hear Mrs. Duncan now, exclaiming over your being a real actress."

Alice smiled slyly. "This is all about you staying close to Nashville, so you can get there quickly when your lieutenant returns."

"Perhaps," Hattie said.

"Then it's a plan," Alice said.

"It feels good to have one," Hattie admitted, her mood brightening. "War or no war."

Chapter Nineteen

DECEMBER 10, 1864

The waning December light slanted through the sunroom windows in the Duncans' spacious Indianapolis home, illuminating Anne's daughter Jo as she executed an unsteady toddler's twirl in the holiday dress Hattie had stitched for her.

Gently, Anne took hold of her arm. "Stand still, Peanut. Your Aunt Hattie needs to pin your hem."

"Pretty, pretty." Her whirling interrupted, Jo clapped her chubby hands.

"A pretty dress for a pretty girl." Seizing the moment of calm, Hattie stuck three pins along the skirt's hem.

"You picked the perfect color," Anne said. "Red becomes her. I don't know how we'd have found someone to make her holiday frock if you weren't here. I'm all thumbs when it comes to sewing."

"You're allowed to be bad at something." Hattie circled Jo, eying the hemline "I could never believe all you did for yourself when you lived with Franklin. I shudder to think the results I'd get trying to bake a loaf of bread, let alone the pies and cookies you churned out."

"Kept my mind from my troubles," Anne said. The wistful look that had come over her after Franklin first left was gone, Hattie noted. Her friend was nothing if not resilient. And as Mrs. Duncan had been quick to point out, Anne's hasty marriage had been fraught nearly from the start.

"I'm glad you and Jo have moved in with your parents," Hattie said. "I know you like to do for yourself. But in that little house down the street, you'd have worked yourself to the bone just with housekeeping. Your suitors would be put off."

Anne laughed. "Men aren't exactly lined up at the door."

"Give them time," Hattie said.

"It's myself I'm giving time to," Anne said. "I'm in no hurry to rush into another marriage though I admit it will feel good to have the divorce final. I'm grateful to Papa for urging me forward on that count. There's a good deal to be said for putting an end to things so you can have a new beginning, even if you're not quite sure what that will be."

"Indeed." Crouching, Hattie adjusted a pin. Having told herself she'd done all she could in the trail of malfeasance she'd followed from Montreal to New York, she was feeling something close to contentment. The festive spirit that pervaded the Duncans was a boon in that regard. Between her one-year-old granddaughter and Alice's promise to spend the holidays there, Mrs. Duncan had vowed to put on the best Christmas ever, never mind that the war raged on.

Squirming away, Jo reached for the Duncans' tabby cat, which had tried to slink by undetected. The cat darted across the room. Jo raced after it, squealing.

Anne lunged, grabbing her daughter by the shoulders. "Not so fast, little lady. You can't be tearing about the house in that dress."

Jo tugged at the frock that had delighted her only moments ago. "Kitty," she said, frowning.

Hattie laughed. "Capricious, isn't she?"

"Indeed." Anne unfastened the dress's buttons and wriggled it over Jo's head. Wearing only her petticoat, Jo sauntered off in pursuit of the cat, which seemed to have vanished.

"It's good to hear you laugh," Anne said, handing the dress to Hattie. "You seem so pensive at times. Though I suppose that's to be expected, with your lieutenant off in the field. I know reports of fighting at Franklin haven't helped."

Not two weeks ago, Union and Confederate forces had engaged in a bloody battle at Franklin, south of Nashville. All reports indicated that most of the casualties were on the Confederate side, but it was also said Union troops had been forced to leave their wounded behind as they pulled back to defend Nashville.

"At least John's not in the infantry," Hattie said. "Working in military intelligence, he should be ahead of the fighting. Still, my thoughts are often with him, I admit." She set the dress in her lap, then gazed at the snow falling in fat clumps outside the window. "And with George. Surely he has written by now. But with John away, I suppose his letter is languishing on his desk at the Army Police Headquarters."

"There must be some associate there who could forward a letter," Anne said.

"They'd had quite a lot of turnover before I left," Hattie said. "Colonel Truesdail is still there, I presume. But I shouldn't bother him with something so trivial."

"Papa has a number of connections in the military," Anne said. "He could make some inquiries."

"I hate to have him do that, all over a letter."

"You could go to Nashville yourself."

"Have I worn out my welcome so quickly?" Hattie teased.

"You know we'd have you stay forever if you'd stand for it," Anne said. "But if you feel you need to leave, I won't hold you back."

Hattie cut a length of red thread. "It's tempting. But without John there, I fear it would only make me melancholy. If I go anywhere, it should be to visit my father."

Anne raised an eyebrow. "Your father? I thought he disowned you after finding out you'd been spying for the Union."

"He did. But while he was in Montreal, George corresponded with our mother. She informed him that Father was quite unwell." Hattie held her needle close, threading it. "George considered stopping to see him on his way to Oregon, but it was simply too risky. He needed to get as far away from Montreal as fast as he could."

"So you'd go in his place."

"I feel I should." Hattie pulled the thread through her needle and knotted it. "But I can't say I'm looking forward to it."

"Then you'd best go sooner rather than later. So you don't spoil your holiday."

Cornered beneath a chair across the room, the cat yowled. Rising, Anne pulled Jo away, scooping her up in her arms. "I swear you get heavier by the day," she said. "You'd best stop growing, or your pretty dress won't fit by the time Aunt Hattie finishes it."

"Then I'd best finish quickly. A bit of lace here, a bit of ribbon there." She touched the places on the dress she planned to embellish. It was satisfying, fashioning a bit of clothing that came out just the way she intended. Always a happy ending.

~ ~ ~

Two days later, Hattie decided to make good on her plans to visit her ailing father. She wouldn't have to stay long. And if he refused to see her—well, rejection from her parents was nothing new. And maybe, just maybe, her mother would share some news of George.

But as she got off the spur line train from Indianapolis at La Conner's tiny station, she was already doubting her decision. Heavy with clouds, the skies looked foreboding, and a cold, brisk wind stung her face. She'd been away long enough to have forgotten how bitter a winter day could feel in the prairie town where she'd grown up.

Intending to stay only until the eastbound train came through later in the day, she'd brought no luggage. On foot, she set out down the town's main street, where her father's big grain elevators cast long winter shadows. It was in those elevators, and in those he controlled in every farming town within a fifty-mile radius, that her family's wealth lay.

Farmers hated the prices Edgar Logan charged, taking a large chunk of what they earned whether the year was lean or prosperous. He'd also seized on the opportunity of war to expand his profits in a traitorous scheme to supply grain to the enemy. Hattie had discovered this when she decoded a letter from Pinkerton's mailroom.

Ruts were frozen into the road, and after nearly turning her ankle on one of them, Hattie paid closer attention to her steps. She didn't see the schoolboy until she'd almost run into him.

"Hey, lady." The boy dodged around her, his cheeks red from the wind. "Watch where you're going."

"Sorry," she mumbled. Then she straightened. She was no longer the ostracized schoolgirl. "Though I expect your mother would be dismayed to know you'd spoken so rudely to a stranger."

The boy's look of confidence crumpled. "You ain't gonna tell her, are you?"

Hattie offered a measured smile. "So long as you promise to treat the next stranger you meet with more kindness, I expect we can keep your remarks between the two of us."

He grinned, revealing a crooked tooth. "Thanks, Miss." Then he took off running.

Ahead, occupying an entire town block, was the house where Hattie had grown up. Since leaving home, she'd seen more elegant abodes, including an estate outside of Nashville where she'd posed as a seamstress as part of her spying. But in a little town like La Conner, the Logan property stood out like the proverbial sore thumb. Hattie had come to hate the house, which for all its elegance had always felt dark and cold.

She ascended the walkway. At the paneled oak door, she squared her shoulders, then rapped the brass knocker. She was about to knock again when the door opened slightly, revealing the thin, careworn face of Sallie Higgins, her mother's maid. How she'd managed these many years Hattie didn't know. Lydia Logan was not an easy woman to work for.

"Miss Hattie." Pressing her hands to her apron, Sallie offered a nervous smile. "You've come home."

"George told me Father was sick." As she gazed past Sallie into the dark hallway, it occurred to Hattie that her father might no longer be among the living.

Sallie peered over Hattie's shoulder. "George is here too?"

"No," Hattie said. "He went West."

"That's what your mother said. He wrote her a letter. But with your father suffering so, I thought he might come."

Relief flooded over Hattie, knowing George had written. "I've come in his place."

A thin voice called out from behind the parlor's closed door. "Who's there, Sallie?"

Sallie's gaze darted toward the parlor. "It's Miss Hattie, ma'am," she called over her shoulder. "Come to see her father."

There was a moment's silence. "May I come inside?" Hattie said. "I'm letting in the cold."

"Can't get much colder in this house than it is already." Sally glanced nervously at the parlor door, then stepped aside, allowing Hattie in.

Tentatively, Hattie stepped into the foyer, dark save for the flickering light of a single sconce. Motionless, she waited for her mother to come storming from the parlor. But there was only silence.

"Mr. Logan is upstairs," Sallie said softly. "Hasn't been out of bed in a week. The doctors say it won't be long now." She shook her head. "Horrible, the cancer."

Lifting her skirt to her ankles, Hattie proceeded up the grand mahogany staircase. Reaching the top, she turned down a hallway of closed doors. She rapped lightly on the paneled door of her father's room. No response.

She twisted the brass knob, cool to her touch, and let herself in. Like the rest of the house, her father's bedroom was dark, the velvet drapes sealing out any light that might have come in through the windows. An oil lamp on the bedstand cast a weak circle of light that barely reached the bed.

As a child, Hattie had associated her father's room with the smells of shoe polish and mustache wax, but now the odor of camphor assaulted her nose. Stepping close, she scarcely recognized her father. His face was gaunt and gray, with gray stubble protruding from his normally clean-shaven chin. His eyes were closed, but they fluttered open as Hattie approached.

"Father." The lump that rose in her throat surprised her. "It's me. Hattie."

He blinked. "Hattie," he repeated in a voice so gravelly she had to strain to hear.

So many thoughts arose in her, so many memories of the times he'd ignored her, the times he'd failed to stand up for her against her mother's withering criticism. She hardly knew him, and yet he was her flesh and blood. He'd had his reasons, she supposed, for allowing greed to consume him, but she couldn't fathom what they were.

He closed his eyes. For a moment, she thought he was drifting off to sleep. Then he opened them again. "All grown up," he murmured.

"Indeed," she said. Having scarcely known her as a child, he knew nothing of the person she'd become. Their last communication had been the letter he'd sent to the prison in Richmond. *No daughter of mine.* The words still stung.

Coming here on the train, she'd rehearsed in her head what she'd say to him. That they'd chosen different sides in the war. That her work for the Union was honorable and just. But seeing him like this, she couldn't see the sense in saying any of it.

He shifted ever so slightly, raising his bony hand from beneath the sheets. His fingers fumbled for hers, his touch light, ethereal. An almost-memory rose. A child, too young to know better, pressing her hand to her father's. For a moment, he'd taken it, and she'd felt, however briefly, that she was loved and protected.

A flight of fancy, she thought. Wishful thinking. And yet if she hadn't ever known that sort of affection, how could she have found herself missing it?

"My...my daughter," he said.

Unbidden, tears streamed down her face. "Yes, Father."

His eyes closed, and his hand dropped from hers. She stood a moment, watching as his breathing settled into the rhythm of sleep. She studied his face, trying to imagine a younger man with hopes and dreams and aspirations. A man capable of love.

"Goodbye, Father," she whispered.

Turning, she left the room, her footsteps heavier than before. Her father would spend his last days in this oppressive castle of his own making.

She descended the stairs. The hallway was silent and empty. Sallie was in the kitchen, she supposed, the only part of the house that ever felt truly warm.

As she neared the front door, her mother's reedy voice called from behind the parlor door. "Hattie Logan. Come here right now."

Hattie froze in her steps. When she was very young, she'd obeyed such commands. Even knowing that her mother would upbraid her for some fault or another, there was a part of her younger self that had sensed that even the harshest attention was better than no attention at all.

But as she'd grown older, her mother's commands for an audience were just as likely to send Hattie running in the other direction, a fact that no doubt contributed to her mother's whisking her off to the Ladygrace School for Girls to refine her manners.

She owed Lydia Logan nothing. The last time Hattie had visited, her mother had ordered her out of the house, threatening to summon the town constable if she failed to comply.

But curiosity now got the best of her. It was not like her mother to cower behind a closed door. Head held high, Hattie strode toward the parlor and swung open the door.

Stuffed with Moroccan furniture, Turkish wall hangings, German crystal, and Chinese porcelain, the parlor looked grossly out of place in the little farming community. In the midst of it, Lydia Logan sat in a wing-backed chair. Shoulders slumped, she looked shrunken and hard, like a wizened apple.

"He's dying." She looked not at Hattie but at the embers glowing in the fireplace. I don't know what will become of me."

Her assertion was at once predictably self-centered and also ludicrous in that the Logans' fortune was surely more than enough to sustain an elderly widow, even one with extravagant tastes.

"There's the plantation," Hattie said, speaking of her grandfather's Louisiana cotton enterprise. "You've always loved it there."

"None of it will ever be the same," her mother said. "Not with what they've done to us in this war."

"I suppose not," Hattie said. The luxury her mother had enjoyed her whole life was built on the backs of enslaved persons who were now emancipated.

Lydia turned her gaze on Hattie. She'd been a striking woman once, her beauty captured in an oversized portrait in oils that hung on a parlor wall, shrouded in shadow. "I've had a letter from George," she said. "It seems he's in Oregon. I can't fathom why."

That her mother would offer this information, knowing how eager Hattie would be to hear it, came as a surprise. "I suppose he's gotten a fresh start."

"We should all be so lucky." Her mother sniffed with what struck Hattie as disdain. But perhaps it was envy.

Hattie stepped toward her mother. From her handbag, she took out a slip of paper on which she'd written the Duncans' address. "Here's the address where I can be reached when...when you've news to share of Father."

Her mother waved off the paper. "That won't be necessary." Any hint of sadness, of vulnerability, had faded from her voice.

"Very well." Hattie slipped the paper into her purse. "Good day, Mother."

Three strides and she was out the door, closing it firmly behind her.

Chapter Twenty

December 24, 1864

Christmas came to the Duncans' home with as much joy and frivolity as could be mustered during wartime. On Christmas Eve, Alice arrived on the train from Buffalo. Hattie met her at the station. Riding in the stage back to the Duncans' house, they had shared what had transpired in the weeks they'd been apart. Alice had Hattie in stitches, imitating her Irish mother's brogue.

"She wasn't disappointed you didn't stay for Christmas?" Hattie said.

Alice shook her head. "I love my ma, but after a while, we get on each other's nerves. Besides, she has a man friend she'll be spending Christmas with. I didn't need to be in their way. What about your folks? I remember George saying your father was sick."

"Near death, actually," Hattie said. "I just got back from seeing him."

Alice set her hand over Hattie's. "I'm sorry. I remember when I lost my da. Crushed me, it did."

"It's different for me," Hattie said. "I'm not exactly welcome at home. All the same, I'm glad I went. My mother says she's gotten a letter from George."

Alice clapped her hand to her mouth, then let it drop. "Thank heavens. What did he say?"

"I'm not sure," Hattie said. "Mother wasn't exactly forthcoming."

"Doesn't matter," Alice said. "He's safe. And if he's written your mother, there's sure to be a letter waiting in Nashville when your lieutenant returns."

Her lieutenant. Hattie had thought more and more of him these past few days. Visiting her childhood home had made her think how different her life could be with someone like John Elliott. A man she admired, a man who respected her for who she was. She could imagine a home they made together, filled with light and love.

As Hattie had expected, the Duncans welcomed Alice with open arms. As soon as Hattie introduced her, Mrs. Duncan began plying her with questions about the performances she'd starred in. The banter continued through a hearty Christmas Eve dinner of roast pork and potatoes, Alice happily obliging with tales that drew much admiration all around.

Even with Alice visiting, there were fewer seats at the table this year. The Duncans' youngest son, Henry, was in Washington City, celebrating with his cousin's family. Missing, too, was Anne's oldest brother, Richard, who'd assisted Hattie's escape from a Richmond prison. An officer in the Union Army, he hadn't been able to get a furlough.

This was a disappointment, especially to his fiancée. But now that General Sherman had delivered the last major city in Georgia—in a telegram to the president, he'd declared it a Christmas gift that came with guns, ammunition, and 25,000 bales of cotton—Richard's post in Northern Georgia seemed relatively secure.

After dinner, the remaining Duncans, along with Hattie and Alice, gathered in the parlor. With Anne at the piano, they sang carols. Hattie held Jo in her lap, rocking side to side with the music as the child's eyes grew heavy.

The warmth in the air came from more than the fire blazing in the hearth. War had divided the Duncans, taking two sons away. Anne's husband was missing, perhaps gone for good. Yet they'd welcomed Hattie and Alice into their home as if they were family. With such love all around, it was easy to believe in a bright future once the nation emerged from the dark night of war.

~ ~ ~

On Christmas morning, Hattie and Alice enjoyed a lazy breakfast with the Duncans. They had fruit-filled Stollen bread, a tradition Mrs. Duncan said had been passed down through her German mother, washed down with rich, dark coffee—the real thing.

"We've so much to be thankful for," Mrs. Duncan said as the servants cleared the table.

Dressed in the resplendent red dress Hattie had made, Jo tugged at her mother's hand. With the two of them leading the way, they all retreated to the front room.

A Christmas tree filled one corner of the room, floor to ceiling, tinsel sparkling in the light from candles secured to the branches. "Santa came," Jo said, pointing at the packages crowded under the tree.

"So he did." Anne nudged her forward. "Now you shall be Santa's helper, handing out gifts."

"Just mind the candles," Mr. Duncan said. "We don't care to celebrate with the house afire."

At the mention of fire, Hattie caught Alice's eye. Last night, as they'd readied for bed, Alice had told her a contingent from Buffalo had pursued several suspects in the New York City fires over the Canadian border. One of the men they'd seen at Delmonico's—loud, burly Robert Cobb Kennedy—was apprehended. The rest got away. Frustrating, but Hattie hoped the arrest would make the attackers think twice before attempting a similar plot in another Northern city.

Mr. and Mrs. Duncan arranged themselves in a pair of horsehair chairs. Hattie and Alice occupied a settee. Crouching near the tree, Anne handed one gift at a time to her daughter, whispering instructions.

Jo toddled dutifully to each recipient, delivering the gifts. One by one, the packages were opened. A ruby broach from Mr. Duncan to his wife, a gold watch chain from her to him. A handbag in a cheery floral print from the Duncans to their daughter, and from her to them, a tea set imported from Canton.

Hattie and Alice unwrapped tiny bottles of Paris perfumes from Anne. Alice had brought a box of chocolates from Buffalo, which they shared all around. After that came an intermission, so Anne could wash away the chocolate smeared over Jo's hands and face.

Clean-faced again, the child resumed her distributions, now with Hattie's gifts. With the money George had given her dwindling, she'd obtained scraps of fabric from a servant so she could stitch pouches for her hosts and friends. There were oohs and ahs all around at Hattie's careful stitching, the one useful skill she'd learned at boarding school, and everyone seemed pleased with the patterns she'd chosen.

By the time she'd finished her deliveries, Jo had to be reminded that the remaining gifts under the tree were for her. She tore into boxes of candies and fruits, then unwrapped a porcelain doll which she clutched to her chest, loudly proclaiming it "mine."

Soon she abandoned the doll for a pull toy shaped like a hound dog, complete with wagging tail, which she walked in circles about the room.

With all the gifts dispersed, Hattie relaxed in her seat. Smells of roasting turkey and boiled ham wafted from the kitchen. In his chair, Mr. Duncan, head drooping, began to snore.

"I can't think of a more pleasant way to spend Christmas," Alice said.

"Nor can I," Hattie said. "Unless of course word came that the war has ended."

"Ah, that would be lovely indeed," Mrs. Duncan said. "I do hope that Richard is having a bit of enjoyment this holiday."

"He should at least have received a package like the ones we made for our soldiers," Anne said. Last week, she and Hattie had volunteered with the local sanitary commission to package up fruit, nuts, socks, and wool hats to be delivered to Union soldiers on the front lines.

"And your lieutenant, Hattie," Mrs. Duncan said. "I hope he received a package too."

More than that, Hattie hoped he was safe. For once, she'd been glad he'd been sent away from the city. Recently, the Confederates had tried to take Nashville. Union soldiers had turned them away, but there had been casualties on both sides.

Jo began to fuss. Anne bent to help her untangle the pull cord of her mechanical dog toy from its wheels. Mrs. Duncan nudged her snoozing husband, startling him awake. "If you're going to nap, dear, you should do it properly, in your bed."

He blinked several times, looking a tad disoriented. "Properly," he repeated. "Yes." He stood. "If you'll excuse me, ladies."

Mrs. Duncan stood too. "I'd best see to the preparations in the kitchen. Last year the chestnuts were underdone and the plum pudding burnt around the edges. We mustn't have that disaster again."

Abandoning her pull-toy, Jo reached for her new doll, clutching it to her chest. Anne scooped her up in her arms. "Someone is quite overdue for her nap."

"No, mama," Jo said. "More presents."

"We're finished with the presents."

"Are we?" Alice said. "I wouldn't mind another even if it's for someone else."

"Now Alice," Hattie said. "We mustn't be greedy."

As Anne and Jo left the room, she gazed out the window. From the gray sky, a steady snow was falling. "Snow for Christmas," she said. "We don't always get that in Indiana."

"We do in Buffalo," Alice said. "Tons and tons of it. My favorite part of Christmas used to be snowball fights with the neighborhood kids."

"George and I would do that, too, when the snow was deep enough. But it was only the two of us, and I'm afraid I got the worst of it. George has a superb throwing arm."

"I wonder if there's snow in Oregon," Alice said.

"Probably just rain, close as he is to the ocean." Studying Mr. Duncan's atlas, Hattie and Alice had located Astoria, situated near where the Columbia River emptied into the Pacific.

"I wish your mother had shown you his letter," Alice said.

"There'll be one waiting for us in Nashville," Hattie said. "I'm sure of it. As soon as John gets home, we'll have it."

"And you'll be off to Nashville, leaving me to fend for myself." Alice's pout seemed mostly feigned.

"The war's tide is turning," Hattie said. "The Confederates have been turned back from Tennessee. The Federals have Savannah. Soon it will be over, and we can all be together. In the meantime, you've got your engagements to keep you occupied."

"I suppose," Alice said. "Although I received some distressing news before coming here. You remember I have a commitment in Washington City in March?"

"The benefit for John McCullough?" Hattie said.

Alice nodded. "At Ford's Theatre. I'm to play Florinda in *The Apostate*. But recently I learned that Wilkes is cast as the male lead. I can't bear the thought of taking to the stage with the cad."

"Then say you won't do it," Hattie said. "They've time to find someone else."

"Oh, but McCullough would be so disappointed," Alice said. "He begged me to perform in his benefit. Besides, I'd rather not give Wilkes the satisfaction of having run me off."

"You are an actress," Hattie said. "You can make nice while seething inside."

"That's precisely what I intend to do," Alice said. "And maybe Wilkes will let slip about the company he's been keeping of late. That man he met with in Boston, who turned up at Delmonico's in association with the plot to burn down New York."

"Headley," Hattie said. "But that's guilt by association. Hardly enough to accuse Wilkes of wrongdoing."

"What about the money you saw him get at the bank?" Alice said. "And that lovely sometimes-widow Sarah Slater we've known him to be with."

"That's what's got you perturbed," Hattie said. "The veiled lady."

Alice's eyes flashed. "You suspected her too."

"But without any real evidence," Hattie said.

Alice folded her arms at her chest. "And here I thought you were a spy."

In the hallway, the door knocker sounded. "Now who could that be, on Christmas Day?" Hattie said.

"Maybe it's a delivery boy. With some ingredient or other for the Christmas feast."

"He should have gone around to the back." Too late, Hattie realized how much this sounded like something her mother would say.

"Probably not a path shoveled yet, with the snow," Alice said.

There was the creak of the front door's opening. A moment later, Anne poked her head into the room.

"Hattie, there's someone at the door who wants a word with you."

"With me?" Hattie stood. "Who?"

"Never seen him before," Anne said.

"And you opened the door to him?" Hattie said.

"It's Christmas," Alice said. "Not even a stranger should have to stand outside in the snow."

Anne withdrew. Hattie stepped from the front room into the foyer. A man stood on the rug near the door. Looking down, he was brushing snow from his trousers.

Hattie stepped forward. "You asked for me?"

He looked up, and she saw the warm smile and gentle eyes she'd come to cherish.

"John!" She rushed into his open arms, reveling in the warmth of his embrace. Snow from his coat melted against her cheek, wet also by her joyful tears.

"I've missed you so." His voice was gruff with emotion. He drew her into a kiss, and in that glorious moment, the world seemed to right itself.

Their kiss would have gone on longer had they not been standing in the Duncans' entryway, with light from the gas scones illuminating them for all to behold.

Reluctantly, Hattie pulled away. "How did you get here? I thought you'd be gone another week at least."

"The Confederates nudged us along a bit sooner than anticipated," he said. "I sent you a telegram."

"I never got it," Hattie said.

"Intercepted." Hattie whirled around, and there was Anne, standing near the staircase, beaming. "I've been known to open correspondence before. As have you, Hattie Logan."

"She wired me straightaway, proposing that I come here and surprise you for Christmas," John said. "Colonel Truesdail granted a few days' leave, and here I am."

Anne hurried forward, arms outstretched. "Now that you two have your greetings out of the way, I'll take your coat and hat, Lieutenant Elliott."

He removed his cap, shook off the droplets of water, and handed it to Anne. "Quite the snowstorm you arranged for my arrival," he said, shrugging out of his overcoat and handing it to Anne.

"I was afraid your train would be delayed," Anne said. "And our surprise would be ruined."

"I always knew you could keep a secret," Hattie said. "But one this big..." She shook her head. "I had no idea." She looped her arm around John's. "Come along with me," she said. "There's someone else I'd like you to meet."

Anne hung John's hat and coat, and the three of them proceeded to the front room. As they entered, Alice stood. She was grinning from ear to ear. "So your handsome lieutenant truly does exist. I was beginning to suspect you'd fabricated him just to keep us guessing."

Hattie pursed her lips in mock indignation. "Don't tell me you were in on this too." She looked up at John. "It seems my detective skills have atrophied from lack of use."

"I doubt that," John said. "It's just that you've chosen to associate with women as clever as you are."

"Lieutenant John Elliott," Hattie said, remembering her manners. "Allow me to introduce Alice Gray. She befriended me years ago, and we reconnected in Montreal."

"Alice." John tapped his breast pocket. "That explains the letter."

Alice grabbed hold of his arm. "A letter from George! You brought it."

"Indeed I did."

"Come along, all of you, and let's be seated," Anne said.

Hattie, John, and Alice arranged themselves on the settee, and Anne sat in one of the horsehair chairs. John slipped an envelope from his pocket. "It's addressed to the both of you," he said. "Who shall be the first to read it?"

Alice snatched the envelope from his hand. "We'll read it together."

She tore open the envelope's flap. Hattie leaned close as she unfolded the pages inside and read George's missive aloud.

Dearest Alice and Hattie,

After a roundabout journey, I've settled in Astoria, Oregon. It's a remarkable town with thriving lumber and fishing industries. And the size of things here! Trees wide as a house and so tall they seem to scrape the sky. Fish large enough for a week's worth of meals, and the rivers so thick with them I'm told the waters are nearly choked with them when a run is on.

The town is booming, and I've found work as a printer's devil. Not the choicest trade, but my salary is sufficient to cover my room and board. I'm making inquiries about fishing and lumbering. Once I'm fully situated, I intend to send for the both of you, if you're still inclined to associate with a ruffian such as myself.

In the meantime, I'll watch eagerly for correspondence at the address given herewith. And fear not, I've seen neither clay *nor* martins *in this part of the world.*

With all fondness,

George

"How wonderful to know that he's well," Anne said.

"And safe," Alice said.

"But what's this about clay?" John said. "And martins?"

"It's a long story," Hattie said.

"Involving poison," Alice said. "And saboteurs by the names of Clay and Martin."

"I shall want to hear all about it," John said. "At your earliest convenience."

Hattie touched his hand. How kindly he spoke. "First, you must tell us how you arrived here safe and sound," she said. "I was so concerned about your being sent away from Nashville. Especially with the Confederates crossing over into Tennessee."

"It was because of their pending incursion that someone needed to go to the southern part of the state," he said. "As Hood advanced with his troops, there was a call for more coordination among Federal scouts and pickets. And as ever, there were Confederate spies to be reckoned with, including one rather charming lady in Franklin who made a habit of plying Union officers with food and drink, then extracting their secrets to share with the Confederates."

"I hope she wasn't *too* charming," Hattie teased.

"You mustn't worry about that," Alice said. "From the way your lieutenant looks at you, it's clear where his affections lie."

And so it was. The perfect Christmas, Hattie thought. The perfect start to the next chapter of our lives. If only...No, she was tired of *if only*. There was only this moment, this place, this feeling of love all around.

Chapter Twenty-One

DECEMBER 28, 1864

J ohn's three days of furlough passed all too quickly. And he wouldn't be returning to Nashville as Hattie had initially assumed. Instead, the Army Police wanted him in Louisville, where there had been a good deal of consternation involving Kentucky's military governor and his retaliatory killings of Confederate guerrillas.

Much as John would have liked for Hattie to go with him, the posting promised to be difficult, and he needed to give his full attention to it. He would be there a few months at most, he hoped. Then they could be together.

Hattie tried to put this disappointment out of her mind, vowing to make the most of these few days they had together. As the weather warmed and the snow turned to slush, she toured John and Alice around Indianapolis. She took them by the statehouse, where she and Anne had gone to see Indiana's first regiment, the

Zouaves, off to war. They took in a theatrical at Metropolitan Hall. They strolled along the river, and Hattie pointed out the spot where she'd first seen the Sons of Liberty demonstrate their use of Greek fire.

That was all the opening Alice needed to launch into an account of how she and Hattie had dealt with the fire bombings in New York City.

"Hattie knew what was going on," Alice said. "She even went to Washington City, right before Election Day, to get word to Federal authorities."

John rubbed his chin. "I'm confused. I thought the fires were at the end of November, not the beginning."

"The trouble was initially planned for Election Day," Hattie said. "We learned of it with Frederick Curtis."

"When you wired asking who could help, I thought of him immediately," John said. "He's well-connected with the Confederates. Risks his life every time he goes South. If they ever find he's been trading secrets, they won't hesitate to kill him."

"He certainly knew where to find the ringleaders," Alice said. "And he treated us to a magnificent meal to boot."

"He also warned us the police were unlikely to act against the men behind the plot," Hattie said. "At least two of them are well-known in New York. Another was a man we'd followed from Montreal, a man we suspected of trying to harm George."

"So Hattie took her concerns straight to Washington City," Alice said.

"Washington, eh?" John said.

"It's not so impressive. I simply called on an old friend. She owed me a favor, and her father is well-connected."

"Sure enough, General Butler showed up in New York with his troops," Alice said. "Election Day went off without a hitch."

"And the men you've overheard planning the operation were arrested?" John said.

"Unfortunately not," Hattie said. "I managed to have a word with General Butler about apprehending them, but he showed little interest."

"If you'd come to Nashville's Army Police with the names of men plotting an insurrection, you can be sure we'd have been taking notes," John said.

"At any rate, it turned out the plot was not put down, only delayed until the day after Thanksgiving," Alice said.

"And the only reason it didn't do more damage than it did was that the Greek fire, by virtue of its chemical elements, requires air to burn, something the renegades failed to take into account," Hattie said.

"Surely at that point, arrests were made," John said.

"One arrest," Alice said. "When I was visiting my mother in Buffalo recently, word was that the others had escaped through there into Canada."

"It seems wrong that criminals can get away simply by crossing the border," Hattie said.

"You'll be pleased to know there's another who didn't get away," John said. "John Beall was apprehended near Niagara last week. He was caught trying to throw a passenger train off the rails."

"Beall?" Alice said. "Who's that?"

"He commandeered a Lake Erie ferry in a plot to free thousands of Confederate prisoners," Hattie said. "Murray Wilson was trying to hunt him down."

"Oh, right," Alice said. "Maybe Wilson's work at the bank aided in his capture."

"I hope so," Hattie said. "It's good to know there's been at least some progress in stopping Rebels from harming civilians. I only wish I could have done more."

"You mustn't blame yourself for the ones who got away," John said. "It's inevitable. The enemy is trained in subterfuge, just as we are."

Hattie drew a deep breath of wintery air. "I for one would readily exchange subterfuge for an ordinary life."

John took her hand. "As would I. When the war's over."

She looked up at him, unable to contain any longer the thought that had been circling in her mind ever since his arrival. "Why must we wait? George is settled in Oregon. We could all go there now."

There was affection in his gaze, but his forehead furrowed. "But I've my new post."

"Let someone else go to Louisville," she said. "We can start a new life in Oregon. There must be a police force there. You have the experience." She turned to Alice. "And surely there's a theatre too. If there isn't, you can start one."

Alice laughed. "George said you've always been one for big dreams. Aside from that requiring a good deal of cash, there's another wee problem. My theatrical commitments."

"You don't want to perform with Wilkes. Leave for the West, and you won't have to deal with him."

Alice's expression turned serious. "I'm surprised at you, Hattie. I'd have not thought you one to run away from adversity."

"True enough." John gave her hand an affectionate squeeze. "You're more inclined to run toward it."

"You know Wilkes is up to no good," Alice said. "Him and Sarah Slater both. You said so yourself. Now you want to go off and leave them to their mischief?"

"If it's mischief they're up to, someone else can uncover it," Hattie said.

"Would one of you ladies care to enlighten me?" John said. "I know of the theatrical Booth family. Which are you referring to?"

"John Wilkes," Alice said. "The rogue."

This was not a topic Hattie cared to engage in, especially not in the hours she had left to spend with John before he left for Louisville. But the genie was out of the bottle, so to speak. "When I first met Alice, she was romantically involved with John Wilkes Booth."

"Quite unwisely, as it turned out," Alice said. "There seems no end to the women he'll pursue."

"A hazard of fame and fortune, I suppose," John said. "But if you've got Hattie on his trail, she'll get to the bottom of it."

"It isn't his mischief with women that concerns me," Hattie said. "I happened upon him in Montreal, making a substantial withdrawal from the bank where George was employed. My curiosity was aroused, and I followed him."

"Him and the veiled lady," Alice said.

"A veiled lady," John said. "You said your friend Pauline suspected a veiled lady of trying to poison her, didn't you, Hattie?"

"Yes, but—"

"And someone tried to poison George," Alice said. "In Montreal, where we first saw Sarah Slater."

"She's the veiled lady," Hattie said. "But her involvement in anything untoward is all supposition. George would be the first to say so."

"What about her being with Wilkes in New York?" Alice said. "And how perturbed he became when confronted about it?"

"You said yourself he has a wandering eye. It's no surprise he was dining with an attractive woman. At any rate, I don't care to discuss the man any longer. I'd rather we consider our future."

Alice stopped walking. She set her fisted hands on her hips. "And what sort of future will we have, pray tell, if everyone with talents like yours abandons their duty prematurely?"

Hattie stopped short, and John beside her. "I...I don't suppose I'd thought of it in those terms."

"Perhaps you should," John said gently. "The war is at a critical juncture. You have talents that will help the Union. Which leads me to a matter I've been meaning to discuss. An opportunity for you to put your skills to work while I'm in Louisville."

They began walking again. "All right," Hattie said. "I'll admit I'm intrigued."

"There are concerns within the Bureau of Military Information about some unusual activities in the county south of Washington City," John said. "The War Department's contraband division needs an additional person to help investigate."

"Contraband." Alice giggled. "Sounds as if she'd be smuggling."

"In this case, the contraband consists of messages transported by couriers across enemy lines," John said. "I mentioned to Colonel Truesdail that I know someone who has done just that sort of work. Someone who also has an aptitude for decoding."

"As long as they aren't looking for someone to simply sweat away her days unsealing and resealing envelopes," Hattie said.

"The only way to know for sure is for you to go to Washington City and see for yourself," John said. "If the position's not to your liking, you can always come back."

"Washington City!" Alice said. "That means you'd be there when I perform with Wilkes in March. I can't tell you how much that would mean to me, to have a friend in town."

"And there's the inaugural ball," John said. "The colonel has hinted that we'll receive invitations."

"So you'd be coming to Washington City in March too?" Hattie said.

"Quite possibly." He gazed at her, eyes sparkling. "And at the ball, I'd most definitely want a beautiful woman at my side."

"How about two beautiful women?" Alice said.

He laughed. "I doubt my influence with the president goes that far. What do you say, Hattie? I know the ball would be but slight recompense for us foregoing your plans. But you'd be doing a service to the country."

When he put it like that, she could hardly refuse.

Chapter Twenty-Two

JANUARY 9, 1865

After John and Alice left Indianapolis within twenty-four hours of each other, the wisdom of Hattie's going to Washington became clear. Much as she enjoyed the Duncans, she felt aimless there.

When John wired to say the Bureau of Military Information had accepted his recommendation and was looking for her to arrive at her earliest convenience, she found herself eager to get going. The prospect of a normal life hadn't lost its allure, but she couldn't simply ignore the war and hope it went away. She needed to help bring it to an end, and if this operation would help toward that end, she was more than willing to serve.

She left Indianapolis on the first Friday in January, saying a tearful goodbye to Anne and little Jo with repeated promises to return as soon as her work was finished. The following Monday, she found herself back at the War Department, where she and

Anne had gone to work in Allen Pinkerton's secret mailroom at the start of the war.

Upon arrival, she was ushered directly in to see John Babcock, another former Pinkerton spy who'd stayed on with the Bureau of Military Information after Allen Pinkerton's departure from government service.

Babcock rose from his desk to greet her. "Hattie Logan. Last I saw you, you'd come from escaping a Richmond prison. We sent you to Tennessee, and now you're back with the highest of recommendations."

"I'm pleased to be of service if you've a place for me."

"Oh, we've a place all right, though it comes with little pomp or prestige. And the...ahem..." His gaze darted away and then back again. "The fact of your gender creates some obstacles."

Hattie squared her shoulders. "I can hold my own among men, I assure you."

"It's not that I doubt your tenacity. But it seems improper to place one woman among a group of men.

"Then I'll work alone."

"I've come upon a better solution. The Treasury Department has several women in their employ, filling clerk positions vacated by men who've gone off to fight. I've pulled some strings to get one of them reassigned here. I think you'll be pleased with my choice."

Hattie nodded. "As you wish, Captain Babcock."

A flush rose on his face. "I have no actual military rank, you know. I'm not certain how I came to be assigned one."

"You've proven your value here at the War Department," Hattie said. "As I hope I shall too. Who knows? Someday, women serving here might achieve actual military rank."

"Perhaps," he said, but he looked skeptical.

She followed him out of his office. Toward the back of the building, he led her to a familiar door. Swinging it open, he revealed the closet-like space that had once been Pinkerton's mail room. The table, the chairs, the stove—all was as Hattie remembered. And there was a familiar face, too.

"Constance!" Hattie said. "What a pleasant surprise."

Constance rose from her chair, nearly toppling a stack of envelopes as she stood. "I thought you'd never get here. Captain Babcock promised I'd have assistance, but I was beginning to think he'd only said that to lure me from my previous post."

"I'd never mislead a lady," Babcock said. "If my dear mother taught me nothing else, it was that. And now, if you two will excuse me, I'd best get back to my work. Hattie, Constance will fill you in on the specifics of your assignment."

He backed out the door, closing it behind him. Hattie removed her cloak and hung it on the rack, then took a seat beside Constance. "I hardly know what to do with myself without Lucy barking orders," she said.

Constance picked up an envelope. "She's a lively one, isn't she? I see her now and again about town. Doesn't have the time of day for me though."

"I can't say I'm surprised," Hattie said. "Lucy has always had a high opinion of herself."

"I thought being in prison might have brought her down a notch," Constance said.

"It did at first," Hattie said. "But she found her footing."

Constance turned the envelope over and removed the letter folded inside. "She gave up you and poor Thom Welton. That's what I heard."

Hattie nodded curtly. "Water under the bridge." The quiver in her voice surprised her. She pressed her palms to her skirt. "Well, let's be about our business. All I've been told is that we're looking for unusual activity in a nearby county."

"King George County," Constance said. "Babcock has been tight-lipped on the specifics. But so far, the work is much like what we did at Pinkerton's." She patted the stack of envelopes. "We open letters, we pass along suspicious information. Although it seems there are fewer letters now."

"I suppose they've gotten more discerning about which correspondence is suspect," Hattie said.

"Right," Constance said. "Remember how weary we got reading about bonnets and pound cake?"

Hattie smiled. "I never managed to convince you those could be code words."

"Bonnet for General Lee, pound cake for Mr. Lincoln? I still maintain that's a stretch." Constance spread out the letter she'd opened on the table. "We're to watch for mentions of soldiers on leave. Especially in King George County. Also, anything mentioning a Mr. Lohmann or a Mr. Ruth."

"Samuel Ruth?" Hattie said. "The man in charge at the Richmond, Fredericksburg, and Potomac Railroad?"

"That's right. You've heard of him?"

"I met him once, traveling to Richmond with Lucy. That was before I went there with Thom Welton. I got the impression that he was working in Virginia on the Union's behalf, slowing down trains and disrupting routes."

"That sounds dangerous," Constance said. "From what I'm told, Mr. Lohmann and Mr. Ruth are key figures in what Captain Babcock calls the Union line in Virginia, passing information by courier to officials here in Washington. Generally, they don't risk writing things down, but there is the occasional coded letter, I'm told. Oh, I almost forget—we're to watch for coded messages, too, coming out of Richmond. There's a Southern woman there spying for the Union. Can you believe it?"

"I can," Hattie said. "And if it's who I think it is, I've met her. Elizabeth Van Lew. She's from a wealthy Richmond family, and she makes no secret of her support for the Union."

"How is it she hasn't been arrested?" Constance said.

"Oh, they've tried," Hattie said. "But the charges never seem to stick. She's a smart woman, and a kind one too. If it weren't for her, I don't know that I'd have escaped that prison in Richmond."

Elizabeth Van Lew had also been the one who told her that Thom Welton had been executed. But Hattie said nothing of that to Constance. Even now, it pained her to speak of those times when she'd thought, having lost her first love, that her life was all but over.

Going to work on the stack of letters, Hattie was grateful for the improved efficiency of their operation. Due to the steaming kettle they used to open the envelopes and the iron they used to reseal them, the windowless room was still too warm, But without as many letters to go through, and with only the two of them working, it wasn't as unbearable as it had been under Pinkerton's watch.

As they worked, Hattie filled Constance in on what had become of Anne. She glossed over the fact that Anne's husband had proven a traitor to his country, siding with the Confederates in their attempt to gain control of Lake Erie. Instead, she said only that theirs had been a hasty marriage that had ended almost as quickly as it had begun. She also entertained Constance with tales of little Jo's antics, emphasizing how contented Anne seemed with her life now that she'd gotten over the shock of her husband's leaving.

In turn, Constance told Hattie of the developments in her own life. Saddest of these was the fact that her father had been killed in the war, leaving Constance and her mother to raise Constance's four young brothers.

"Quite the handful they are," Constance said. "And an expense. We'll have Father's pension, of course, but it's a good thing the government saw fit to hire me over at the Treasury Department. Not that it was much fun trimming dollar bills. I'd much rather be here with you, kettle and iron and all."

"I'm glad you're here too," Hattie said. "I wasn't sure what to expect, coming here."

"But how did you come here?" Constance stood at the kettle, an envelope balanced between her hands, holding it over a plume of steam.

"By train," Hattie said.

"You know what I mean." Constance tossed the envelope onto the table. "Last I knew, you went from Pinkerton's to some sort of position at a theatre."

Hattie reached for the steamed envelope. "Grover's National. That seems so long ago now."

"Three years, has it been?"

"I suppose so. Well, from the theatre, Miss Warne called me back to do some work with Pinkerton's."

Constance eyed her. "Some spying, you mean."

"You could say that. Eventually, I ended up in Richmond with Thom Welton. You know about that."

"Couldn't help but know. It was the talk of the town after you two got arrested. Lucy too. But you say you escaped prison?"

"With some help," Hattie said. "After coming north, I went to General Sharpe, asking to be sent to Nashville. He referred me to Captain Babcock, who referred me to the Army Police there."

"Why Nashville?" Constance asked.

"I suppose you could say I had a score to settle," Hattie said.

"And did you? Settle it, I mean."

"Not the way I intended." Hattie offered a smile. "But I did eventually succumb to the charms of the lieutenant who oversaw my work there."

"I thought you must have love in your life," Constance said. "There's a glow about you."

"And what of you?" Hattie said. "Have you a beau?"

Constance shot her a sly look. "Perhaps."

Hattie laughed. "Ah, a woman with secrets. I should have expected that."

Chapter Twenty-Three

When Hattie informed Anne's family that she was headed to Washington City, Mrs. Duncan insisted she stay with her cousins there.

"No more boarding house rooms for you," she'd said, waggling her finger at Hattie. "I'll wire Patty Trent straightaway to let her know you're coming."

"Oh, but the Trents have Henry staying there already," Hattie had protested, naming the youngest of the Duncan clan, who was working in Washington City and had recently become engaged to marry his cousin Julia.

"You'd be doing Patty a favor," Mrs. Duncan said. "Julia's all a-flutter over the wedding. Your steady influence would do her good."

Steady wouldn't have been how anyone would have described Hattie a few years ago. She only wished George could hear it. And she'd quickly given up objecting to Mrs. Duncan, who was a force to be reckoned with when she set her mind to something.

Arriving at the Trents at the end of her first day of official duties, Hattie was glad she'd acquiesced. In truth, she'd long since tired of boarding house rooms. And the Trents were every bit as gracious as the Duncans, with equally comfortable accommodations. Hattie had stayed with them once before, when she'd returned to Washington after escaping prison, luxuriating in the clean sheets and warm bed.

This time, Henry was occupying the guest room, so Mrs. Trent had arranged for an extra bed to be brought into Julia's room. Julia could not have been happier with the arrangement.

Up in their room following Hattie's first day at the War Department, Hattie was ready for a good night's rest. She nestled under her covers, her eyes heavy, as Julia searched her wardrobe for a dress to wear tomorrow.

"I suppose all the handsome couriers are falling over themselves for a word with you." Julia pulled out a green gown. "Mother says this one brings out the color in my eyes. But there's too much lace for my taste."

Despite her fatigue, Hattie rolled to her side, propping her head on her hand. "It is a lovely shade of green. But I agree about the lace."

Julia hung the dress back in her wardrobe. "And what of the handsome couriers?"

"I've yet to see one," Hattie said. "But Constance assures me they exist. One in particular she seems to fancy."

"Like you with Thom Welton," Julia said. Then her smile faded. "Oh, I'm such a ninny. I shouldn't have brought him up. Your first love, and it all ended so badly."

"The memory isn't as painful as it once was," Hattie said.

Julia's expression brightened. "And you've your lieutenant now. I can't wait to meet him when he comes for the inaugural ball."

"If he comes," Hattie said. "It's not for certain he'll be invited."

"Oh, but he must come. Papa will pull some strings if necessary." She pulled another gown from the wardrobe, the fabric decorated with pale orange flowers. She held it up to her chin, checking her image in the mirror. "Too peachy for January?" she said.

"I don't think so," Hattie said. "It's cheery."

"These teas mother drags me to are such a bore," Julia said, laying the dress over a chair. "Thank heavens you're here to amuse me with tales of your spying."

"It's not real spying I'm doing here. Just sorting through correspondence."

"You don't fool me. In her letters, Anne hints at some exciting adventures you've had."

Hattie yawned. "There's much to be said for less excitement and more ordinary living."

Julia looked shocked. "You can't mean that. Not with the important work you've been doing."

It was important, Hattie reminded herself, rolling away from Julia, who was about to snuff out the lamp. Already, she'd seen mentions of Confederate soldiers on leave in King George County, south of the Potomac—an unusual number of them, she noted, especially at a time when the Rebels were desperate for fighting men. And Constance claimed to have learned, from a source she coyly wouldn't name, that a Federal patrol vessel had recently intercepted torpedoes and barrels of explosives in that same county.

All very curious, Hattie thought as she dozed off to sleep. A puzzle to be solved.

~ ~ ~

Only two days passed before Hattie met Roger Montgomery, the courier Constance spoke of with such high regard. He arrived late on Wednesday afternoon, bringing a batch of correspondence from Virginia. He was of average height, his face ruddy and his hair dark.

"So this is the lady Captain Babcock recruited." He bowed gallantly in Hattie's direction. "Sergeant Montgomery at your service."

"Don't be flattered," Constance said. "He tries to charm all the girls." But her admiring gaze suggested that Montgomery's charms had not been wasted on her.

"I beg to differ." Montgomery drew himself up. "It's just that it's so rare to come upon two such lovely flowers in one room." He tossed a stack of envelopes on the table, then spread them around as if he were mixing a deck of cards for a trick.

A rather careless way to handle the missives, Hattie thought, but she kept her opinion to herself.

"Most of these won't be of interest," he said. Hattie supposed this was for her benefit, as if she didn't already realize how much ordinary information a spy might need to go through in search of the one clue that made all the pieces fit. "Though there are these."

He reached into his satchel and pulled out two sweet potatoes, one in each hand. He tossed them on the table next to the letters.

"Vegetables?" Constance said.

Hattie reached for one of the sweet potatoes. Examining it, she noted a thin line circling the top. She wedged her fingernail inside the line and ran it around the circumference, then pried off the potato's top. She reached inside and pulled out a wadded piece of paper.

"Aren't you the clever one," Montgomery said. He sounded disappointed she'd discovered the paper without his guidance.

"Let me try." Reaching for the other sweet potato, Constance followed Hattie's example, extracting another wadded-up paper. "Voila!" she said.

Montgomery shook his head. "Why Liz and Fanny see the need to resort to vegetables is beyond my ken. A woman thing, I suppose."

Hattie couldn't contain her surprise. "I should hope you're careful about announcing the names of our friends behind enemy lines."

His gray eyes narrowed. "I'm always careful, Miss—"

"Logan," Constance offered. "Hattie Logan."

He nodded curtly. "You may not realize, Miss Logan, that a courier such as myself, whom the enemy trusts, is most valuable indeed. And as for those two women, their activities are hardly a secret. Liz Van Lew—"

"Elizabeth Van Lew," Hattie said. Calling her Liz seemed disrespectful.

"Crazy Bet, they call her in Richmond," Montgomery said. "As for Fanny Dade, I assure you the Confederates are well aware of her activities, as she is of theirs. A Rebel spy, recently exposed in this city, now resides adjacent to her home." He shrugged. "A peculiar arrangement, but there you have it."

"Roger carries Confederate correspondence between Richmond and Montreal," Constance said.

"Montreal," Hattie said. "You have dealings with the Confederates there?"

"Been going back and forth every week or two, starting last summer." He tossed the blank envelope back into the pile. "I assumed the name of James Thompson, though I never used it in registering at a hotel."

"Why not?" Constance asked, gathering up the letters he'd spread across the table.

"To convince the Rebels that I wished to conceal it," he said smugly.

A bit too eager to convince them that his work was legitimate, Hattie thought. "How is it that the Confederates came to entrust you with their correspondence?" she asked.

He laughed. "Are you suggesting, Miss Logan, that I appear anything other than trustworthy?"

"Of course not," Hattie said. "I wonder, Sergeant Montgomery, if during the course of your work in Montreal you've happened upon a gentleman named Robert Martin. Or a widow, Mrs. Sarah Slater."

He rubbed his chin. "Can't say that I have. Why do you ask?"

"I've some connections in Montreal myself," she said. "How about Clement Clay?"

"Oh, I've had many dealings with Clement Clay. At Niagara Falls, at Toronto, at St. Catharines, and at Montreal. He'd do anything under the sun to achieve a Confederate victory."

"Like setting fire to New York," Constance said. "Was he among those you implicated in that plot?"

"The New York fires," Hattie said. "You had a hand in that investigation, Mr. Montgomery?"

"In a manner of speaking. There was much conversation in Canada about the firing of New York. Two days before the attempt was made, I left Montreal to bring news of it to this Department." He shook his head. "But by the time I arrived, the damage had been done."

"How fortunate it wasn't worse than it was," Hattie said, determined to keep her role in the matter under wraps.

"More recently, I stopped an attempted raid on Buffalo."

"You were involved in the capture of John Beale?" Hattie said. "When he tried to derail the train headed to Buffalo?"

"I don't know him by that name," Montgomery said. "But I warned government officials that the Confederates were about to set out on a raid of that sort, and by that means the raid was prevented."

"Amazing," Constance said. "To be in the thick of things as you are."

"Amazing," Hattie repeated. It was only exaggeration, she told herself, intended to impress. Still, she couldn't help wondering if there was a good deal more to Roger Montgomery than what he let on. Then again, the War Department trusted him. Why shouldn't she?

Hattie set to work steaming envelopes while Constance and Montgomery bantered back and forth a bit. Finally, the courier took his leave.

"Now that's the sort of man I could fall for," Constance said after he'd gone. "Smart. Dashing. Adventurous."

"He does have a way about him," Hattie said. "But you mustn't tumble head over heels for a man just because he pays you attention."

Constance stiffened. "Easy for you to say. Men fall all over you."

"I wouldn't say that," Hattie said.

"Well, it's true. You had Thom, and now you have that lieutenant whoever back in Tennessee. Me, I'll probably end up an old maid living with my mother."

"You've got your whole life ahead of you, same as me. I'm only saying be careful who you choose to spend it with."

Hattie set a stack of steamed envelopes on the table, then picked up the crumpled paper she'd extracted from the sweet potato. She unwadded it, then pressed it flat with her hands on the table. The handwriting was clear, the message direct.

Two here last night met with Conrad. Turned back. Fear line exposed. F.

"Line exposed," Hattie said. "That doesn't sound good."

"It surely doesn't," Constance said.

"The F must be for Fanny, the woman Sergeant Montgomery mentioned," Hattie said. "Captain Babcock should have a look."

Setting the paper aside, she recalled what Montgomery had said about Fanny Dade. A rebel spy, exposed in Washington City and now living adjacent to Mrs. Dade, who secretly favored the Union. A strange arrangement, to say the least. And a dangerous one.

But she'd managed to get her message out, signed with only a single initial. And yet Montgomery had been almost flippant in naming her. No wonder she'd hidden her message instead of only speaking it to him, which with a trustworthy courier would have been the safer method.

Constance reached for the second wadded paper and pressed it open in front of her. She read aloud from the slanted script.

"One wedding last week, another next. We wish you could be with us here, dearest cousin. Regards to your husband and son." She looked up from the paper. "It's signed Eliza A. Jones. I thought Roger indicated it was from Elizabeth Van Lew."

How quickly Constance had taken to familiarity with Roger Montgomery, Hattie thought. But she wasn't inclined to lecture her yet again on the virtues of being prudent with her affections. Hattie herself hadn't always been prudent in that realm.

"I've met Miss Van Lew," Hattie said. "She strikes me as far too clever to use her real name in correspondence."

"Hattie Logan, there is much you haven't told me." Constance sounded peevish.

"It was ages ago," Hattie said. "She came to my rescue while I was imprisoned in Richmond, alerting me to an escape effort. It took some convincing, but the men let me in on their plans. Otherwise, I might still be locked up."

"Miss Van Lew may be clever in that regard, but I don't see why she went to such trouble to conceal a message about family weddings."

"May I have a closer look?" Hattie said.

"Weddings." Constance handed her the paper. "That's all it says."

Hattie studied the message, the hand steady, the lines evenly spaced.

"I wonder…" Her voice trailing off, she stood and carried the paper to the kettle steaming on the stove.

Constance watched as Hattie held the letter over the steam. "Careful," she said. "That heat could ruin the ink."

"Or expose it." Hattie squinted at the paper. "When I was at Pinkerton's, one of the men in the deciphering division showed me how their work was done. You've heard people talk about reading between the lines, right?"

Constance nodded.

"Well, the meaning can be quite literal. Senders write an ordinary message using ordinary ink. Then, between the lines, they write the real message using some sort of acid-based liquid. Lemon juice, vinegar, that sort of thing. When the liquid dries, it's invisible. But when the paper is heated, a chemical reaction reveals the hidden message."

Constance got up and looked more closely at the paper. "I don't see anything hidden."

Frowning, Hattie pulled the message from the heat. "There must be something there. I can't imagine Miss Van Lew going to the trouble of concealing this paper in a hollowed-out sweet potato unless she had something important to convey." She looked up at Constance. "There must be someone here at the War Department who works on deciphering. Did Captain Babcock mention anything about that to you?"

Constance shook her head.

"I'm going to ask him," Hattie said. "This message warrants his attention."

"We're not to disturb him unless the information is critical and timely. I doubt a wedding qualifies." Returning to her seat, Constance plucked an envelope from the pile on the table. "Or maybe you just want to get out of the steaming."

Hattie chose not to reply. She set Fanny's message atop the message from Miss Van Lew, then slipped out the door and into the War Department proper. It was cooler in the open area, owing in part to the marble floors. As always, there was a good deal of activity, with clerks coming and going, some carrying telegraphed messages.

She approached Captain Babcock's office, pleased to see he was still in. He'd warned he was sometimes away at General Sharpe's field headquarters at City Point, a Union stronghold in eastern Virginia.

Looking up from the papers spread about his desk, Babcock gestured for her to come in. She complied, shutting the door behind her.

She held out the messages. "I know you asked us to deliver our work at day's end. But Sergeant Montgomery just brought a fresh set of correspondence, and these two items seemed of immediate interest. They were..." There was no way to put it but bluntly. "Concealed in vegetables."

Babcock took the papers from her outstretched hand. "One of the best local couriers in our line from Richmond is a farmer," he said. "He and a female spy in Richmond devised the vegetable method for concealing the most sensitive information. You were right to bring them to my attention."

Hattie was quiet while he read the messages. "Fear line exposed," he said, reading from Fanny's note. "I don't suppose Montgomery mentioned how the...vegetable containing that message came into his possession."

"Not exactly. But he mentioned that Fanny Dade and Elizabeth Van Lew sometimes rely on vegetables."

Babcock frowned. "He gave their full names?"

"Rather flippantly, I'm afraid."

Babcock sighed. "I'm sure I don't need to tell you that we expect better of the people in our employ. We must protect our sources. Especially the ones who risk their lives in enemy territory. I'll have a word with Sergeant Montgomery, but I'm not sure how much good it will do. Sometimes the circumstances of our work require us to take less than stellar characters into our confidence. I fear Montgomery falls into that category. But he has been a reliable courier, and the Confederates do seem to trust him."

He set Fanny's letter aside. "We can only hope her alarm about our line being exposed is misplaced. I'll have our scouts look into it."

"Sergeant Montgomery mentioned a Rebel spy, exposed here in Washington, now residing adjacent to Mrs. Dade's home," Hattie said. "A peculiar arrangement, he said."

Babcock leaned back in his chair. "The circumstances are indeed peculiar." He was silent a moment. "I'll share the details with you, Miss Logan. Knowing the full picture may help in your work. But I must ask that you be discreet. Until we better understand the situation, the less said about it, the better."

"I understand, sir."

"The Rebel spy in question goes by the name of Conrad. His work here in Washington was discovered, and he was forced to vacate the city. We suspect he still has at least one informant here, possibly in the employ of Lafayette Baker's secret service."

Baker. George's former employer, who was engaged in high-stakes cotton speculation. What a tangled web, Hattie thought.

"Our scouts tell us Conrad set up camp across the Potomac," Babcock continued. "He's at Boyd's Hole Farm, a property owned by Mrs. Fanny Dade. Mrs. Dade is a long-standing friend of the Union in King George County. How or why Conrad chose that location isn't known to us, but we suspect that Mrs. Dade somehow lured him to the site, knowing she could keep an eye on him there. Her home is also a safe house for Union officers who've escaped from Confederate prisons. Miss Van Lew, who you mentioned earlier, is the one who set up the escape route."

"Miss Van Lew befriended me when I was imprisoned," Hattie said. "She helped assure my escape and safe passage north."

"I remember that now." Babcock picked up the second paper, the one with the innocuous lines about weddings. "This came from Miss Van Lew, you say?"

"That's what Sergeant Montgomery indicated. Owing to how it was concealed, I suspected there might be more to the message, written in a way that's not ordinarily visible. But when I heated the paper, no hidden words came to light."

"It's the Sacred Three you need," He handed the message back to her. "Our cipher clerks. Only one of them is here at present though. The others are at General Sharpe's City Point headquarters, putting their minds to work on encrypted messages there."

"I've worked some ciphers myself," Hattie said. "Back when I was in Mr. Pinkerton's employ."

"That's welcome news," Babcock said. "With the others away, poor David Bates is swamped with work. But I expect he knows how to make Miss Van Lew's real message appear. You'll find him in the telegraph office."

Hattie pressed Elizabeth's message to her chest. "I'll go there immediately. Thank you, sir."

She proceeded to the telegraph office, which was next door to the office of Secretary of War Edwin Stanton. Formerly, the room had been a library, and shelves of books still lined the walls. Save for the clicking of the telegraph keys, a hushed silence pervaded the office. At various desks, several men, most of them young, bent studiously over their work.

Approaching the nearest desk, Hattie asked where she might find David Bates and was directed to a desk in the farthest corner of the room.

She wove past the workers, only a few of whom looked up as she passed. Nearing the corner, she said, "Mr. Bates?"

The man who looked up at her, his eyes earnest and his face clean-shaven, might have passed for a schoolboy. "Yes?"

"I'm Hattie Logan," she said. "Mailroom clerk." Not the most elegant title, but this was how Babcock had instructed her to refer to herself should anyone ask. "Captain Babcock suggested I see you for help with this letter."

Bates set down his pencil. "Have a seat, Miss Logan." He nodded at the chair beside his desk.

Sitting, she handed him the wrinkled paper from Miss Van Lew. "The person who sent this is a trusted informant. So there's reason to believe that she's saying more than what appears on the surface. Thinking she'd used an acid substance to hide the actual message, I heated the paper. But nothing appeared."

"If that's the case, you've come to the right place." He set Miss Van Lew's letter on his desk, then reached into a drawer, removing what appeared to be a medicinal vial. He unscrewed the cap and from the same drawer removed a thin brush. He dipped the brush in the vial. Then, leaning over the message, he swabbed the brush in measured strokes above the penned words. At first, nothing happened. But gradually, pen strokes emerged between the lines.

"Impressive," Hattie said as the words darkened. "What sort of substance is that?"

"Can't say exactly. But I'm told it contains some combination of gum Arabic and ferrous sulfate."

"What makes the ink invisible?"

He shrugged. "An old formulation, I'm told, used by our forefathers in the War of Independence." He handed her back the letter.

Hattie held the paper close, peering at the marks as they darkened. "They're not words," she said, holding the paper out for him to see. "Only numbers."

"Ah," he said. "Then that requires the Polybius." He nodded at a stack of papers. "Put it there," he said. "At the bottom. I'll get around to it when I've finished the others."

She drew the paper back. "If you show me how to use the Polybius, I'll decipher it myself. I've used a Vigenère's Square before."

"You've successfully deciphered a message using the Vigenère's?"

"Yes. I worked in Pinkerton's mail room in the early days of the war. One of the men who worked on deciphering showed me how to use it."

"Using a keyword," he said.

"Mostly," she said. "But one time I figured the keyword out on my own."

"If that's the case, the Polybius will be a cinch for you."

He withdrew a sheet of paper from his desk. On it was a grid of handwritten letters in seemingly random order. Above each row and column was a number. "This is the grid we're currently using. First, the sender locates a letter, then writes the corresponding number above the column followed by the corresponding number from the row containing the letter."

Hattie touched her finger to the grid, on top of the H. "So if I were writing my name, I'd start with the number of the column, here." She slid her finger to the top of the grid, landing on the number 3. "Then I'd follow with the number of the row, here." She moved her finger back to the H, then to the left until she reached the number 4, which began the row. "Thirty-four," she said. "Two numbers for each letter."

"That's right," he said. "A laborious method, but it works."

She took back Miss Van Lew's message along with the Polybius Square. "I'll return the square as soon as I've finished with it."

"Very good, Miss Logan," he said. "You'll be doing me quite the…" His voice trailed off. "Don't look now, but there's Mr. Lincoln, going into Mr. Stanton's office."

Hattie swiveled in her chair. Through the door's glass window, she caught a glimpse of the president, unmistakably with his tall, lean frame and stovepipe hat.

She turned back to David Bates. "I used to see him when I worked here before. Once, he even conversed with my friend and me, out in front of this building."

"That's our Mr. Lincoln. He comes into this office too. Reaches into a batch of wired messages with his long arm and fishes them out one at a time. When he's read them all, he'll say 'down to the raisins,' whatever that means."

"We're fortunate to have such a personable man leading us through these dark times. I'm glad he won re-election."

"As am I," Bates said.

She stood to leave. "Thank you for entrusting me with the Polybius, Mr. Bates. I enjoy a challenge and would be happy to help with any further deciphering should you find yourself in need of assistance."

He swept his hand over the papers piled on his desk. "Careful what you wish for, Miss Logan."

She left the telegraph office, shutting the door behind her. Passing Mr. Stanton's office, she glanced through the open doorway at Mr. Lincoln. Sitting at a large desk that looked as if it had been cleared to accommodate him, he studied a paper, brow furrowed.

How often he must get discouraged, she thought, considering how the war had dragged on. Her troubles—worries over who'd tried to harm her brother, questions about the future, disappointment at being separated from John Elliott—seemed trivial by comparison.

Chapter Twenty-Four

JANUARY 23, 1865

Within two weeks of arriving at the War Department, Hattie had found her stride. Using the Polybius Square, she'd deciphered Elizabeth Van Lew's message. In it, Miss Van Lew reported that Confederate forces were regrouping in the Carolinas in order to defeat Sherman and Grant. She also said Richmond's iron works had discharged 1,500 employees, having no money to pay them. This information she reported back to Captain Babcock, who took it to General Sharpe at City Pointe.

The next time Roger Montgomery came through the War Department, he brought more vegetables. Hattie opened them and withdrew the papers. She used the reagent to reveal hidden numbers penned by Elizabeth Van Lew. Then she used the Polybius Square to reveal their meaning.

Within a large turnip, she uncovered a message about machinery from three Richmond factories being moved south. Within a rutabaga, she discovered a ciphered note about a Richmond laboratory laying off 2,000 workers. This was yet more evidence that the Confederates intended to move the front lines of the war away from Richmond. Could that also mean the war was nearing its end? Hattie hoped so.

Shuttling between the War Department and General Sharpe's headquarters, Babcock was glad for each scrap of information that came through, especially if it hinted at the evacuation of Richmond. That would signal a dramatic turn in the war.

But the next time Montgomery brought more letters, Hattie noticed his usual swagger was gone. "The line has been broken," he said grimly. "The Confederates have arrested Lohmann and Ruth."

Hattie's heart sank. Mr. Lohmann and Mr. Ruth were vital to the Union's spy network in the South.

"I hope they won't come after you too," Constance said.

"Likewise," Montgomery said.

"Remember the message I took to Captain Babcock a couple of weeks ago?" Hattie said. "The one from Mrs. Dade?"

Constance nodded. "Something about two people being at her property."

"She said they'd met with the Confederate spy living at her farm," Hattie said. "And she warned that the line had been exposed."

"No one told me," Montgomery groused. "And here I've been risking my neck."

"I'm sure Captain Babcock looked into the matter," Hattie said. "But Mrs. Dade's claims are likely difficult to substantiate without compromising her position. Boyd's Hill Farm. That's the name of her property, isn't it?"

"Right," Montgomery said. "It's just across the Potomac."

"In King George County?" Hattie said.

"Right smack in the middle of it," Montgomery said. "Well located for escaped Union soldiers heading North. Though with the line exposed, I doubt her farm will be of any use to them now."

"What will happen to Mr. Lohmann and Mr. Ruth?" Constance asked.

"Hard to say," Montgomery said. "For the time being, they're locked up in Castle Thunder."

Hattie shuddered at the thought. Conditions at Castle Thunder had been harsh when she'd been confined there three years ago. She hated to think how much worse they'd be now that the South was running short on food.

The arrests were worrisome, to say the least. Montgomery assured them he'd be taking extra precautions. When Constance asked what that meant, he said only, "We shall see."

"What about Fanny Dade?" Hattie asked. "Have suspicions fallen on her as well?"

"I don't doubt that she'll be drawn into it, one way or another," Montgomery said.

Hattie thought of the people who'd helped her when she'd escaped from prison, unsung heroes all. She hoped Fanny Dade was being careful.

~ ~ ~

Despite the arrests, the mail kept coming, now through an eastern line that hadn't been discovered. The messages continued to suggest an unusual level of Confederate activity in King George County.

"I hope that doesn't mean the Rebels are going to try again to take Washington City," Constance said. "My nerves still haven't recovered after they got so close last summer."

"They'd have a hard time getting past General Sherman and General Grant," Hattie said. "Plus they've got Richmond to worry about. From what Miss Van Lew writes, there are serious questions as to whether it's defensible."

But none of that explained what the Rebels were up to in King George County. After what they'd attempted on Lake Erie and again in New York City, Hattie couldn't help feeling wary.

With so much to concern her—and with so little of it being anything she could discuss with anyone outside the War Department—she couldn't have been more delighted to receive a letter from John Elliott. After retrieving it from the Trents' letterbox, she fairly ran up the stairs to the room she shared with Julia.

Happily, Julia was out with her mother at a social engagement. She'd want to know every word John had written, and Hattie wanted to hold his words close, at least for the moment. Gently, she lifted the envelope's flap, not wanting to sully the letter by tearing into it.

Sitting on the bed, she pulled three folded sheets of paper from the envelope and began to read. In his careful hand, John wrote of his arrival in Louisville. His room at the Galt House Hotel had been quite comfortable, he said, up until the fire.

The fire. Her hand on her chest, Hattie reread that sentence, making sure she'd understood correctly. The blaze had broken out on January 10, John said, only a few days after he'd arrived. Within an hour, the entire hotel was engulfed in flames. Two bodies were later pulled from the rubble, but the rest of the guests had escaped with their lives.

"Thank God you're safe," Hattie whispered aloud.

Before fleeing the blaze, John said he'd managed to grab his revolver and a change of clothes. *Along with a remembrance of you*, he wrote, *which is dearer to me than anything.* Tears welled in her eyes at these words. What remembrance would that be, she wondered, for she'd given him nothing but her affection.

Having comfortably resettled in another hotel, he assured her that he was well. As to his work in Louisville, he was characteristically circumspect. She could tell he didn't want to openly criticize General Burbridge, the military commander under whom he served in Louisville. But she knew from what he'd told her before that Burbridge was engaged in a campaign of retribution aimed at suppressing the Confederate guerrillas who'd been terrorizing Kentucky. Wherever the outlaws committed an outrage—sabotaging railroads and telegraph lines, intercepting and destroying the mail, killing civilians—he ordered Union soldiers to arrest all Rebel sympathizers within a five-mile radius in order.

Even more troubling, John said, was the governor's demand that for every unarmed Union supporter Confederate guerillas killed, four Confederate prisoners would be executed. John had his own grudge to settle with Rebel guerillas. But the killing of innocents as an act of revenge troubled him.

There is much consternation among the citizens here, he wrote. *The reasons behind the orders may be sound, but in the hasty and arbitrary enforcement, justice is poorly served. There is talk that the hotel blaze was set as an act of retribution. That seems entirely possible.*

Toward the end of his letter, John mentioned Hattie's friend Edith Greenfield, a doctor who had worked with Hattie to expose the Confederates' Lake Erie plot. Edith was now directing a women's prison in Louisville, John wrote. He had yet to meet up with her, but he'd heard she was running a tight ship.

That would be Edith. Either you toed the line, or you got out of the way.

Hattie smiled at what John had written in closing, the single word *Fondly* warming. And he'd added a postscript: *Tickets to inaugural confirmed. I hope a lovely lady such as yourself will see fit to accompany me.*

Hattie closed her eyes, envisioning herself in John's arms, the two of them waltzing gaily as if the war had only been a figment of their imaginations.

Grateful to have an address where she could write, she sat down immediately to pen a reply. After expressing her relief that he was safe and well, she wrote of the Trents' hospitality and Julia and Henry's plans for their wedding once the war had ended. Of her work at the War Department, she was careful not to say anything that could compromise her efforts should her letter fall into the wrong hands. *I stay busy with my work and look forward to the day when we can be together.* That was the most she dared say.

~ ~ ~

Days later, word circulated through the War Department that Roger Montgomery had been arrested. Hearing this, Constance sank to her chair, her hands pressed to her heart. "It can't be," she said. "Not Roger. He's too clever."

"It may only be a rumor," Hattie said. "You mustn't fret until we know that it's true."

But Constance did fret in what seemed an endless loop of speculation. Finally, Hattie suggested she go home early. If nothing else, her boisterous brothers would be a distraction.

The next day, new details emerged. Montgomery had indeed been arrested, not by Confederates but by Union officials.

"I don't understand," Constance said. "Surely they don't suspect him of wrongdoing."

"It's likely a ploy," Hattie said. "An arrest in Union territory erases any doubts about his loyalty to the South. Soon enough, we'll get word he's escaped. The escape will be a ruse, of course. His captors will be in on it. But with any luck, the Confederates won't know that."

"What if something goes wrong?" Constance said. "What if he's shot by a guard who doesn't know the circumstances?"

A legitimate concern, Hattie knew. "We have to trust they know what they're doing," she said.

For the remainder of the week, Constance was on pins and needles, waiting for word of Montgomery's fate. In the meantime, attention turned to the case of Samuel Ruth. After a hasty trial in the South, the railroad superintendent had been set free.

On the surface, this seemed like good news. But Hattie worried about the circumstances of Ruth's release. From King George County, Fanny Dade had been brought to Richmond to testify in his trial. According to the Richmond papers—widely circulated in the War Department—Fanny had revealed all sorts of details about the Union's line of spies in the South.

Was Fanny's allegiance to the North so flimsy? Was she a double agent? Or had the Confederates threatened her, perhaps through the spy who'd encamped on her property?

It was impossible to know. At least Samuel Ruth was free. Hattie had met him once, traveling to Richmond. With the acts of sabotage he'd managed to pull off in his position as railroad superintendent, he'd done much to aid the Union. That was all over now that he'd been exposed.

Strangely, neither Fanny nor Elizabeth Van Lew was imprisoned. That, too, was good news, but Hattie couldn't help but wonder why. It was almost as if the Confederates, having discovered the Union line, now wanted its route forgotten. What could be their reasons for not wanting to draw attention to it? Might they be planning to use the safe houses for their own purposes, allowing safe passage for fugitives fleeing to the South?

I'm reading too much into it, Hattie told herself. But her questions remained.

Then one day, as if out of nowhere, Roger Montgomery re-turned, bringing a fresh batch of mail. Constance rushed to greet him. "I – we – were so worried about you. Were you truly in prison?" Her gaze landed on his left arm, confined to a sling. Touching it, she said, "Oh, but you've been injured."

Flashing a half-smile, he tossed a stack of envelopes on the table. "A flesh wound," he said. "Smarts a bit, but I doubt they'll have to amputate."

Constance gazed up at him. "They tried to kill you when you made your escape."

"Sergeant Montgomery was held in a Union prison," Hattie said. "No one intended to kill him."

"True enough," he said. "I shot myself, actually. Adds to the realism of the ploy. No one in the South will doubt my allegiance now."

"How clever," Constance said. "And how daring."

Hattie didn't believe him. Likely his injury—if there even was one—had come about in an ordinary way, and he'd chosen to work it for maximum effect. She'd seen this propensity for exaggeration among other spies. Her friend Pauline Cushman had made up so many stories about her escapades that Hattie doubted whether Pauline herself could separate fact from fiction.

She pressed her lips together, choosing not to question Mont-gomery further. If he desired his moment in the sun with a fawning admirer, who was she to deny him?

Chapter Twenty-Five

FEBRUARY 18, 1865

I n the bedroom they shared, Julia twirled in her new gown, modeling it for Hattie.

"Magnificent!" Hattie said. "That shade of blue makes your skin look positively creamy."

Standing still, Julia fingered the velvet trim on her bodice. "But is it too much blue?" she said. "With the embellishments?"

"Different shades," Hattie said. "An altogether elegant effect."

"What about the gold baubles?" Julia touched one of the myriads of little gold balls attached along the bodice trim. "Too much?"

"Not at all. You'll be the belle of the ball," Hattie said. "Best take care you don't outshine Mrs. Lincoln."

Julia's brow furrowed. "I wouldn't want to offend her. She has so few friends here as it is."

Hattie laughed. "I'm only teasing. I don't know Mrs. Lincoln as you and your mother do, but I can't imagine she'd begrudge a young woman her moment to shine."

Pressing her hands to her tiny waist, Julia studied herself in her full-length mirror. "Can you imagine? We'll be telling our grandchildren one day how we danced the night away at Mr. Lincoln's inaugural ball. Papa says the preparations are well underway at the Patent Office."

"Hard to imagine dancing there," Hattie said. "When it's so recently been used as a hospital for the Union wounded. When we visited Henry there, I remember being struck by how many beds they'd managed to squeeze among the patent exhibits."

Julia tipped her head, smiling at her image in the glass. "Those days are over. Besides, Papa says it's just the top floor that's being transformed for the festivities. On a raised dais, Mr. and Mrs. Lincoln and their most distinguished guests will sit on blue and gold sofas." Her eyes sparkled with mischief. "It's that little detail about the blue and gold that inspired my gown."

"How astute," Hattie said.

"I must credit Mother for that," Julia said. "Oh, but here I am, going on and on about what I'll be wearing, and I haven't even asked about your plans. Will your lieutenant be bringing one of your frocks when he comes?"

Hattie smiled at the image of John Elliott traveling from Louisville with a ballgown. "I won't be troubling him with that," she said. "Besides, my fancy dresses are with Anne."

"Then you must have her send one straightaway," Julia said.

"I don't want to trouble her. And in truth, I'm not especially fond of any of those gowns. I acquired them in haste to play the part of a wealthy Confederate widow. A ruse to entrap a Rebel spy."

Julia's eyes widened. "And it worked?"

"The plot was foiled," Hattie said, keeping her explanation as simple as possible. "And last I heard, the spy was in prison."

"How exciting," Julia said. "But it doesn't solve the problem of what you'll wear to the ball."

Hattie shrugged. "There's my green dress. Nothing fancy, but I rather like the shade."

Julia looked horrified. "But that's an everyday dress. You've worn it at the War Department any number of times. You can't wear it to the biggest social event of the season—maybe even of the decade."

"I'm sure it will be a magical evening regardless of how I'm dressed."

"You'd be Cinderella without her fairy godmother's intervention. We can't have that." Julia fell silent a moment. Then, skirt swishing, she went to her wardrobe and swung open the door. "You must wear one of my gowns. You're my size, after all."

"Oh, I couldn't," Hattie said.

"Whyever not? I have far more than I need." She pulled out a pale yellow skirt with a matching bodice trimmed with brown lace. Holding it up, she eyed it critically.

"So gracious of you, Julia," Hattie said. "But truly, I'm fine with wearing one of my tried-and-trues."

Undaunted, Julia walked the dress over to where Hattie sat. "Stand up," she said.

Hattie complied. Despite her age, Julia spoke with an authority that came from years of wrangling her younger brothers.

Turning Hattie toward the mirror, Julia held the dress to her chin. "What do you think?"

"It's quite...yellow," Hattie said. "The color suits you fine. But on me..." Her voice trailed off.

"Right." Julia sashayed back to the wardrobe and hung the yellow dress back up. She ran her finger along the hanging clothes, stopping at a dress with a pale green skirt. She removed the dress, carried it to the mirror where Hattie stood, and held it up to her. "Not the most stylish, but the color's better."

"The green is nice," Hattie said. "But the skirt...it's so wide that if I'm not careful, I'll get stuck in a doorway."

"I see your point." Lowering the dress, Julia grabbed Hattie's hand and tugged her toward the wardrobe. "You pick one out."

Hattie had little choice but to go along. Running her fingers over the hangers, she had to admit that Julia was right on one count. The night would be magical, spent in John Elliott's arms. It would be nice to look special.

But the dresses in Julia's wardrobe had been tailor-made for her at a younger age, and though Hattie took out a few more to consider, Julia had to agree that none seemed quite right. Hattie was about to give up when, at the very back of the wardrobe, a gown caught her eye.

Reaching inside, she pulled the dress out and held it up to her chin. "This one will do."

Julia let out a little gasp. "But it's red."

"A delightful shade." Hattie fingered the silk. Red was John Elliott's favorite color.

"It does look stunning against your skin," Julia said. "And it brings out the highlights in your hair. But you can't wear a red dress. You're not married. I only have it because it belonged to Mother's sister, and Mother thought I might like to wear it after I'm wed."

Hattie gazed at her image in the mirror. "Whoever made that rule about not wearing red must have been an old married lady who wanted to keep the color all to herself."

"It's not the latest fashion either," Julia said.

"I don't care about fashion," Hattie said. "Or silly rules about what unmarried ladies can and can't wear." She folded the dress over her arm. "If your offer still stands, this is my choice."

Julia smiled. "You are scandalous. And you'll be the talk of the ball, that's for certain."

Whether people talked about her or not was of little concern to Hattie. She only hoped she and John would remember the ball as long as they lived.

~ ~ ~

The gown decided upon, Hattie immersed herself in less frivolous matters. Despite the compromised line, Elizabeth Van Lew managed to keep spying, sending her messages through the eastern route. David Bates was only too happy to leave their deciphering to Hattie. He was immersed in a project that consumed nearly his entire attention, though he was tight-lipped about what it was.

Preparations were being made to evacuate Richmond, Miss Van Lew wrote. At the same time, Confederate General Robert Lee was planning a surprise attack near Petersburg, Virginia, once the weather improved. Even in the South, the winter months had been plagued with cold and rain, but Miss Van Lew wrote that the Confederates still had their scouts out, surveying the Union-held territory around Petersburg.

Hattie brought these messages to Captain Babcock. Reading it, he thanked her for her sound judgment in doing so. As she turned to leave, he called out to her.

"Miss Logan? I wonder if you might give Mr. Bates a hand with another project. He is loathe to admit it, but he's having difficulty with the Confederates' Court cipher."

"The Court cipher—that's using the Vigenère's Square?"

"Yes. Mr. Bates mentioned your having had some experience with it."

"I have," Hattie said. "And I enjoy a puzzle. I'll check with him right away."

Pleased at the chance to put her skills to use on a greater challenge than Miss Lew's numerical cipher, she went directly to Mr. Bates. She found him hunched over his desk, pencil in hand, intent on the paper before him. He seemed not to notice her standing in the doorway, so she rapped lightly on the door.

He looked up, and she saw the weariness in his eyes. "Oh," he said. "Come in, Miss Logan. I didn't mean to ignore you. Please don't tell me you've brought another message I won't be able to figure out."

She peered at the papers he'd been bent over. On one was a message with what looked like several nonsensical words. On the other, Bates had copied the nonsense words into blocks of five letters each.

"That was sent using the Vigenère's, wasn't it?"

"Right." His hands behind his head, he leaned back in his chair, stretching his back. "But they've changed the keywords, and danged if I can figure out what the new ones are."

"They're no longer using COMPLETE VICTORY?" she said. Those had been the keywords for the last message she'd deciphered using the Vigenère's—a message that had mentioned her father's involvement in smuggling grain to the South.

Dropping his hands, Bates shook his head. "I thought so at first. The first three letters seemed to fit. But not the rest. MAN-CHESTER BLUFF doesn't work either," he said, naming another keyword the Confederates had used in the past.

"How frustrating," Hattie said. "Perhaps if we both put our minds to it, we could figure it out."

His expression relaxed. "That would be a great help."

"You have an additional square?" she said.

"Somewhere." He rifled through the stack of papers on his desk, then opened one desk drawer after the other. "Ah," he said at last, producing a paper from the bottom drawer. "Here it is."

He handed her the paper. On it was a printed table consisting of letters. At first glance, the effect was dizzying. The alphabet ran along the table's top row and left column. Letters repeated along diagonals. A row of Zs divided the table from the top left corner to the bottom right. Above the Zs, the diagonals ascended to A. Below, the diagonals started with As and descended to Zs.

"I'll copy the message," Hattie said. "That way we can work simultaneously."

"Good idea." He passed her a pencil and a sheet of paper along with the paper he'd been struggling over.

She sat in the chair beside his desk and carefully copied the message, one letter at a time.

To Hon. J.C. Breckenridge, Sec'y of War: I recommend that the tsysmee fn qoutwp rfatvvmp ub waqbqtm exfvxj and iswaqjru ktmtl are not of immediate necessity, uv kpgfmbpgr mpc thnlfl should be lmqhtsp. R. E. Lee

She checked her work against the original, then returned the message to Bates.

"At least it's not all encoded," she said. "That helps a bit."

"A bit," he repeated. "But not enough."

Hattie took the Vigenère's Square and the message she'd copied back to the mail room. Struggling with an envelope flap, Constance looked up when she came in. "I thought you'd wandered off and got yourself abducted by the Rebels," she said.

"Captain Babcock asked if I'd give Mr. Bates a hand with a ciphering problem," Hattie said. Taking her seat, she set the Vigenère's Square and the copied message on the table in front of her.

Constance leaned in for a look. "*I recommend that the tsys-mee-fn-qout-wp*," she read aloud. "What's that supposed to mean?"

"I haven't a clue. But I aim to find out."

"Using this?" Constance pressed her finger to the Square. "Show me how you do it."

"I can't," Hattie said. "At least not right away. It's a more complex cipher than the one Miss Van Lew uses. It requires knowing what keywords the sender used. But Mr. Bates said the Confederates have changed their keywords, so we need to figure that out first."

Constance shook her head. "Beyond me." She returned to her envelope flap.

By late afternoon, Hattie was starting to wonder whether the task was beyond her too. Line by line, she pulled out the gibberish. She divided the letters into columns—first two letters each, then three, and then four. Each time, she studied the results, looking for patterns that might indicate words.

She filled paper after paper with columns of letters, but nothing came clear. She rubbed her fingers over her forehead, where a dull ache was forming.

"No luck?" Constance said.

Hattie shook her head. "I have no idea what the new keyword could be."

"Put it away for the day," Constance said. "In the morning, it might all look different."

"Ever try falling asleep with a bunch of letters swirling around in your head?" Hattie said.

Constance glanced at the papers Hattie had filled with her scratching. "I see your point."

Hattie reached for another blank piece of paper. Rather than copy down yet another configuration, she wrote down the keywords the Confederates had used before, MANCHESTER BLUFF and COMPLETE VICTORY.

Bates had told her that in Richmond, the Confederates used cipher cylinders to encode their messages. But recipients in the field would have to do their decoding manually as she and Bates were attempting. That meant keeping things as simple as possible. With this reasoning, it would make sense that whatever the new keyword was, it would be similar in some way to the previous ones.

She sat up straighter, then tapped her pencil from letter to letter in the two known keywords. "Fifteen," she said aloud.

Constance looked up from the message she was reading. "Fifteen what?"

"Fifteen letters. That's how many the old keywords had, so I'm guessing the new one has fifteen letters too."

"If you say so." Constance went back to her reading.

Despite her fatigue, Hattie's excitement grew. On a clean sheet of paper, she copied the first fifteen garbled letters: *tsysmee fn qoutwp.* Then she rewrote them in three columns of five letters each: *tsysm eefung outwup.*

"Easy, but not easy enough," she muttered.

"Come again?" Constance said.

"Nothing." Hattie bent closer to the paper. Bates had said the first three letters of the old keyword, COMPLETE VICTORY, had seemed promising. She copied the next string of fifteen letters, dividing them into three columns too: *rfatv vmpub waqbq.* Above the *tsy* from her first set of letters and above the *rfa* from the second, she wrote COM.

She grabbed the Vigenère's Square. "C to T," she said softly, moving her fingers across the square. "C to R." With each letter, she repeated the process. She jotted down the results: *rem* for the first set of fifteen letters, *pro* for the next set. Then she began trying words that might fit. Remain, remember, remove.

"Removal!" She felt like a schoolgirl who'd found the Easter egg the others had given up on.

Constance came over to look.

"It fits here." Pointing, Hattie read aloud from the message. "I recommend the removal."

"The removal of what?" Constance asked.

"I don't know yet," Hattie said. "But I've got enough now to make a good guess." Working from the word *removal,* she ran her fingers over the table, jotting letter after letter. "C-O-M-E-R-E-T. That's the start of the new keywords."

"Comeret," Constance said. "You sure it's not *comet?*"

"Positive. But think what would come after *removal.*"

"Of?" Constance said.

"Right." Hattie trailed her fingers over the table again. "O gives us R. F gives us I. So now we've got C-O-M-E-R-E-T-R-I. Come something." She drew a line between the first E and the R. "Retri—" She thought a moment. "Retribution." She scribbled the words, then counted the letters. "Come Retribution. Fifteen letters. Those are the new keywords."

"Well done," Constance said. "You should be pleased with yourself."

And she was. But as she rushed to deliver her findings to David Bates, a sobering thought came to her.

Come Retribution. That sounded as if the Confederates had something dark in mind. Something more ominous than victory.

Chapter Twenty-Six

MARCH 3, 1865

With Hattie's discovery of the keywords, she and Bates were able to decode the entire message with relative ease. Confederate officials were to start moving property, machinery, stores, and archives out of Richmond, Confederate General Lee advised. In addition, they should secure all powder.

Babcock was pleased with this revelation. He took the message to City Point headquarters himself, ensuring that General Grant could use it in planning his next battle. Hattie and David Bates were the heroes of the day.

Still, Hattie worried about the threat COME RETRIBUTION signaled. It didn't help when Constance told her that her mother's landlady, a Southern sympathizer, had muttered something about their prospects improving after the fourth of March.

But Bates said not to worry. Keywords didn't have actual meaning. They were simply combinations of letters that could easily be remembered and repeated. As for Constance's landlady, well, Southern sympathizers were forever looking for better prospects. And as of now, those prospects were diminishing rapidly.

So Hattie turned her attention to John Elliott's arrival. He'd written to say that he'd procured tickets for the two of them to attend Lincoln's inauguration tomorrow as well as the inaugural ball Monday night.

To quell her excitement, Hattie had busied herself making a few alterations to the dress she was borrowing from Julia. Now it fit perfectly.

On Friday evening, she went to the station to meet John's train. It was packed with people milling about, most no doubt here because of the inauguration. She pressed her way through the crowd to the platform. Rain had fallen steadily all day, and wind whipped her skirt, which she was forced to lift slightly, owing to the amount of mud that had been tracked onto the platform.

Holding her umbrella high, she peered over the crowd to get a view of the locomotive chugging toward them. The whistle blew, and her heart thrilled. The train pulled to a stop at the platform, its engine smell mixing with the odor of wet wood and woolens.

The crowd seemed to contract on itself, drawing close as passengers began to get off. Hattie scanned every face. Finally, she spotted John, handsome as ever in his uniform. She hurried toward him, glad for both her umbrella and her wide skirt, which forced people out of her way.

Moments later, she was in his arms, relaxing into his embrace, and the world felt whole again.

~ ~ ~

The next morning, Hattie hired a buggy to take her to the National Hotel, where John was staying. Despite the early hour, carriages jammed the streets, causing her to arrive later than she'd hoped.

John was waiting for her in the lobby. Smiling, he took her hand. "You look ravishing. The rain becomes you."

She brushed a damp curl from her forehead. "I'm glad you think so. Even with the buggy, I feel rather soggy."

"Perhaps we should watch the parade from my room," he said. "If you don't think that would be too untoward."

"You're a respectable officer," she said. "And we did share a bit of forest floor back in Tennessee, with no undue harm to my honor."

"So we did," he said.

Weaving their way through the knots of people gathered in the hotel's lobby, they started for the staircase. From the corner of her eye, Hattie caught a glimpse of a man she recognized. Slim, handsome, jet-black hair that curled slightly.

She stopped walking.

"What is it?" John said.

"Over there." She nodded toward the hotel's entrance. "That man walking toward the door. That's the actor John Wilkes Booth."

He peered that direction as the actor exited the hotel. "The man Alice says is up to no good."

"Yes. But I suppose it's no surprise he's in the city. He and Alice are performing at Grover's National on the eighteenth."

They started up the stairs. "As I recall, there was a woman in-volved with Mr. Booth," John said.

"Several women," Hattie said. "The one that concerned me veiled her face, dressing as a widow."

"You thought she might have had something to do with your brother being poisoned," John said.

"Right. But in the end, there's nothing I can prove." She looked up at him. "Some things you just have to let go."

"True enough."

They came to the second-floor landing. His hand on her elbow, he steered her toward the right. Halfway down the hall, he took out his key and unlocked a door.

"Nothing fancy," he said, swinging open the door. "But I slept like a rock last night."

She entered his room, which smelled pleasantly of hair oil and leather. The bed was neatly made, and at the tall window, the drapes were tied back, allowing in the morning's gray light.

John stepped close, and she felt his warm breath on her shoulder as he helped her out of her wrap. His lips brushed her neck, and a shiver ran through her.

"I won't lie," he whispered. "You tempt me greatly." He drew back just enough to look into her eyes. "But I intend to make an honest woman of you as soon as this war is over. If you'll have me, that is."

She felt herself melting into his embrace. "That sounds like a marriage proposal, Lieutenant Elliott." She drew a breath, looking deeply into the gaze of the man she'd come to love. "If it is, I accept."

They kissed, and she wished the moment would never end. But of course it had to.

As they pulled apart, he drew her toward the window. "If we're not careful, we'll miss the parade."

He raised the sash, letting in a rush of cool air. From the street belong came the lively notes of a march. Despite the dampness, enthusiasm was in the air. People jammed the sidewalks, craning their necks toward the parade. In the windows of buildings all around, ladies waved handkerchiefs and men waved their hats at the bands, marchers, and floats making their way down Pennsylvania Avenue from the Executive Mansion toward the Capitol.

Hattie and John stood side by side, shoulders nearly touching. "Look," she said, pointing. "A company of colored troops."

"What a difference a war makes," John said.

When the presidential carriage came into view, the crowd raised a cheer. It was hard to imagine that just a few months ago, the president's re-election prospects had been dim. Through plots and schemes, the Confederates had tried to unseat Lincoln and diminish the Union's prospects. But they'd failed. Knowing she'd helped thwart their efforts, Hattie felt a swell of pride.

And yet as she watched the president's carriage pass, she also felt a sense of foreboding. "I hope nothing untoward happens."

John turned toward her. "Why would you think that?"

"The Confederates recently adopted new keywords for their secret communications. COME RETRIBUTION."

Furrows formed between his eyebrows. "That does sound men-
acing."

"And there's talk among Southern sympathizers here about
their prospects improving after today. I worry that harm might
come to Mr. Lincoln."

John rubbed his chin. "There may be reason for worry. Southern
officials have planted the idea that the Union had to kill Jefferson
Davis. Now, with the war turning in the Union's favor, harming
Lincoln could be the retribution the South has in mind."

"You mean they'd make an attempt on Mr. Lincoln's life, then
justify it by saying the Union tried to do the same to their president?"

"It's possible. I'm told one of Mr. Lincoln's aides has been concerned about his safety for some time."

"Before his first inauguration, there was a plot to assassinate
him," Hattie said. "Miss Warne was the first to learn of it. She and
Mr. Pinkerton devised a plan to foil it."

"And Mr. Lincoln took a good amount of ribbing in the press
for his evasive measures, as I recall," John said. "Which I'm told
now makes him less likely to embrace efforts to protect him."

She drew a deep breath. "I fear the lengths his enemies might go
to."

"As do I." John squeezed her hand. "But the hostilities are winding down. Within a few weeks, the threat may be over."

She looked up at him. "You truly think the war may end within
weeks?"

"Smarter men than I are saying so."

Her shoulders relaxed. After all these years of pain and sorrow and division, a new beginning was within reach. A new life for her and John Elliott.

~ ~ ~

On the streets, the traffic was so heavy that Hattie feared they would never reach the Capitol's east lawn in time to hear the president speak. And yet even with the crowds, the mood was buoyant. Joy and confidence were in the air.

With breaks now and then in the clouds, the Capitol's newly built dome shone off and on as Hattie and John drew near. "There must be ten thousand people here," Hattie said as they edged forward.

"Likely there will be twenty thousand more before the day's over," John said.

Nearing the front of the throng, John showed his tickets to an attendant, who unfastened a cord, allowing them access to the Capitol's portico. Though crowded, they were able to move more easily here, finding a place to stand with only one row of people ahead of them.

Below, a platform had been erected with seats for the dignitaries. In the crowd beyond the cordoned area, Hattie saw dark faces mingled with the white. How much this day must mean to the Negroes, after all Mr. Linocln had done to free them from the bonds of slavery.

With the rest of the crowd, Hattie and John waited for the president and his party to emerge from the chambers where members of the Senate were being sworn in. Hattie shifted side to side, her feet aching from standing so long in one place.

Finally, the dignitaries came from inside the Capitol to take their seats on the platform. Hattie stood on tiptoe, straining for a glimpse of Mr. Lincoln, looking dapper in his top hat and tails. As ever, Hattie was struck by how his craggy face looked both intelligent and kind. In an ermine-trimmed black dress, Mrs. Lincoln was at his side.

When the officials were seated, the crowd's murmuring ceased, and the ceremony began. At the moment the president stepped forward, setting one hand on a bible and raising the other to take the oath of office, the clouds parted, and the sun cast a warm, brilliant light over the scene.

In a clear, strong voice, the president delivered his inaugural address. Hattie listened intently, wishing she could commit every word to memory. He spoke of the war which after nearly four years still engrossed the nation's energies. He mentioned the insurgent agents who had plagued this city at the time of his first inaugural address.

"Both parties deprecated war," Lincoln said. "But one of them would make war rather than let the nation survive, and the other would accept war rather than let it perish. And the war came."

In a nutshell, those were the circumstances of the conflict that had altered the course of Hattie's life. She'd heard no other words that so readily captured the heartache, pain, and triumph that had been visited upon the nation.

The president went on to acknowledge slavery as the root cause of the war, and he invoked the Living God as the source of the divine attributes that would bring healing once the offense was removed.

"Fondly do we hope—fervently do we pray—that this mighty scourge of war may speedily pass away," Mr. Lincoln said, echoing the deep longing Hattie had felt these past few months.

"With malice toward none; with charity for all; with firmness in the right, as God gives us to see the right, let us strive on to finish the work we are in," he concluded. "To bind up the nation's wounds; to care for him who shall have borne the battle, and for his widow, and his orphan—to do all which may achieve and cherish a just and lasting peace, among ourselves, and with all nations."

The crowd cheered. The president stepped back. With four ruffles and flourish, the Navy Band struck up a tune. "Hail to the Chief," John whispered, leaning close. "The president's song."

As the spritely song continued, Hattie sensed movement behind her. She turned, as did John. A man was pushing his way forward, the same man they'd seen leaving the hotel that morning. Booth.

John stepped forward, blocking Booth's way. "There will be no rushing from here. At the appropriate moment, onlookers will disperse in an orderly manner."

Booth eyed John's uniform. Then he glanced toward the platform, where the president was shaking hands with the dignitaries gathered there. "I have...a commitment to keep."

John took another step forward, forcing Booth to step back. "Your commitment will have to wait."

Booth glared at him. Then he shrank back, disappearing into the crowd.

"What an arrogant man," John said. "I'm glad Alice parted ways with him."

"As am I," Hattie said.

They watched as the presidential party moved from the platform back into the Capitol. Slowly, the crowd began to disperse. As Hattie and John moved toward the steps leading away from the portico, she kept an eye out for Booth. Wherever he'd been headed in such a rush, he must have found another way out, for she didn't see him. He hadn't seemed to recognize her from their encounter in New York. Just as well, she thought. He might be a beloved actor, but the less she had to do with him, the better.

The festivities continued with a presidential reception at the Executive Mansion. If there had been a crowd of thirty thousand at the inauguration itself, there seemed at least that many jammed in front of the Lincolns' residence, filling the lawns and the sidewalks as they waited to be let inside.

Hattie and John joined a queue. As the line snaked forward, they spoke of how they'd separately passed the recent weeks, filling in the details they'd only been able to allude to in their letters. John told her of yet another fire in Louisville, destroying a military prison housing Confederates. He didn't have to say aloud what Hattie suspected, that this was yet another case of suspected arson.

He also told her about Kentucky's new military governor, who promised to free Negro "contrabands" who'd been kept in pens.

The governor was also stationing men around Louisville to guard the city against guerrilla attacks.

"The populace as a whole won't like that," John said. "But it will restore justice and order."

Hattie told him what she could about her work with David Bates. "I introduced him to Constance last week," she said. "Every day since, he has come by to speak with her. But she seems stubbornly committed to another."

She also filled him in on Julia's wedding plans, assuring him that she would prefer a far simpler affair.

They arrived at a passageway leading into the Executive Mansion. A sharp-eyed guard advised the crowd to move along. Then he held his arm, stopping a man behind Hattie.

"No coloreds allowed inside," the guard said.

"But Mr. Lincoln is expecting me," the man said.

Hattie whirled around to see a face she recognized from newspaper photos. "Why, this is Frederick Douglass," she told the guard. "The famous Negro orator. You must admit him. Mr. Lincoln wouldn't stand for him being left out. Or any of his people, for that matter."

The guard grabbed Mr. Douglass's arm. "I doubt either one of you speaks for the president. I've got my instructions. No coloreds inside."

As he yanked Mr. Douglass toward the passageway, another guard stepped up to take his place. "Move along," the new guard said, making a shooing motion with his hands. "There's thousands behind you determined to tromp through here before the day ends."

Hattie tugged John's sleeve. "We've got to see that Mr. Douglass gets admitted."

He nodded, and they proceeded down the passageway where the guard and Mr. Douglass had disappeared. From behind, the crowd filled in the space they'd left.

"Imagine, trying to keep a man as well-known as Frederick Douglass from greeting the president," Hattie said as they strode quickly ahead.

"Not to mention all the other Negroes who admire Mr. Lincoln," John said.

At the end of the passageway, they caught up with the guard and Mr. Douglass. The guard was pointing toward the exit. Mr. Douglass was standing his ground.

Approaching them, John withdrew a badge from the inner pocket of his jacket. "Provost guard," he said. "I've been sent to escort Mr. Douglass to see Mr. Lincoln."

The man squinted at the badge, engraved with the words PROVOST GUARD. Then he looked up at John. "Sent by who?"

"Captain Babcock," Hattie said, certain her supervisor wouldn't mind her invoking his name for a good purpose. "Military Intelligence."

The man eyed her. "Military intelligence, you say?"

"They're aware of all my comings and goings, I'm afraid," Douglass said, his dark eyes twinkling.

"Indeed we are," John said. "After you, Mr. Douglass." John gestured back toward the passageway.

The guard let go of Mr. Douglass's arm, and they set off toward the entrance. "Anyone asks how he got in, I'm sending them straight to you," he called after them.

"Thank you kindly, sir," Douglass said to John. "And madam. Your intervention came at a timely moment."

"It's an honor to meet you," Hattie said. "While at boarding school, I read your narrative on having been a slave. Your words impressed me greatly."

"I'm glad of it," he said. "Once we're inside, I hope you'll direct me to this Captain Babcock you mentioned so that I might express my gratitude to him as well."

"I'm afraid he may be...indisposed," Hattie said.

"But we'll be happy to direct you to the president," John said.

As they drew near, the new guard turned to them. "Just one minute," he said.

Without breaking stride, John flashed his badge again. "Provost guard. Taking this gentleman directly to Mr. Lincoln. Stand aside."

The new guard looked confused. "Provost, you say?" He scratched his head.

With John pushing through the crowd, they proceeded past him. "Provost guard," John repeated over and over. The crowd fell away like the Red Sea parting for Moses.

At last, they reached the East Room. Compared to the jostling crowd outside, it was awash in elegance, the ladies and gentlemen finely dressed. There was a queue of common folk, too, moving past the Lincolns, shaking hands.

"Do we insert ourselves in the line?" Hattie whispered. "They might take offense."

Just then, Mr. Lincoln glanced over at them. His expression brightened. "Ah, here comes my friend Douglass." He waved his long arm, beckoning them close.

As they approached, Mr. Lincoln reached out his hand. Mr. Douglass grabbed it firmly and shook it.

"I saw you in the crowd today, listening to my address," Mr. Lincoln said. "I value no man's opinion more than yours. What did you think?"

"A sacred effort, Mr. President," Douglass said.

"I'm glad you liked it," the president said.

Mr. Douglass moved on, allowing John and Hattie to step forward. Mr. Lincoln reached his hand out for what must have been the thousandth time that day.

Hattie clasped it, her hand small against his large palm. Standing this close, she saw how careworn he looked.

"I much admire you, Mr. Lincoln," she said. "For all you've done for the Union."

"We've all made our sacrifices, haven't we?" he said. She saw a remorsefulness in his expression she'd not noticed before, as if he knew all too well that there would be greater sacrifices to come.

Chapter Twenty-Seven

MARCH 6, 1865

Every moment of John's three days in Washington City felt magical, but nothing could surpass attending the inaugural ball with him.

He arrived by carriage to fetch Hattie from the Trents' house. Mrs. Trent, dressed in her most elegant gown, called up the stairs. "Hattie, your lieutenant has arrived."

Taking one last look in the mirror, Hattie patted the French twist Julia had arranged in her hair.

"You've spoiled that gown for me, you know," Julia said. "I'll never be able to wear it without thinking how fabulous it looked on you."

"You look quite stunning yourself," Hattie said. "Henry may have a hard time keeping you to himself."

"I only have eyes for him. And judging from what I've seen of you and your lieutenant, you know precisely what I mean." Julia took her arm. "The whole family loves John Elliott, you know. I don't know that I've ever heard Papa carry on so about a man's suitability for courting."

"I'm sure it helps that he's not *your* suitor," Hattie said. "But I'm glad to hear your family is impressed. Going forward, it may be that in putting up with me, they'll have John Elliott to contend with as well."

Julia's eyes widened. "He's asked you to marry him?"

"When the war's over," Hattie said.

Julia set her hand on her hip. "And how long were you planning to wait before telling me?"

"It wasn't so much that I was trying to keep it a secret. It's just that I can't quite believe it myself."

"No wonder you look so radiant." Julia tugged her forward. "Come along. We mustn't keep our admirers waiting."

They descended the stairs. At the foot of the staircase, John stood looking up at her, handsome as ever in his dress uniform. Reaching the foyer, she took his arm.

"You'll be the belle of the ball," he said, leaning close. "In red, no less."

"I thought you'd like it," she said softly, warmed by the intentness of his gaze. "Even if it is a bit scandalous for an unmarried woman."

"A betrothed woman," he said.

They said their goodbyes to the Trents, then joined Henry and Julia in the carriage. Rolling away from the house, John's hand wrapped over hers, Hattie thought there was nowhere in the world she'd rather be.

~ ~ ~

The last time Hattie had visited the Patent Office building, she'd had the misguided idea that she might work as a nurse. But the carnage Julia was dealing with as a volunteer had convinced Hattie her talents lay elsewhere.

Since then, officials had closed the hospital, concerned about the spread of contagious diseases within the city. Formerly housed in beds positioned between glass cases in the Patent Office's galleries, sick and wounded soldiers were now treated in pavilions on the outskirts of the city.

Arriving at the rotunda, John presented their tickets. With Julia and Henry trailing behind, Hattie and John ascended the grand staircase to the top floor. Beneath a stained glass dome and a ceiling painted with gold-edged frescoes, they joined the promenade through the south hall. Over Julia's chatter, Hattie heard strains of military music.

Entering the north hall, Hattie paused to marvel at its transformation. Gas jets strung from the ceiling cast a warm glow over the smartly dressed men and women gathered there. Along the length of the walls hung bunting fashioned from Union flags.

"I'm glad we were able to greet the president at the Executive Mansion the other day," Hattie said. "I don't see how we'd ever come near in this crowd. There must be thousands here already. It feels a bit like the sidewalks of New York City at the busiest time of day."

"Though with everyone dressed much more stylishly," John said.

Spotting a friend, Julia veered away from them, Henry at her side. The band struck up a quadrille, and the couples who chose not to dance crowded to the sides of the hall.

In a far corner, Hattie spotted an unmistakable figure dressed in black trousers and a black skirt. Bloomers. She knew only one person who wore them consistently.

"That woman over there." She nodded toward the corner. "That's Edith Greenfield."

"So it is," John said.

"Let's say hello," Hattie said.

They wove among what seemed like hundreds of finely dressed couples to where Edith stood. At her side was a gentleman who, like Edith, was small in stature but sprightly in appearance.

Letting go of John's hand, Hattie rushed to greet her. "Edith! It's wonderful to see you."

Edith's stern expression broke. "Why, if it isn't Hattie Logan and John Elliott," she said as John came alongside. "I'd been meaning to get over to see you in Louisville, Lieutenant. But my work at the prison has kept me quite busy."

"I'm sure it has," John said.

Edith reached for the hand of the gentleman standing beside her. "Hattie, John—this is Doc."

Doc what, Hattie wondered, but Edith offered no clarification. He reached to shake hands, first with John and then with Hattie. "Pleased to meet you both," he said. "Miss Logan, Edith has spoken in glowing terms of your...escapades." He glanced at Edith with what seemed to Hattie to be great affection. "It was Shakespeare, I believe, who spoke of loving someone for the dangers they'd passed."

"Have your brushes with danger continued?" Hattie asked Edith.

Edith shrugged. "Of late, the dangers have taken the form of men who would like to relieve me of my duties. They insist I'm too hard on the troublesome inmates. They seem indisposed to any sort of restrictions on the fairer sex, regardless of how they flaunt their disloyalty. But I have gleaned some facts of interest from some of my more obstinate prisoners."

"The Army Police are indebted to Dr. Greenfield for her dispatches regarding guerrilla activity," John said. "She has helped us avert trouble on more than one occasion."

"And what of you, Hattie?" Edith said. "Are you steering toward trouble these days, or away from it?"

"Some of each. Most recently, I've been doing clerical work with the War Department, trying to do what I can, in whatever small way, to hasten the war's end."

Edith nodded curtly. "A worthy goal."

Out of the corner of her eye, Hattie caught a glimpse of a familiar woman dressed in a pale blue gown. "My goodness," she said. "I believe that's Abigail Rice over there. Remember, Edith—it was at her cottage that you treated me after I escaped from prison."

"You never told me you'd been injured," John said.

"It was only a sprained ankle," Hattie said.

"Ah, but you were of a mind to give up on everything," Edith said. "Despondent over a lost love."

"And you advised me that even so, life would go on, and I'd best make the most of it." Hattie reached for John's hand. "You were right, Edith."

Edith sighed. "If only I could hear those words from my superiors."

Looking in the direction where she'd spotted Abby, Hattie saw that she was now barely visible through the crowd.

"I'd like to say hello to Abby. Good to see you again, Edith. And to meet you, Doc."

She led John toward the general area where she'd spotted Abby. They maneuvered around a group of laughing gentlemen. On the far side of them stood Abby, plump and smiling.

Catching Hattie's eye, Abby cried out. "Hattie Logan!" Abandoning the man at her side, Abby hurried toward her. "Oh, my heavens. How long it's been." She stopped short, looking Hattie up and down. "You look amazing, my dear."

"As do you," Hattie said. "That shade of blue becomes you."

Abby laughed. "We both look a fair bit better than the last time we met. As I recall, you were up to your knees in the Rappahannock River when I lost sight of you."

"There were so many cavalrymen, weren't there? When I got to the other side of the river, I asked after you, but the commander said there was no way to find you among the two thousand soldiers gathered there. The next day, they put me on a train to Washington. I could only hope you'd somehow found your way back to Boston."

"I did," Abby said. "Though I won't say it was easy. Enough adventure to last a lifetime for me."

They introduced the men, and Hattie learned that Abby was betrothed as well. There would be quite a few wedding bells ringing once the war ended.

As they caught up on each other's lives, Hattie picked and chose what to tell, mindful of not compromising her work. She was telling Abby about Pauline Carlton when the band struck up the flourishes and trills of "Hail to the Chief."

From a hallway at the far end of the room, Mr. and Mrs. Lincoln entered. Straining to get a look, Hattie saw that the president wore white gloves, but his attire seemed otherwise rather ordinary—a plain black coat and trousers. Though plump like Abby, Mary Lincoln cut an elegant figure in a white silk dress with a wide hooped skirt. Over her shoulders, she wore a lacy shawl. Purple and white flowers adorned her hair.

The Lincolns took their seats on a raised platform, and the merrymaking began in earnest. Well-wishers streamed toward the president, and the band struck up a polka. Abby and her fiancé took to the dance floor. Turning to Hattie, John bowed. "I don't believe I ever mentioned that I dance a fair polka. May I have the pleasure?"

"Most certainly." She bowed as she'd learned at the Ladygrace School for Girls. Taking John's hand, she followed him onto the dance floor.

He was indeed a fine dancer. From the polka, they moved into a schottische and then a reel. As he twirled her about, she felt light as a stream of gossamer.

At midnight, the supper room was opened. Hattie and John followed a stream of revelers toward a long banquet table. The buffet was like nothing she'd ever seen, the bill of fare so extensive she scarcely knew where to begin.

The array of meats alone was dizzying—beef a la mode, veal Malakoff, turkey, pheasant, quail, venison, duck, lobster, and ham. The array of sweets was equally spectacular, with cakes and tarts on a table that ran along the entire length of the banquet room. There were spun-sugar ornamentals, too, including models of a sailing ship and Washington's Capitol.

For all the elegance, there was a bit of a melee when it came to the meal. Men filled trays with food to take to waiting parties, and with all the slopping of jellies and stews, Hattie had to pick her way among mashed cakes and oily spills to reach their table. Hungry from all the dancing, she ate heartily. Miss Whitcomb would have disapproved. But John only smiled, and when she'd cleaned her dessert plate, he shared half his cake with her.

Full and satisfied, Hattie was happy to return to the dance floor. The band struck up a waltz. According to the headmistress of the Ladygrace School for Girls, unmarried ladies were to refrain from waltzes, owing to the closeness with which couples danced.

But with John's arm gently circling her waist, Hattie cared little about Miss Whitcomb's advice. As they circled the dance floor, she locked eyes with John. Love. This was love.

Then, out of the corner of her eye, she spotted Lucy Hamilton. Of course she would be here. Her father was an influential politician. But it was the man Lucy danced with who gave Hattie pause. John Wilkes Booth. How in heaven's name had she gotten herself mixed up with such a cad?

Expertly, John whirled her away, Lucy and Booth disappearing from Hattie's sight. Just as well. Celebrating the promise of new beginnings, she had no desire to mingle with anyone distasteful.

Chapter Twenty-Eight

MARCH 13, 1864

T hat night, Hattie and John danced nearly till dawn. But however magical, no night lasts forever.

A day later, she was back at the railway station, whispering a tearful goodbye. She told herself that with Kentucky's new governor, John would be safe. Still, the threat of guerrillas loomed large in her mind as she watched the train shrink from view.

The war was nearing its end, she reminded herself. As she resumed her work at the War Department, that fact became ever clearer. Yet the mood was more wary than festive. Desperation had a way of emboldening one's enemies. She needed no other reminder than the Confederates' new keywords, COME RETRIBUTION.

Still, it did her good to think that even as John was helping to restore order in Louisville, she was helping to uncover bits and pieces of information that gave the Union's generals a clearer picture of what they would face as they closed in on Richmond.

Constance, however, seemed less and less happy with their work. Hattie thought this was mostly because Roger Montgomery had made himself scarce. He was only being careful, Hattie told her, but Constance was sure it was her. To make matters worse, David Bates had asked her to the inaugural ball. She'd turned him down, but from the way she moped about, she seemed to regret it.

Thankfully, Hattie soon had Alice to distract her. Five days before she was scheduled to perform with Wilkes in The Apostate, she arrived in Washington. From the station, Hattie took her to meet the Trents. Julia was quite taken with her charms, as were her younger brothers, Sam and Halsey.

And of course Mrs. Trent was enthralled, even offering to have the boys bunk together so Alice could stay with them. Only by assuring her that her room at the National Hotel was both comfortable and convenient to Ford's Theatre, where she'd be performing, was Alice able to quell Mrs. Trent's persistent offers.

Having a good deal to catch up on, Hattie and Alice agreed to meet the next afternoon for tea in the National's dining room. It was an elegant venue, but quiet at that hour, giving them ample opportunity to talk.

Alice wanted to know every detail about the inaugural festivities, and Hattie was happy to oblige. She also shared the news of John's proposal, albeit without a ring.

"I knew it," Alice said. "You were meant to be together."

"And what of you and George?" Hattie said. "He's written precious little to me, but I suspect he's filled your mailbox with letters."

"He has." Alice spooned sugar into her tea. "Long letters of all the goings on in his little town. When I'm done performing here, I'm heading for Oregon."

"So soon?" Hattie asked.

"Not really." Alice stirred her tea. "It's been months and months. You aren't angry, are you? After I talked you out of going there yourself?"

Hattie sipped from her tea. "I admit it would be a nice escape. But you and John were right. This is the best place for me now. When the war ends..." Her voice trailed off. How often she'd repeated those words.

Alice cupped her hand over Hattie's "When the war ends, you and John shall be married. And then, I hope, you'll come to Oregon. George says he's already getting friendly with the police chief there. He could use some assistance."

"I expect John would have some interest in that," Hattie said. "I don't suppose George has said anything in his letters about our father."

Alice clapped her hand to her mouth. "Oh, I meant to tell you right away, and here I've blathered on about everything else. Your mother wrote to George recently, saying your father had passed. Knowing I'd be seeing you, George asked if I'd tell you. He thought it the sort of news that's best delivered in person." She studied Hattie's face. "But I have to say, you don't look horribly distraught."

Hattie swallowed back a lump in her throat. "I lost my father long ago."

Alice drank from her cup. "Life can be complicated, can't it?"

"Indeed. As with you and Wilkes being thrown together at your performance. Are you prepared for that?"

"As prepared as I'll ever be, I suppose. If I hadn't such respect for John McCullough, I'd have bowed out long ago."

"Wilkes was at the inauguration," Hattie said. "At the end of Mr. Lincoln's address, he rushed toward the platform. John stepped in his way and dissuaded him from going any closer."

"I can't imagine what he was doing there," Alice said. "I've never known Wilkes to do anything but complain about Mr. Lincoln. And with what we saw in Montreal and New York, he seems awfully close with the Confederates." She shuddered. "After our performance, I hope I never see him again."

"In the meantime, he certainly seems to be making himself seen," Hattie said. "I spotted him at the inaugural ball, too, dancing with Lucy Hamilton. She used to work with me in Mr. Pinkerton's mailroom."

"I hope you enlightened her on the hazards of a man like Wilkes."

"I didn't get the chance. Not that Lucy would have listened to my counsel anyhow."

Alice set aside her empty teacup. "Much as I hate to, I'd best get on to rehearsal."

"I'll walk with you to the theatre. It's on my way home."

Alice tilted her head, smiling. "You're still curious about our Mr. Booth, aren't you?"

"It's just that he keeps turning up in all the wrong places with all the wrong sorts of people," Hattie said. "But there's no crime in that, I suppose."

~ ~ ~

Leaving Alice at Ford's Theatre, Hattie didn't see the famous actor. But she did see a familiar figure, dressed in widow's weeds, a dark veil concealing her face. Sarah Slater, Hattie thought. The woman she'd seen with Booth in Montreal and again in New York. The woman who'd withdrawn large sums of money from her brother's bank.

Probably she was only hanging about with Booth again. Hattie wondered what Lucy Hamilton would have to say about that.

None of her concern, Hattie told herself. And yet she couldn't shake the feeling that, like Booth, Sarah Slater was up to no good.

It wouldn't hurt to see where the woman was headed, Hattie decided. If nothing else, it would satisfy her curiosity. And so she proceeded after her, keeping enough distance between them to dispel any notion that she might be following.

Two blocks east and one block north, the woman turned toward a narrow, three-story residence with two dormers jutting out from the roof. Slowing her pace, Hattie watched as she mounted a flight of stairs to the entrance. She rapped on the door. A slim, pale-eyed man let her in. He looked familiar.

Delmonico's. That's where Hattie had seen the man before, dining with Sarah Slater and John Wilkes Booth. Who was he, she wondered.

As Hattie turned to leave, a red-haired girl who looked to be no more than twenty came alongside her. "Are you lost, Miss?" she asked, a touch of Irish in her voice.

"Perhaps," Hattie said. "I was told a Mrs. Brown operated a boardinghouse in this neighborhood. I don't suppose you know where it is."

"Haven't heard of a Mrs. Brown," the girl said. "But I only came here myself last November. Are you looking for a room?"

"I am," Hattie said. "But rooms seem hard to come by here."

"I'm boarding at Mrs. Surratt's." The girl pointed to the three-story house with the dormers. "I'd suggest you take a room there, only she's had quite a few people coming and going of late." The girl leaned in as if to share a secret. "One is a famous actor." She took a carte de visite from her purse and showed it to Hattie.

The image was of a seated man, a fisted hand at his hip, looking resolute. "Why, that's John Wilkes Booth. Quite the well-known figure."

"He's performing here this week." The girl slipped the photo back into her pocket. "I'd love to see him, but Mrs. Surratt frowns on girls going unaccompanied to the theatre. It's only when her son invites me that I'm allowed to attend."

"Her son is your beau, then?" Hattie asked, grateful that the girl was so chatty.

"John Surratt? Goodness no. He's taken up with another woman." The girl leaned close again. "She dresses like a widow, but from what I've observed, she doesn't much act like one. Here one day, gone the next." She shrugged. "I'm glad of it since it leaves John Surratt in need of a theatre companion. We'll be attending a performance tomorrow night. That's why I've been out, you see."

She raised a small shopping bag. "I simply had to have a new pair of gloves. You never know. Mr. Booth might stop by. And we'll be seated in the very box that the president normally occupies when he goes to the theatre."

"What a privilege," Hattie said.

"I suppose it is," the girl said. "Though I believe the Surratts would as soon spit on Mr. Lincoln as look at him."

In this, they were hardly alone, Hattie knew. But then why rent his box?

"Which show will you see?" she asked.

"A double bill at Ford's Theatre," the girl said. "*Jane Shore* and *The Love Chase*."

"Why, I've been thinking of attending that same performance," Hattie said, though it was only now that she had reason to attend. "Perhaps I shall see you there." She extended her hand. "Hattie Thomas," she said, giving the alias she sometimes used.

The girl shook Hattie's hand gently but firmly, an indication that she'd had the same sort of finishing school training Hattie herself had suffered through. "Nora Fitzsimmons," she said. "A pleasure to meet you. I hope you find what you're looking for."

"I've no doubt I shall." Then, conscious of how long she'd been standing there, Hattie turned and hurried off.

~ ~ ~

Perhaps it was all innocuous—Booth and the Surratts and the woman Hattie was certain was Sarah Slater. But she couldn't put to rest the feeling something was amiss. And if she'd learned nothing else in recent months, it was that, logic aside, her inklings and intuitions deserved her attention.

With this in mind, she passed by Ford's Theatre on her way home. At the box office, she purchased two tickets for tomorrow's double bill.

Julia had plans with Henry, but Hattie had no trouble convincing Constance to go with her to the show. It was a chance to get out of the house, away from the commotion her four younger brothers wrought. Besides, she told Hattie, she'd never been to the theatre before.

Wearing her finest dress—as far as Hattie could tell, Constance owned only three—she was in awe when they entered the theatre.

"Never in my life," she said as they passed through a door tucked beneath rows of concrete arches.

"There's nothing like the theatre," Hattie said. "I don't know how I'd have managed without it, growing up. It was my escape. That and books."

Constance sighed. "I love a good book. But I like reading in quiet, you know, and that's in short supply at our house."

They passed through the lobby and into the auditorium, where gaslit sconces lent a fairylike glow. They ascended the stairs to the second level, known as the dress circle. Many of the red-up-holstered seats were already occupied by well-dressed ladies and gentlemen, and the air smelled heavily of perfume and tobacco.

Hattie and Constance settled into their seats, a few rows from the top. All the seats were arranged to afford good views of the stage, but Hattie had chosen these because they also allowed a glimpse into the upper box on the right side of the theatre, where the box office girl confirmed the president sometimes sat.

Sure enough, when Hattie looked over at the box, she saw Nora, the girl she'd met near the boardinghouse, along with the man she now knew to be John Surratt. With them was another man. Like Surratt, he seemed young, but he was broad-shouldered with a full face and a thick head of hair.

Rounding out the party was a girl who looked to be about ten years old. By any measure, it was an odd group. None of them looked as if they were related, and the men seemed to be ignoring the girls entirely.

Constance studied the program. "First up is *Jane Shore*."

"That makes sense," Hattie said. "It's a tragedy. Better to end the evening on a comic note."

The lights dimmed, and the curtains opened. Constance as she leaned forward in her seat, intent on the story that began to play out on the stage. Having read the complete works of Shakespeare from her parents' library, Hattie vaguely recalled Jane Shore as a character in *Richard III*. There was ample court intrigue to cap-ture the attention of even the most jaded theatre-goer.

"What a web of lies she lived," Constance said when the lights came up for intermission. "And all those men! No wonder she got wrapped up in a conspiracy."

"Indeed," Hattie said. But her attention was on the state box. A third man had entered, his back to the auditorium as he spoke to Surratt. Then he turned, and his profile confirmed Hattie's suspicions. Wilkes.

He gestured toward the door that opened from the state box to the dress circle. With a sour look on her face, Nora stood. She took the child's hand and exited through the door.

Hattie stood. "I'm going to walk about a bit," she told Constance.

"Go ahead." Constance stared at the stage as if she might miss some action by looking away. "I'll be right here."

Hattie edged along the back of the dress circle to a door that opened into a lounge. There she spotted Nora and her young companion. She walked casually toward them.

"Miss Fitzsimmons," she said as she drew near. "A pleasure to see you again. I trust you're enjoying the show?"

"Fair enough." Nora spoke through a frown. "The plot was awfully complicated, don't you think?"

"There were a fair number of men to keep track of."

"I couldn't tell who was on whose side," Nora said.

The girl tugged her hand. "Can we go back now?"

"Not yet," Nora said. "Mr. Surratt will fetch us when the men are finished."

Finished with what? Hattie wondered.

"But I want to sit down," the child said.

"In good time." Nora turned her attention back to Hattie. "Mr. Booth came by our box. He has some business to discuss with Mr. Surratt and Mr. Wood, so he asked us to leave them to their discussion."

"They have business together, the three of them?" Hattie asked.

Nora waved her hand in the air. "They're always murmuring in low tones to one another. I think it makes them feel important."

"Men can be like that," Hattie said. "Forever making plans."

"That's for certain," Nora said. "Those three do quite a lot of running back and forth between the boardinghouse and Mrs. Surratt's tavern across the river. Their poor horses must tire of the trip."

Across the river was King George County. An area rife with Confederate activity, as Hattie well knew.

"All the better for them to enjoy a respite here at the theatre," Hattie said. "Where we can all forget for a few hours that there's a war being waged."

"Not that it's looking to end well," Nora said. "Although Mrs. Surratt says the tide may turn when we least expect it."

"True enough," Hattie said.

The lights dimmed. Nora tugged her young companion's hand. "Come along, Mary," she said. "I suspect the men have forgotten all about us, so I suppose we must return on our own. The show is about to start."

"But we just saw a show." With her free hand, the child rubbed her eyes. "I'm tired. I want to go home."

"Hush now," Nora said. "It isn't every little girl that gets to go to the theatre and sit in the president's box." She turned to Hattie. "Good to see you again."

"Likewise." Hattie curled her fingers, waving goodbye. Then she started back to her seat, pondering what Nora had told her.

Chapter Twenty-Nine

MARCH 16, 1865

At work at the War Department the next day, Nora's revelations were still on Hattie's mind. Enlivened by last night's outing, Constance prattled on about the shows they'd seen. Much as she'd enjoyed *Jane Shore*, she'd been even more enthralled by the brief comedy that followed, *The Love Chase*.

Recounting the twists and turns of the plot, she even failed to comment on her most recent worries about Roger Montgomery, who hadn't brought them any letters in over a week. And when David Bates looked in on them, Constance was more pleasant with him than she'd ever been. In turn, he seemed to hang on her every word.

This left Hattie more time with her thoughts. More than the theatricals, she pondered what had gone on in the state box. Why had Wilkes been there? For that matter, why had the state box been reserved in the first place? It couldn't have come cheap.

On the other hand, it could have been just an ordinary outing, a treat for the young woman and child who boarded with the Surratts. As for Wilkes being there, Nora had made clear he was friendly with the Surratts. No crime in that.

She knew what George would say. No evidence. Let it go.

~ ~ ~

David Bates returned that afternoon. This time, he had Alice in tow. "This lady says she needs to speak with you, Miss Logan," he said. "She says it's urgent."

Hattie stood. "What is it?"

"I don't know about urgent," Alice said. "But it's important. Is there somewhere we might talk in private?"

They were standing in the most private place Hattie knew of within the War Department, but she could hardly ask Constance and Mr. Bates to vacate the room.

She reached for her cloak. "Let's step outside. Excuse us, please."

Deep in conversation, neither Bates nor Constance seemed to notice as Hattie and Alice slipped out the door and into the larger office space.

"It was quite the challenge finding you," Alice said, their footsteps echoing on the marble floor. "No one seemed to know you were here. Finally I was directed to Mr. Bates."

"We keep rather quiet about our operations," Hattie said.

"Oh, right." Alice leaned close, her voice dropping to a whisper. "Wilkes is up to something. A little while ago, as we were getting ready to start rehearsing, Ned Davenport stopped by. You've heard of him, yes?"

"I know he's an actor," Hattie said. "As I recall, he's in a show at the Washington Theatre, isn't he?"

"Right. It wraps up this week. He mentioned that tomorrow they'll be performing for the soldiers at Campbell Hospital."

"How kind of them."

"That's not all." Alice lowered her voice a notch. "He said Mr. Lincoln plans to attend."

"Not so surprising. He and Mrs. Lincoln visit the hospitals often."

"Well, Wilkes was surprised, I can tell you that. Or maybe agitated is a better way to describe it. He pressed Ned for details."

"What sort of details?"

"When the show would start. When it would finish. Where they intended to seat the president. And you should have seen the look on his face. Fierce, that's what I'd call it. I don't know if Ned noticed, but I certainly did. After Ned left, Wilkes began to pace. He was muttering to himself. Then he announced that he had business to attend to. So the rehearsal disbanded. That's when I decided I'd best find you straight away."

They fell silent as a clerk hurried past them. When he was out of earshot, Hattie said, "You think he intends some harm to Mr. Lincoln."

Alice nodded. "You should have seen the look in his eyes."

Reaching the exit, Hattie pushed open the door, and they stepped into the open air. A blast of wind rustled their skirts as they descended the stairs. Close, so close, to the war's end. To the fresh start she craved, with John Elliott. Why get herself mixed up with what was only a supposition?

"You said Wilkes never liked Lincoln," Hattie said. "So perhaps it was just the mention of him that—"

"It's not like before," Alice said. "Wilkes is obsessed over the fate of the Confederacy. He hardly talks of anything else. He despises Lincoln's freeing of the slaves. This country was formed for the white man, not for the black man, he says. He thinks African slavery is one of the greatest blessings God ever bestowed on this country."

"He's far from the only one who thinks that way." Hattie thought of her mother, and her mother's father, with his sprawling Louisiana plantation that depended on the unpaid labors of men and women he treated like cattle. A whole way of life that would end if the Union prevailed.

"You've seen the sorts of people Wilkes associates with," Alice said. "He has such a high opinion of himself. He could easily be persuaded that any harm he caused would make him a hero."

A hero. No surprise that Lucy was attracted to him, even if his ideas were opposed to her father's.

They turned a corner, walking into the wind. With its chill, Hattie's breath caught in her throat. She thought of Mr. Lincoln's craggy face, the sincerity of his gaze. Of how he'd taken time, years ago, to speak with her and Anne. Of how he'd welcomed Frederick Douglass, and of what he'd done for his people. Of how his words had inspired her to hope.

She thought, too, of the keywords she'd discovered. COME RETRIBUTION. "Do you have any sense of what Wilkes might do?"

"No. Only that it seems centered on Mr. Lincoln's being at the hospital tomorrow."

Hattie slowed her steps. There was no real evidence. No logical reason for alarm. Still, she felt her unease growing.

"Then we need to make sure he's not there."

"But how?"

"I'll go to the Executive Mansion," Hattie said. "Try to talk my way in. Mr. Lincoln has spoken with me before. Perhaps he'll do so again."

"Shall I come with you? Rehearsal won't resume until evening."

"I'd welcome your company. But if I'm not successful, we need to have another plan. One that involves convincing someone in charge that Wilkes needs to be brought in for questioning. And for that, we'll need proof, not just supposition."

"You want me to track him down?"

Hattie shook her head. "You mustn't confront him. You've too much history with him, and we know he has a temper."

"Then what? I want to do something."

Hattie thought of where she'd last seen the veiled lady, the house where Wilkes hung about. "There's a boardinghouse," she said. "At the corner of H and 11th. The other day, I followed Sarah Slater there."

"You never told me," Alice said.

"It was on a whim," Hattie said. "And you've been busy with rehearsals. I recognized the man who let Sarah Slater in. He was with her and Wilkes at Delmonicos. I spoke with one of the boarders and learned his name is John Surratt. His mother owns the boardinghouse."

"Did you see Wilkes there?"

"No, but the boarder showed me his carte de visite. She's young and impressionable. Says he visits often. She's quite taken with him."

"She'd best be careful, mixing with the likes of Wilkes."

"I don't know how much she mixes with him. During intermission at the theatre last night, he and John Surratt sent her away."

"Wait—which theatre?"

"Ford's. The boarder—Nora is her name—told me she'd be attending with John Surratt. I was curious, so I bought tickets for Constance and me."

"So you do suspect they're up to no good."

"I've no proof. They rented a state box. Wilkes came by during intermission, and they sent Nora and another girl away so they could talk."

"Plotting what they'd do to the president at Campbell Hospital."

"That can't be," Hattie said. "You said Wilkes only learned about his plans today."

"Oh," Alice said. "Right. All the same, it's suspicious."

"Agreed," Hattie said. "Desperate men are prone to desperate actions. What time tomorrow did Mr. Davenport say they'd be performing at the hospital?"

"Two o'clock."

Hattie nodded. "You to go to the boardinghouse. Hang around a bit and see if there's any unusual activity. I'll do all I can to see that the president is elsewhere at that time tomorrow."

~ ~ ~

Hurrying toward the Executive Mansion, Hattie could almost hear George chiding her. No solid evidence. No plan.

If Captain Babcock were here, she'd have consulted with him. But he and Mr. Stanton were in the field with General Grant, and they weren't expected back anytime soon. She would have to trust her instincts and hope that was enough.

Getting word to the president was easier said than done, she knew. Still, from what Julia's father said, more people had access to Mr. Lincoln than was proper. There were protocols, to be sure, but the president was known to overlook them. His humble roots were the problem, Julia's father said. Mr. Lincoln had a soft spot for the common person.

Arriving at the portico, Hattie hoped this was true. Expressing concern for the president's safety would likely get her nowhere. Criticized for having disguised himself on the way to his first inauguration to avoid an assassination plot, Mr. Lincoln wasn't inclined to concern himself with such matters.

Indeed, there was only one man standing guard at the entrance. Drawing herself up in a confident manner, Hattie walked directly toward him. "I've come from Indiana to see Mr. Lincoln," she said. "My brother served in the war but has been denied his army pension."

"War Department's over there." The guard pointed in the direction Hattie had come from. "They handle pension requests."

"But my family knows Mr. Lincoln from his early days." Drawing on skills she'd learned performing onstage at her finishing school, she spoke with a quiver in her voice. "They assured me Mr. Lincoln would see me. If you'll only tell him—"

"There's a war on," the guard interrupted. "In case you haven't heard. Mr. Lincoln's quite busy."

She stamped her foot, a gesture that had come to her all too naturally when she was young. "I'm well aware. I just told you my brother served. And nobly, too. Wounded at Gettysburg. He came home with—"

Hearing footsteps, she broke off midsentence. "Why, it's Governor Morton!" Turning from the guard, she held out her hand. "Hattie Logan. I'm a friend of the Duncans. I brought you a note last year. About certain—" She glanced at the guard. "Certain activities being planned in your city."

"Ah, yes." With a slight dip of his head, he took her hand and shook it firmly. "We made a number of arrests based on the information you provided. What brings you to Washington City, Miss Logan?"

"I'm hoping to get an audience with Mr. Lincoln," she said.

"As am I," he said. "Come along. We shall see him together."

Falling in step beside Indiana's governor, Hattie brushed past the guard. He looked none too happy, but he made no further attempt to stop her.

"Thank you," she said to the governor once they were inside. "I was under the impression that Mr. Lincoln took callers, but the guard wasn't inclined to let me in."

"Mr. Lincoln used to see people more freely," Governor Morton said. "But things got out of hand. Now he holds hours twice weekly, between ten and three. He says they're his public opinion baths, though I've also heard him refer to them as beggars' operas."

Hattie's steps slowed as she took in her surroundings. Only days ago, she and John Elliott had passed through here to greet the Lincolns, but that had been amid such a crush of people that she hadn't been able to properly take it all in.

Today, the mansion was quiet, with only a handful of servants and staff in view. The furnishings were elegant—Mary Lincoln had spent quite a lot of money, Mrs. Trent said, purchasing new carpets, draperies, and lighting for the mansion. But more than that, Hattie stood in awe of the history that had been made here.

"Mr. Lincoln's big White House, as he calls it," the governor said, pausing beside her. "Impressive, isn't it?"

"Quite," Hattie said.

"The first floor is primarily for receptions." The governor swept his hand through the air. "Red Room, Blue Room, Green Room, East Room. The grand staircase over there, that leads to the private residence. For official business, there's a separate set of stairs. Shall we?"

She nodded. They proceeded through the vestibule, then around a corner, doubling back to an inauspicious room containing a single set of stairs.

"What is your business with Mr. Lincoln?" Hattie asked as they started up the steps

"Our boys in Company C of Indiana's 140th Volunteers captured a Confederate flag in a battle last month. The captain passed it on to me, hoping that I would in turn pass it on to the president. I thought I might present it to him at a little ceremony at my hotel."

Hattie paused mid-step. "When will that be?"

He tipped his head, looking at her. "I'm not sure. That's what I've come to ask."

"How about tomorrow afternoon at 2 o'clock?" she said, continuing up the stairs.

He looked at her quizzically. "Why do you suggest that?"

"There's a play being staged at Campbell Hospital tomorrow. Two o'clock. The president plans to attend. But I fear there's a plot afoot to harm him if he does."

"What sort of plot?"

"I don't know all the details," she admitted. "But there's an actor involved. And I have...well, not enough evidence to go to the authorities. Still, I'm worried."

"So you've come to talk the president out of going?"

"Something like that. It sounds vague, I know."

He glanced her direction. "You were right about that plot in Indianapolis. But it's no easy task convincing the president to take steps to ensure his safety. Heaven knows I've tried. So has his personal secretary John Hay. But Mr. Lincoln says he can't imagine any man wanting to harm his person."

"Yet I fear they do," she said.

"I suppose he feels that if he paid attention to every crackpot threat that came his way, he'd never leave the confines of this place."

Discouragement fell over her. Was this how the president would receive her—as bringing a crackpot threat?

They reached the second floor. Governor Morton motioned for her to follow him across a spacious corridor. "Mr. Lincoln's office," he said, indicating an open doorway. "Ah, but he's not in."

Her heart sank. "Perhaps we should wait for his return?"

"Who knows when that will be. He gets called away so often." The governor pulled a gold pocket watch from his pocket, flipped open the case, and checked the time. "And I've got another appointment soon."

"I'll wait myself then," she said. Now that she was here, her task felt more important than ever.

The governor looked her up and down. "His aides might not let you in."

"Still. I have to try."

Disappointment must have shown on her face. "Let's get you a proper introduction at least."

He slipped his watch back into his pocket, then motioned for her to follow him down the corridor. They passed an open doorway. Inside, Hattie glimpsed a desk piled high with papers.

The governor poked his head inside. "Mr. Nicollay is out too," the governor said. "He's Mr. Lincoln's personal secretary. That leaves his assistant, Mr. Hay."

They proceeded to the very end of the corridor, where a door opened into a narrow office. Along one wall, a fire burned in the grate, warming the space.

"John?" the governor said.

A man looked up from his desk. In spite of herself, Hattie smiled. Another John. This one was surprisingly young, little older than she was, from the looks of him, clean-shaven and earnest.

"Governor Morton." Hay stood, coming around his desk to shake hands with him. "To what do we owe the pleasure of a visit from you and this lovely young lady?"

"This is Hattie Logan," Morton said. "A...a friend of the family. I...we've come to ask the honor of Mr. Lincoln's presence at a flag ceremony. A Confederate flag, that is. Some of our Indiana boys captured it in a rather fierce battle recently, and they asked if I'd present it to the president."

"Well, then." Hay's manner was pleasant, but his forehead tensed. He reached for a notebook that lay open on his desk. "Mr. Lincoln has quite a few commitments coming up, given the state of things. Perhaps next month."

"Oh no," Hattie said. "That won't do. You see, there's a—"

"A ceremony already planned," the governor interrupted, giving her a sharp look. "For tomorrow. Two o'clock."

Hay shook his head. "Not much notice, I'm afraid." He scanned the notebook, pencil in hand. "Mr. Lincoln is scheduled to attend a performance at Campbell Hospital tomorrow afternoon."

No, Hattie wanted to shout. *He mustn't go.* Hadn't the governor said Mr. Hays was concerned about the president's safety? But there was the problem of Mr. Lincoln's attitude toward the matter, she realized. His tendency to discount any threats made to him.

"Perhaps his schedule could be changed," the governor said.

"And disappoint the soldiers at the hospital?" Hay shook his head. "I think we both know the president better than that."

"Well, then," Morton said. "We won't take any more of your time, Hay. I know you're busy. Let Mr. Lincoln know about the flag, would you?" He glanced at her. The look in his eyes said this was the best he could do.

"Surely you could pick another day for your ceremony." Hay flipped pages in the appointment book. "There's an opening the week after next."

Hattie stepped forward. "If you please, Mr. Hay. We all know how hard our boys have fought for the Union. We women too—we've done all we can for the cause. For my part, I—"

"Miss Logan," the governor said. "I don't know that we should bother Mr. Hay any further."

She didn't want to defy him, but she felt she had no choice. "I worked with Mr. Pinkerton's Agency early in the war. As a spy."

Hay quit flipping pages. "A spy, you say?"

"For the Union. And while I'm not here in any official capacity, I have concerns about Mr. Lincoln's safety if he goes to Campbell Hospital tomorrow."

Hay's eyes narrowed. "What sorts of concerns?"

She drew a breath. She could mention Booth, the boarding-house, the veiled lady. But with nothing firm, she risked him thinking this was but another of the crackpot threats Morton had mentioned, which was of course why he hadn't mentioned her concerns. Even she had to admit that, taken together, there was little more than bluster and circumstance to implicate Booth.

"Nothing that would hold up in a court of law," she said. "Not even enough to interest the police. But there's a man who piqued my interest in Montreal and again in New York. A man with links to the Confederates. Now he's here, and he has shown more interest than he should in Mr. Lincoln's plans to be at Campbell Hospital tomorrow."

Hay looked at her sharply. "That all sounds rather vague, Miss Logan."

The governor shifted again. "You should know that Miss Logan once brought me some information that proved to be quite cred-ible."

"I wouldn't have come here if I wasn't gravely concerned," Hat-tie said. "I know the president gets all sorts of threats. I know he prefers not to worry over them. But just this once, might you be able to dissuade him from his plans tomorrow?"

"I must say, even without specifics, you make a convincing case," Hay said. "But even if I choose to believe you, my powers to persuade the president are limited."

"But you'll try?" Hattie said.

Hay closed the appointment book. "I'll propose a change of plans, based on the heartfelt request of a young woman whose sincerity strikes me as beyond question."

"And the flag ceremony," the governor said. "Let him know how much it would mean to Indiana's soldiers."

"Yes," Hay said. "But I can't promise anything."

Not the surety she'd hoped for. She would need to do more. But what?

Chapter Thirty

MARCH 17, 1865

Leading out of the city toward Maryland, the road to Campbell Hospital was lightly traveled. In the carriage she'd hired, Hattie passed only a few travelers, most of them farmers bringing produce into Washington.

Nearing the hospital, the carriage passed a tavern. Several horses were hitched up outside, saddled and awaiting their riders. But Hattie saw no buggies. She wasn't sure if that was a good sign or a bad one. When Alice went by Mary Surratt's boardinghouse yesterday, she'd seen a swarthy man loading a trunk into a buggy. Wherever he'd gone with it, it wasn't here.

Turning for a last look at the tavern, Hattie saw a rider approach. From the carriage window, she caught a glimpse of his face, slim and framed by a hairline that was notably receding for a man of his young age. John Surratt, who'd taken Nora to the theatre, who'd dined with Wilkes and Sarah Slater at Delmonico's. If he was at the tavern, there was a good chance Wilkes was there too.

Hattie settled back in her seat. She thought about asking the carriage driver to turn around. But a woman entering a tavern alone was sure to attract attention.

The carriage continued, delivering her in front of the hospital shortly before one o'clock. Getting out, she saw no sign of the much larger carriage in which the president generally traveled. But then it was unlikely he'd arrive this early.

A light mist was falling, spritzing her face and hands as she surveyed the grounds. As with most wartime medical facilities, this one seemed rather insubstantial, consisting of several one-story buildings sided with rough lumber. She headed for what looked like the most central of the bunch. Inside, she asked a nurse if she knew the location of the theatrical that was to be performed that afternoon.

"One of the cast, are you?" the nurse asked. "I thought they'd all have arrived by now."

"I was delayed and had to take my own carriage," Hattie said. "And I'm afraid I neglected to ask where I should meet up with them."

"Next building over," the nurse said, pointing. "The dining room."

Proceeding there, Hattie found workers moving tables against the walls and arranging chairs in rows. At the far end of the long, low-ceiling room, others were draping up curtains over a makeshift stage and drawing shades over the windows.

She went around to the back of the curtains. Several actors were milling about. She approached an older man who matched the description Alice had given her, his head balding, his hair graying, and his eyes a pale shade of blue.

"Mr. Davenport?" she said, approaching him. "I'm Alice's friend."

"Ah, yes." He looked about, momentarily distracted by two workers who'd begun to argue over the pulley that would operate the curtain. Then he returned his attention to her. "Pretending to be an actress. I must say I've never fielded that particular request before. But I'm happy to oblige. Alice is a good woman." He leaned close. "A saint, if you ask me, for playing alongside Wilkes after the way he treated her."

"I won't argue that point," Hattie said. "And thank you for indulging our little ruse."

"Alice wouldn't say a word as to what the two of you are up to. But it's no concern of mine." With an actor's flourish, he waved his hand at nothing in particular.

"Alice says the president will be in attendance today," Hattie said.

"So we've been told. Quite exciting, isn't it?"

"Indeed." She steadied herself. Just because they were expecting him didn't mean he'd show up. "As long as I'm here, perhaps I can be of some assistance?"

"I don't suppose you do hair?" he said. "Florence is in a bit of a tizzy over hers. Her assistant fell ill at the last minute and couldn't be here."

"I'll do what I can," Hattie said, happy for the distraction.

Mr. Davenport escorted her to the kitchen, where an older woman was perched on a stool, gripping a hairbrush. Propped on the table in front of her was a folding mirror, reflecting her creased forehead and graying temples. Hair was pinned haphazardly at the back of her head, making it look more like a rat's nest than any recognizable style.

"I've brought in the cavalry," Mr. Davenport said. "Or at least what passes for it when it comes to hair. Florence, this is Hattie. She's come to help."

The woman turned, and her forehead relaxed. "A hairdresser. Thank heavens."

Hattie stepped forward. "Not a hairdresser by trade. But I can follow directions if you'll tell me what you want."

"Just a simple French twist." She patted the remnants of what must have been her attempt at this. "I'm ashamed to admit it's been years since I've had to do it myself. I know these shows for the soldiers are important, but it's an inconvenience not having our full crew at our disposal." She gave Davenport a pointed look.

"It will all be fine, Florence. And the soldiers will be ever so grateful. Not to mention Mr. Lincoln being in attendance."

"Oh, yes!" Florence fluttered her fingers. "It will all be quite intimate, don't you think?"

Too intimate, Hattie thought. *And dangerous.*

Florence handed her the brush, and Mr. Davenport left her to her task.

The brushing and combing and pinning was a good distraction from her worries, most of which centered on exactly what she'd do if Booth showed up. She'd talked this over with Alice, and the best they'd come up with was Hattie disrupting the performance the moment Booth showed up. Alice didn't like the idea of her coming here alone, given how volatile he was, but she agreed that her being there would only make matters worse.

Florence chattered as Hattie worked, explaining all about the character she played in the drama, a Mrs. Milmay. The plot centered on the murder of a ship's captain who was blackmailing members of a well-to-do family. "Each points a finger at the other, blaming them for the murder," Florence said. "Keeps the audience guessing."

"I expect the soldiers will enjoy it," Hattie said, placing a hairpin at the bottom of the twist she was fashioning.

Florence shook her head, causing Hattie to momentarily stop her pinning. "Poor souls. From what I've seen, half of them are missing limbs."

"Such a sacrifice they've made," Hattie said, making another stab at securing the errant wisp of hair. "Whenever I'm feeling down over how long the war has gone on, I think of all they've been through."

Their talk turned to the theatre. Florence had a passing acquaintance with Alice. "Do give her my regards when you see her next."

"I will," Hattie said. "She's performing tomorrow night. At Ford's Theatre."

"So I saw. A benefit for McCullough. And she's playing opposite Wilkes Booth, isn't she?"

"She is," Hattie said. "Have you performed with him before?"

"Once," Florence said. "He's got talent, I'll give him that. But rather full of himself, I daresay. Then again, that could be said of any number of actors."

Hattie positioned the last two hairpins. She stepped back for a look. She redid another pin, then held up a hand mirror so Florence could see what she'd done.

The actress patted the French twist. "Much better. I don't know where Ned found you, but if he hadn't, I'd have gone onstage looking the part of a scarecrow."

"I'm pleased to have been of some service," Hattie said. Beyond the curtain, she heard the shuffling of footsteps and the murmuring of voices. "It sounds as if your audience is arriving. If you'll excuse me, I'll see if Mr. Davenport needs me to do anything else."

Slipping out from the kitchen, Hattie stationed herself at the edge of the inner curtain. For now, none in the audience would be able to see her, but she had a commanding view of the room. Florence was right—at least half the men in attendance were missing a limb. Some were missing two. Nearly all were bandaged over some part of their body. Some sat in the straight-backed chairs that had been arranged in front of the stage while others—mostly those missing legs—were in wheeled chairs.

It was staggering to think that these men represented only a fraction of those injured in the war, not to mention the hundreds of thousands who'd been killed in battle. Just as many, if not more, had been felled by disease. Her concerns seemed petty by comparison, save the one thing most on her mind at present—the president's safety.

The last of the soldiers took their places. Among them were members of the hospital staff. No sign of Booth. No sign of Mr. Lincoln either. From the far end of the stage, she saw Ned Davenport scanning the crowd. He must be looking for Mr. Lincoln, too.

In front of the stage, a small orchestra began to play. The music should have been soothing, but the sounds grated on Hattie's ears, nervous as she was. The violins reached a crescendo. As they fell off, the lights dimmed, the audience receding into the dark.

Hattie stepped back from the curtain as the actors took the stage. From the wings, she peered into the chasm where the audience sat. As her eyes adjusted to the dark, there was a flash of light as the door at the back of the room opened. A figure stepped in. Mr. Lincoln? No. Not tall enough, and she couldn't imagine he'd come alone.

But it could be Booth. She slipped out from the wings and headed up the side of the makeshift auditorium, hugging the wall and treading softly. But when she reached the place where the latecomer stood, she saw it was only one of the doctors, come to see the show.

She remained there, pressed against the wall, watching the audience for signs that anything was amiss. A good sign, she thought, that Mr. Lincoln hadn't arrived. Maybe Hay had convinced him to attend the flag ceremony after all. Or maybe he'd been detained and would be arriving late.

Her nerves kept her on edge. She caught a line of the play now and then, but for the most part, she was oblivious to what was happening on stage until she realized, quite out of the blue, that Booth might position himself not in the audience but backstage. While in the kitchen with Florence, she'd seen a door that led outside. Booth might enter through there and position himself where she had, with a good view of the audience. Of the president, if in fact he arrived.

She felt keenly aware of how alone she was in this crowd. Should she go back behind the wings or stay where she was? The indecision heightened her nerves. If she chose wrongly, she could do little to intervene.

Mr. Lincoln wasn't here yet, she reminded herself. With any luck, he wouldn't come at all. She needed to stay calm and focus on looking for Booth and his associates. If they showed up, she'd have the proof she needed to back up her suspicions.

The first act seemed to go on forever. She caught enough of Florence's lines to know she played the dowager well, with lines here and there that drew laughter from the crowd.

Finally, the act drew to a close. The soldiers applauded, and the lights came up. Hattie edged toward the front. She slipped behind the inner curtain to where she could see the full auditorium. Behind her, props men bustled about, setting the stage for the second act.

Row by row, Hattie scanned the sea of faces in the makeshift auditorium. Along the opposite wall from where she'd been standing, a flash of movement caught her eye.

Booth. Her heart pounded. There was no reason for Booth to be here. No reason except that he expected Mr. Lincoln to be here as well.

A hand touched her shoulder. She whirled around, her senses on high alert.

"I didn't mean to startle you," Florence said. "But I was hoping you could arrange my hair for the next act. I'm to be lying abed, so it's got to be let down, but it mustn't be in my face."

"Certainly." Hattie glanced toward the other end of the curtain, just in time to see Booth making his way toward the kitchen, where the actors had gathered to ready themselves for the change of scene.

She and Florence entered the kitchen from the opposite direction, through a second set of doors. Actors had taken over every corner of the room, touching up their makeup and hair.

Booth rushed toward Ned Davenport, a riding crop in his hand. Taking up Florence's hairbrush, Hattie circled the actress, putting Florence between herself and Booth. She didn't think he would recognize her, especially not here, but there was no sense taking chances.

Anger flashed in Booth's eyes. "You told me the president would be in attendance."

"So we were told," Mr. Davenport said. "Apparently his plans changed."

Booth paced, flicking his riding crop. "Changed. Why? By whom?"

"By Jove, I don't know, Wilkes. What concern of it is yours?"

Booth stopped his pacing. A crestfallen look came over him. "My hopes are dashed. My prospects ruined."

"I don't see how…" Davenport began.

But Booth wasn't listening. He dashed from the kitchen. On his way out, his shoulder bumped Florence, jostling her. In his haste, he didn't turn to apologize, sparing Hattie the risk of him recognizing her.

"Goodness," Florence said when he was gone. "What's gotten into Wilkes?"

Davenport shrugged. "Haven't a clue."

Brushing out Florence's hair, Hattie's shoulders relaxed. Her appeal to John Jay had succeeded. She only wished she knew what Booth had planned.

At least in coming here, she could now bear witness to Booth's strange behavior. It was the closest she had to proof that he was up to no good.

Chapter Thirty-One

MARCH 18, 1865

Having succeeded in thwarting Booth's plans, whatever they'd been, Hattie should have slept well that night. Instead, she tossed and turned, so much so that Julia commented on it in the morning.

"You thrashed like fish out of water last night," she said, pulling back the curtains to reveal what promised to be a bright spring day. "Did you sleep at all?"

Hattie rubbed her eyes. "A bit."

"You must have something on your mind. Is it your lieutenant? You haven't said a peep about your wedding plans since he left."

"We've spoken of nothing specific."

"Nothing? Not even where you'll be wed?"

"We'll have time for that," Hattie said. "Once the war's over."

"It's all but over now. That's what Papa says."

Hattie sat up, tugging the neckline of her chemise so it covered her shoulder. "Things could change. Something unexpected that sets the Union back."

"You mustn't be so gloomy." Hands on her hips, Julia stepped toward her. "You aren't worried, are you? About John's proposal? That it wasn't...sincere?"

"No, it's not that at all."

"Well, something's eating at you."

"It's just being at the War Department, I suppose. There's quite a flurry of activity these days." She forced a smile. "But as you say, that should all be coming to an end soon."

~ ~ ~

With the performance that night, Alice had no rehearsal. Hattie met her shortly before noon at a restaurant near her hotel. For once, Hattie was glad for the ladies' dining room. It gave them a modicum of privacy.

"Wilkes was a mess at rehearsal last night," Alice said as they settled at their table. "What happened yesterday?"

"The president didn't attend."

"I knew you could do it. You can be quite convincing."

"I don't know about that. It was mostly supposition. But I've got more to bolster that now. Booth came charging into the performance at intermission. He accosted Ned Davenport over the president not being there. Then he went rushing out."

"That makes sense," Alice said.

Their conversation paused as the waiter brought their coffees. Alice dumped two spoonfuls of sugar into hers. Normally, she took it black. "Pre-show jitters," she said.

"You were saying? About Wilkes?"

Alice stirred her coffee. "The way he behaved last night. Not so much of his usual swagger. In fact, he seemed almost fearful. Given what you've said, I can see why he'd be frightened. He must think whatever plot he'd arranged was discovered."

"I hope you're right." Hattie sipped from her cup, the coffee warm and comforting. "I worry that he'll try something else."

"Not the way he behaved last night," Alice said. "Wilkes is volatile, but he's not stupid. He won't risk arrest. You did what you set out to, Hattie. The war is almost over, and whatever threat Booth had planned is averted."

"I wish I knew that for certain."

"If you'd waited for certainty, there might have been a very different outcome yesterday. You mustn't second-guess yourself. As far as I'm concerned, you saved Mr. Lincoln, even if you and I are the only ones who know it."

"All the same, I'm going to Captain Babcock as soon as he returns. With what I saw yesterday, I believe I can convince him that Booth should be watched."

~ ~ ~

The next night, Hattie was back at Ford's Theatre. Sitting beside her, Constance clutched the two guest passes Alice had signed for them. She turned them over and over in her hands, studying Alice's signature.

"Ma won't mind me having come here once she sees these. Autographed by a real actress. And to think she's a friend of yours. What's she like?"

"Bright. And talented. In some ways, she reminds me of you."

"Me? Why, I haven't any talents at all."

"Of course you have."

Constance shrugged. "I can steam an envelope. A lot of good that will do me in the days ahead."

"You got yourself a position at Pinkerton's. And then at the War Department."

"They only brought me to the War Department because you were coming. And getting on at Pinkerton's, that was only luck and gumption."

"That's what Alice says about her start in acting. Luck and gumption. She didn't even know how to read when she got her first role."

"Truly?" Constance said.

"Truly."

"Then perhaps my prospects are better than I think."

"David Bates seems to think so."

"He is rather handsome. And when I told him we were going to the theatre tonight, he asked if I'd go with him one day soon."

"I hope you said yes."

Constance offered a sly smile. "I might have."

Hattie was glad for their banter. It helped ease her tension, with Booth and Alice soon to come onstage. She told herself she was being silly. Alice knew him well, and she was convinced that his plans, whatever they were, had been dashed.

Still, Hattie remained on edge. It didn't help that she'd seen John Surratt coming into the theatre, in the company of the same man he'd been with the other night. But of course Surratt would be here. He was friendly with Booth.

The lights came down and the curtain went up. As best she could, Hattie gave herself over to the show. Alice was magnificent. Her hair darkened for the part, she played Florinda, a Spanish woman who was falling in love with a Moor. But a Christian couldn't marry a Moor, so the man converted.

But it was Booth as the villain Pescara who stole the show. There was such evil in his distorted expression, such a fierce glare in his eyes, that he seemed more demon than man. In the role of Inquisitor, he seized Florinda by the hair and threatened her with the wheel that would stretch her limbs. "Now behold Pescara's masterpiece!" he exclaimed. The audience gasped.

In tragic form, Pescara forced Florinda to marry him instead of the man she loved. Her Moor stabbed himself through the heart. He never knew that Florinda, who stayed at his side as he died, had herself taken a slow-acting poison.

As the curtain closed and the lights came up, Hattie looked over at Constance. Tears streamed down her face. "That wicked, wicked man," she said. "You didn't tell me it would all end so badly."

"All tragedies end badly," Hattie said. "It's so we realize our own lives are better than we think."

~ ~ ~

The next day, Hattie was back at the train station, seeing Alice off to Oregon. As the passengers boarded, she drew her friend into a hug. "You're glowing, you know."

Alice squeezed her tight. "This will be a better journey than any I've made before. To love. And a new life. I hope you and John will soon join us."

"Me too. When the war ends." How many times had she said this?

"It won't be long now," Alice said. "Sherman's giving them hell in the South. And your quick thinking put a stop to whatever malevolence Wilkes and his associates were planning."

"He didn't exactly look defeated onstage last night. More angry and vengeful."

"Wilkes has always played a good villain. Underneath, he's despondent. He left Washington first thing this morning, his tail between his legs. I doubt he'll be back."

"I hope you're right. Even so, I intend to speak with Captain Babcock about what happened at Campbell Hospital."

"What didn't happen," Alice said. "Thanks to your intervention."

"All aboard!" the conductor called out.

Hattie drew Alice into a final hug. "Give George my best," she reminded her as she started for the train.

Alice turned and waved. "I shall! See you soon."

Then she was gone.

Booth was gone, too, Hattie reminded herself as the train pulled from the station. She could relax now.

But the thought of what had happened in New York City plagued her. She'd thwarted one plot only to have another catch her off-guard. But circumstances were different now, she reasoned. Even the naysayers conceded a Union victory was finally within reach. What reason would anyone have then to harm the president now?

At work that afternoon, Roger Montgomery surprised them with a visit.

Constance scarcely glanced at him. "We thought you'd dropped off the end of the earth."

He dropped a pile of envelopes on the table. "I was detained in Montreal. Quite a lot going on there."

"How so?" Hattie said.

"The Confederates. They're up to something, mark my words."

Constance held an envelope to the steam. "Your words don't always bear out."

"What's gotten into her?" Montgomery said, as if Constance had left the room.

"Her horizons have expanded," Hattie said. "And if you expect us to believe your warnings about the Confederates, you should provide some specifics."

"To the likes of you two? Not worth my time."

With that, he turned heel and left.

Constance burst out laughing. "What a proud peacock!"

"I'm glad you've seen his flaws. Still, I wish he'd expounded on what he observed in Montreal."

"What he says he observed. You know how he exaggerates."

She did know this, and she was glad Constance now knew it too. But that didn't stop her wondering about Montreal. Was it only idle talk, or were the Confederates plotting something?

Murray Wilson might know. After work, she stopped at the telegraph office. *Any word of our friends Booth, Slater, Surratt?* She signed the telegram with only her initial *H*. No address. Even the fact of the wire's coming from Washington might raise suspicion should her message fall into the wrong hands.

She expected a response within the day. But none came. Day after day, she checked at the telegraph office on her way home from work. Nothing. She hoped Wilson was all right.

Maybe David Bates would know something. She made a point of asking the next time he stopped by.

"When Mr. Montgomery was here last, he indicated that there had been a good deal of activity in Montreal of late. Have you heard anything about that?"

"Some loose talk," Bates said. "Nothing more. Why do you ask?"

"A good deal of Confederate money passes through there, or so I've heard. Money that's used to fund plots against the Union."

"True enough," he said. "But if anything is being plotted now, I'm not aware of it. Likely the activity involves exiled Confederates withdrawing their personal funds before their government collapses entirely."

"Will they return to the South, do you think?" Constance asked.

He shrugged. "Some might."

"What about those who've violated the laws of war, plotting against civilians in the North?"

"Like the St. Albans Raid, you mean?" he said.

"Or the plot to take over Lake Erie," Hattie said. "Or the attempt to set fire to New York."

"Returning here, they'd face the prospect of prison," he said. "If they're smart, they'll stay away."

Hattie didn't know what to think about that. She'd like to see people like Luke Blackstone, with his plot to infect civilians with yellow fever, brought to justice. It didn't seem fair that by staying in Canada, people like him could get off scot-free.

~ ~ ~

Only days later, word spread through the War Department that the Union had taken the Confederate capitol at Richmond. The mood turned quickly to celebration.

"Miss Van Lew must be overjoyed," Constance said. "No more concealing messages in vegetables."

"Not only her, but all those in her network," Hattie said.

"I can't help but feel we've played a small part," Constance said. "Though I suppose it means an end to our work."

This was true, Hattie knew. When the rest of the Confederacy went the way of Richmond, Union men would come home from the battlefield. They'd reclaim their jobs from women like her and Constance.

Maybe it would be different in the West. Hattie hoped so. She'd gotten used to a life of adventure. She'd gained skills, too, some through hard-won trial and error.

Amid the joy over Richmond, David Bates came with a bit of troubling news. "A plot has been uncovered. One that would have destroyed our government."

"What sort of plot?" Constance said.

"Involving whom?" Hattie said.

"I don't know all the details," he said. "Only that a Confederate soldier approached one of our colonels in Richmond with concerns about Mr. Lincoln's safety."

Hattie's first thought was of Booth. But Alice had said he'd gone to New York. "The president has been warned, I presume, and extra precautions taken."

"Mr. Lincoln is aware of the plot," Bates said. "He's in Richmond at present, seeing for himself the fall of the Confederate capital. The colonel took a statement from his informant, then read it to the president aboard a battleship anchored in the James River. The Confederates have dispatched experts from their torpedo bureau, intending to set off an explosion in the Executive Mansion."

"To kill the president," Hattie said.

"And his cabinet."

Desperate times, desperate men. "I hope all efforts are being taken to stop them."

"I'm told Mr. Lincoln was unconcerned," Bates said.

"Maybe now that Richmond has fallen, the plot has been abandoned," Constance said.

"We can only hope," Hattie said.

But she couldn't shake the worry that Booth and his associates had circled back to attempt a plot against Mr. Lincoln. After work, she went again to the telegraph office. This time, the clerk handed her a telegram from Montreal. "Arrived yesterday," he said. "If you want it delivered, you've got to give an address."

"I know." Taking the wire from his outstretched hand, she stepped aside to read Wilson's reply.

Stepping away from the counter, she read what Wilson had written. *Surratt and Slater send their regards from Montreal. M.W.*

She folded the telegram and slipped it into her skirt pocket. Wilson was safe. Likely the delay had only been him trying to track down an answer to her query.

Leaving the telegraph office, she stepped lighter. Surratt and Slater were out of the country, at least for the moment. Perhaps they saw the writing on the wall. The Confederacy was fast becoming a lost cause. Wherever Booth was, she hoped he saw it too.

Chapter Thirty-Two

APRIL 11, 1865

Hattie stood on the north lawn of the Executive Mansion, Julia and Henry at her side. The evening air was cool and damp, a mist rising from the ground after what had been a warm and exhilarating day. Word had reached Washington that Confederate General Lee had surrendered his Army of Virginia at a courthouse in the little town of Appomattox.

Jubilation spread through the city. Lesser armies would continue to fight, but for all intents and purposes, four years of a nation divided were finally drawing to a close.

A song erupted from the crowd. Hattie and her companions joined in the singing, the words reverberating as night fell over the city. "Look away, look away, look away, Dixie Land." Mr. Lincoln had liked the tune, it was said, before the South claimed it. Now, with victory at hand, they were giving it back to him.

A cheer went up as the song ended. To loud clapping and shouts of *hurrah,* the president stepped onto a second-floor balcony. Henry let out a whistle. Julia gazed up at him, her smile illuminated by the lights burning from the president's mansion, where a multitude of Union flags flapped in the breeze.

Finally the crowd quieted, and the president began to speak. Beside him, a man stood holding a candle, lighting the paper he read from. Even from this distance, Hattie thought Mr. Lincoln looked more worn and haggard.

"We meet this evening, not in sorrow, but in gladness of heart," he said. "The evacuation of Petersburg and Richmond, and the surrender of the principal insurgent army, give hope of a righteous and speedy peace whose joyous expression cannot be restrained."

He spoke of the task of reuniting the nation, of the need to educate children of all races and allowing certain former slaves the right to vote. As he finished with each page of his prepared remarks, he let it flutter to the balcony's floor. At his side, his young son Tad bent to retrieve the papers.

Bringing his remarks to a close, Mr. Lincoln acknowledged that he would have more to say, especially to the people of the South, as events unfolded. Then he lifted a hand to the crowd. The candle was snuffed out, and the balcony went dark.

Julia took Henry's hand. "Isn't it remarkable?" she said. "After all we've been through, a new beginning."

He patted her hand. "For the nation, and for us."

The adoring looks they shared made Hattie wish John Elliott were here. At least they'd be together soon. In his most recent letter, John had written of helping a contingent of Union soldiers track down an infamous guerrilla. Such efforts, he hoped, would soon be over. He wrote that he was as eager as Hattie to travel West and start a new life. Now they could go knowing they'd done all they could to restore the Union.

The crowd began to disperse. Hattie trailed behind Julia and Henry, mindful that they must want a few moments to themselves on this historic night.

A group of laughing, shouting young men, likely intoxicated, cut in front of her, and she lost sight of her companions. No matter. She'd catch up with them sooner or later.

Buoyed along by the masses, she pressed forward into Lafayette Square. With room to spread out, the crowd broke apart. She craned her neck, searching for her companions. Finally, she thought she spotted them on the far side of the green. They seemed to be looking for her too.

She wove among clusters of revelers. Searching for a less crowded path, she veered to the left. Two dark figures were walking away from the square. As she approached, she saw who they were. The square-shouldered man she'd seen with John Surratt in the state box at Ford's Theatre. With him was John Wilkes Booth.

"For six months, we worked to capture," Booth was saying.

To capture. She slowed her steps. A piece of the puzzle came clear. That was what Booth and his associate had planned at Campbell Hospital. To capture the president. Hold him hostage till they got what they wanted. An end to the war on the South's terms. The Union forever divided. Slavery restored to the South.

"It weren't our fault," Booth's companion said. "Someone tipped him off."

"Our cause is nearly lost," Booth said. "Something decisive and great must be done. By God! I'll put him through. That speech we heard tonight is the last he'll ever make."

I'll put him through. That was no idle threat.

"That speech tonight..." Boots clattering on the cobblestones, Booth quickened his steps, his words swallowed up in the sound.

She hastened, closing the gap between them, willing her slippers silent. Closer. Closer still.

"...last he'll ever make," Booth said.

He swung around. She stopped short.

He stepped close, his dark eyes glinting in the moonlight. "To what do we owe the pleasure, madam?"

"Sorry, sir. I mistook you for someone else."

His searing gaze. His anger, now turned on her. "Ah, but you know me now, do you not?"

He wanted acknowledgement. Wanted it above all else, she knew. Well, she wasn't going to give it to him.

"If we've met, it was only in passing."

"In passing." His tone mocked her.

Watching this exchange, his companion set his hand on Booth's shoulder. "Come along, man."

Booth shrugged him off. "A moment, Lewis. To place this lady who saw fit to sneak up behind us. I'm certain I've seen her before. Recently, as a matter of fact."

Hattie locked eyes with him. "Isabelle," she said.

He touched his finger to his chin. "I've known an Isabelle. Sweet young thing. Pretty too. Almost as pretty as you."

She stepped forward, shoulders squared. "Alice."

A derisive smile. "Surely you don't think I'd mistake a stranger for Alice Gray."

"Lucy."

His face darkened. "You are toying with me."

"We're all the same to you, aren't we, us women? Props for your ego. Women you use and cast aside."

"You little slut. How dare you!" He lunged for her.

His companion grabbed his arm. "Ain't no time to be drawing attention."

Hattie stepped back, her gaze fixed on the actor. "He's right. Any man who goes around making—"

"Hattie!"

She turned to see Julia hurrying toward her, Henry at her side.

Booth scowled. "You see, Lewis. I knew her name would come out eventually."

Hattie backed away, not wanting to draw Julia and Henry into this. "Good night, Mr. Booth."

She turned and, without looking back, strode toward her friends.

~ ~ ~

When Hattie went to work the next morning, she learned that Captain Babcock and Mr. Stanton had returned to Washington. Not a moment too soon, considering last night's encounter. She was glad she'd stood up to Booth. She only wished she'd confronted him directly with what he'd said about Mr. Lincoln.

Maybe it was all talk. But she wasn't taking any chances. She went directly to Babcock's office. A queue of people had formed there already, no doubt with matters they considered equal in importance to hers. Better to wait, she decided. If she lingered, Constance would be full of questions. She'd come back later in the day.

In the mail room, Constance sat with a small stack of letters. "This is all we've got to do." Reaching for an envelope, she shook her head. "Don't know what I'll do when they let us go. Factory work, I suppose."

"Maybe they'll keep some women on as clerks," Hattie said. "Now that they've proven themselves useful."

"I wouldn't bet on it." Then her face brightened. "Mr. Bates has asked me to go with him to the theatre tomorrow night. Imagine that. A month ago, I'd never set foot in a theatre. See what you've started."

"I hope your mother lets you go," Hattie said.

"She will," Constance said. "She's all for me meeting a nice man with a good position. And even when there's no war going on, there's always a need for Army clerks like him, David says."

"David, is it now? Sounds as if you're getting awfully familiar."

Constance blushed, a rare occurrence. "What if I am?"

They set about their work. Not a sufficient distraction for Hattie, who was on pins and needles with the information she needed to share. A plot to kidnap the president. Booth's ominous words about putting him through. Sure that would be enough to convince even Mr. Lincoln himself of the threat.

Mid-morning, a rap on the door interrupted the thoughts she was turning over in her head. Looking up, she was relieved to see Captain Babcock.

"Ladies, I appreciate all you've done while I was away. You've kept this operation running smoothly. But I feel it's only fair to let you know that with the war all but ended, the future of the Bureau of Military Intelligence is uncertain."

"Already, we've little to do." Constance patted the shrinking stack of envelopes.

"That's a good development for our couriers and spies," he said. "They've risked their lives to bring us information."

"It has been a privilege to be of service." Hattie's voice quivered more than she'd have liked.

"This war has produced more heroes than will ever be recognized," he said. "I want you both to know that I count you among them."

The lump in Hattie's throat swelled. As he turned to leave, she stood. "If I may, Captain. A word with you?"

"Certainly." He held open the door, and they exited the tiny room into the hum of activity in the office area. Weaving among the desks, she followed him into his office, closing the door behind her.

He gestured for her to sit, but she remained standing. "There has been some unusual activity you should know about."

He frowned. "In the War Department?"

"In Washington City. A plot to kidnap the president. Orchestrated by the actor John Wilkes Booth and his associates."

He ran his hand through his hair. "You're certain?"

"I heard him speak of it last night. I came upon him and another man at Lafayette Square as the crowd was dispersing. Mr. Booth was saying how they'd worked for six months to capture."

"He named the president?"

"Not in so many words. But I've a friend in the theatre. She performed recently with Mr. Booth. During their last rehearsal, another actor told them about a production he would be in the next day at Campbell Hospital. When he said the president was planning to attend, Mr. Booth became agitated, demanding to know the details."

"That does sound like cause for concern."

"So we thought. My friend has been, shall we say, intimate with Mr. Booth in the past. She says he makes no secret of his Confederate sympathies. While visiting my brother in Montreal, I saw him withdraw a large amount of money from a bank known to fund Confederate activities. We came upon him again in New York, and at least one of the men he was with we're sure was involved in the attempt to burn down the city."

"Taken together, it does sound suspicious. Especially given what you overheard last night."

"With the help of Governor Morton, I was able to see Mr. Hay and persuade him that the president's calendar should be changed to forego the Campbell Hospital performance."

"You enlisted the aid of the governor of Indiana?"

"I know it sounds incredulous. But I'd gone to him before with information about the Sons of Liberty. He trusts me."

"And Mr. Hay was able to change Mr. Lincoln's plans?"

"Apparently. I went to Campbell Hospital myself. In case the president was there. But he wasn't."

He smiled. "What would you have done if he was?"

She shifted side to side. "Stepped between him and Booth if necessary. Raised a fuss. I didn't want any harm to come to Mr. Lincoln. But I also knew how hard it would be to convince the authorities that I had cause for concern. Still, I had a bad feeling about what Booth might be up to. I couldn't just ignore it. And Booth did show up at the hospital that day. He came storming in during intermission demanding to know why the president wasn't there."

"You think Booth and his friends intended to kidnap him that day?" Babcock asked.

"That was my assessment, yes. The road to Campbell Hospital is sparsely traveled. If Mr. Lincoln had shown up, I doubt they'd have had any difficulty whisking him away and getting him into Confederate territory."

"Across the river and through King George County," he said. "No wonder we've noted so much activity there. That would've been their escape route."

"I thought they'd been dissuaded from trying anything else," Hattie said. "My friend said Booth seemed fearful. We figured he was worried the authorities were onto him. He had no idea it was just her and me. But then last night, when I heard him say how he'd put Mr. Lincoln through, and how that would be the last speech he'd ever make, my worries all came back.

Babcock's expression darkened. "Mr. Stanton needs to hear about this. Come with me."

Speaking all of this aloud had calmed her. But as she followed him into Mr. Stanton's office, her palms dampened with sweat. Captain Babcock had reason to trust her. Mr. Stanton did not.

Compared to the tiny closet-turned-mailroom, his office was cavernous, furnished not only with a desk but also a sofa and a round table where Mr. Stanton sat. Round-faced, graying, and spectacled, he was looking over papers spread over a richly woven tablecloth. A man Hattie recognized as one of his assistants was at his side.

Both looked up at the sound of Babcock's knock. "This young lady has something I think you should hear, Mr. Stanton."

The War Secretary frowned slightly. "Very well." Speaking in low tones, he instructed the assistant in words Hattie couldn't quite hear. The assistant left the office, closing the door behind him. Hattie and Captain Babcock stepped to the table.

"It's about a possible threat to the president's safety," Babcock said.

"If it's about the plot to blow up the Executive Mansion, we've apprehended the Confederate explosives expert and his men," Stanton said. "On their way to Washington, they got caught up in a skirmish. Our boys took them prisoner. We've got them locked up in the Old Capitol prison."

"It's a different plot, sir," Hattie said. "Involving the actor John Wilkes Booth." Leaving out her more speculative early suspicions, she repeated what she'd told Babcock about Booth's interest in the president's plans to visit Campbell Hospital and his anger when Mr. Lincoln failed to attend as scheduled.

Leaning back in his chair, Stanton templed his fingers beneath his chin. "You were wise to enlist Governor Morton's help," he said. "Without it, Mr. Lincoln might not have been dissuaded. He gives little regard to his safety."

"I'd hoped that was the end of it," Hattie said. "But last night, I came upon Mr. Booth in the crowd that gathered to hear the president speak. He was quite angry about what Mr. Lincoln said. He told his companion that action must be taken, and that this speech would be the president's last."

Stanton leaned forward. "I must say, if I had a nickel for every threat made to the president, I'd be a rich man. Still, you were right to bring your concerns to Captain Babcock," he said. "The next time I see Mr. Lincoln, I'll alert him to the threat."

"Perhaps Mr. Booth should be brought in for questioning," Babcock said.

"And John Surratt too," Hattie said. "You'll find him at his mother's boardinghouse on H Street. I believe he's wrapped up in Booth's scheming. Him and at least one other man who may be boarding there."

Stanton flipped his pencil end over end. "If it were up to me, I'd have them both interrogated immediately. But Mr. Lincoln is very sensitive at present as to how we deal with those who've aided the Confederate cause. Just this morning, when his Cabinet met, I asked what he wants done with the Confederate leaders who are fleeing Canada for England, to place themselves even farther from our reach. We have it on good authority that at least one commissioner is passing through Maine as we speak, bound for Liverpool."

He sighed. "But Mr. Lincoln said that if you have an elephant in hand and he wants to run away, you'd best let him run." Stanton shook his head. "I'm not inclined to be so magnanimous with traitors. But I'm not the president."

Such a delicate balance, Hattie thought as they left Mr. Stanton's office, and yet another complication of the war's ending that she hadn't considered. She only hoped that Mr. Lincoln was right, and that his generosity toward his enemies would be answered in kind.

Chapter Thirty-Three

APRIL 13, 1865

In celebration of Lee's surrender at Appomattox, Washington's mayor called for all buildings in the city to be lit at eight o'clock the next evening. As one of their final duties at the War Department, Hattie and Constance set candles in every window of the building for the night watchmen to light at the appointed hour. At the Trents' house, Julia's mother had the maids set candles in every window too.

As darkness fell over the city, Hattie took to the streets with Julia and Henry, joining the crowd that was making its way down Pennsylvania Avenue. Burning in every residence, business, and government building, the effect of the illuminations was magnificent. At the front of the Willard Hotel, gas jets even spelled out the word UNION.

"I hope Mr. Lincoln is enjoying this," Hattie said. "After all his toils and troubles, we've finally cause for hope."

"As do we all," Julia said. "Henry and I plan to continue cele-brating with a night at the theatre tomorrow. You should join us, Hattie."

"Oh, I couldn't," Hattie said. "I'd feel as if I'm imposing. Be-sides, I've been to the theatre twice already this month."

"You wouldn't be imposing," Julia said. "And it's a benefit for Laura Keene. You've always said how you admire her."

"I'm told she's simply outstanding in this show," Henry said. "And it's the last night she'll be in town."

"And nearly your last night, too," Julia said. "If you're truly intent on leaving next week. I'm going to miss you something terrible, you know."

"I'll miss you too," Hattie said.

"Though not enough to keep you from your lieutenant," Julia teased.

"Or from Oregon." Henry took Julia's hand. "What do you think, darling? Should we join them there? It sounds rather excit-ing."

"Mother would never stand for us moving so far from home," Julia said. "Though I admit it's tempting. What do you say, Hattie? Have we given you sufficient reason to come with us tomorrow?"

"You know my weaknesses all too well," Hattie said. "Just don't let anyone know how easily I can be persuaded."

~ ~ ~

Entering Ford's Theatre the next night, Hattie was glad she'd decided to attend. With the town in such a festive mood, it would have been a shame to stay home. Besides, it gave her an excuse to wear Julia's red gown one last time. Putting it on, the memories of that magical night at the ball came flooding back.

The theatre was packed with people. Earlier in the day, the newspapers had printed notices that Mr. and Mrs. Lincoln would be attending the show. Handbills posted about town announced the same. With so many in attendance, the best tickets Henry could procure were for the dress circle. Julia's older brother, an Army surgeon, was more fortunate, obtaining seats near the stage in the orchestra section for himself and his fiancée. Constance was enjoying fine seats on the lower level, too. David Bates had purchased them as soon as she'd agreed to come with him.

A month ago, Hattie had sat in nearly this same spot with Constance, keeping an eye on John Surratt in the state box. A feeling of heaviness had pervaded the auditorium that night, a sense that whatever relief the audience got from the war was only temporary. Tonight, the mood was light and gay.

Hattie glanced at the state box, decorated with American flags. These adornments had not been there when Nora and her young companion had occupied the box with John Surratt last month. They must have been placed to honor the president and his wife. For the moment, though, the box was empty.

The orchestra struck up a familiar patriotic tune. Hattie sang along with the crowd:

"Honor to our soldiers,
Our nation's greatest pride,
Who, neath our Starry Banner's folds,
Have fought, have bled and died;

They're nature's noblest handiwork—
No King so proud as they. God
bless the heroes of the land,
And cheer them on their way."

As the last notes reverberated through the auditorium, the curtain went up, and the show began. "Our American Cousin" was a farce poking fun at snooty British aristocrats and their visitor, a backwoods American. Hattie found herself laughing more robustly than she had in a long while.

Halfway through the first act, cheering and applause interrupted the show as Mr. and Mrs. Lincoln were escorted along the far end of the dress circle to the state box. With them was a young couple. After they entered the box and took their seats, Hattie could see only the young couple. She supposed the chairs must have been arranged so the president and his wife could watch the performance in relative privacy. Such a trial, Hattie thought, to be so much in the public spotlight.

The show resumed, and Hattie became immersed again in the story. By the third act, the aristocratic British woman onstage was growing wise to the backwoods American who'd hoodwinked her into thinking he was a worthy prospect for her daughter. She upbraided the imposter, and the actor responded with a line that showed his true colors, calling her a "sockdologizing old man-trap." A funny line, delivered with perfect comedic timing, and Hattie laughed along with the crowd.

But as the laughter petered out, a scream pierced the air. It came from the state box. Turning to look, Hattie saw a puff of gray-blue smoke drift from the box over the stage. A loud thump, then more screaming.

Hattie bolted from her seat. A man's legs dangled from the state box balustrade. Then the man was in the air, leaping toward the stage. He landed in a crouch but quickly pushed himself to his feet. Raising his arms in the air, he shouted, "Sic semper tyrannis!"

Horrified, Hattie clapped her hand to her mouth. From her finishing school Latin, she knew the translation—*thus always to tyrants*. And she knew who'd said it.

"Booth!" she cried out.

Pushing past the startled actor who only moments ago had made the audience laugh, Booth dashed from the stage. The theater erupted into chaos, with people pushing and shoving toward the exits.

Hattie started for the state box. Henry was at her heels. Julia stumbled alongside him, sobbing. "The president! The president!"

"Wait here," Henry said as they reached the edge of the dress circle, for Julia was in no condition to venture any farther. As he shoved through the crowd, Hattie wrapped her arm around Julia's shoulder and pulled her close, her tears staining the bodice of the red dress.

Looking below, Hattie saw Julia's brother Charles leap from the orchestra to the stage directly below the state box. "I'm a surgeon!" he called out. A broad-shouldered stranger came alongside and hoisted him to the box. Charles grabbed one of the flags draping the balustrade and climbed inside.

In stunned silence, Hattie and Julia stood among the people who'd flooded the dress circle. The wisp of smoke. The thump. The screams. Booth's leaping from the box to the stage. It sickened her to think what might have happened.

Craning her neck, she saw Henry had reached the state box. With two soldiers from the audience, he was moving people away from the door through which the president had so recently passed.

The state box door opened. The sound of sobbing came from within. Mary Lincoln, Hattie thought.

Men near the door moved inside. Moments later, they emerged, carrying the president, his face ashen. His brow furrowed, Charles lifted Mr. Lincoln's right shoulder. Henry stood beside him, helping to lift the president's torso.

Pressing into the dress circle, a fresh contingent of soldiers moved the crowd back, making room for the president to be carried out. Boots thudded on the stairs as the men descended with Mr. Lincoln. From the lobby, Hattie heard someone shout for folks to move out of the way.

In the dress circle, the soldiers began allowing the stunned theatregoers to file down the stairs. Taking a handkerchief from her skirt pocket, Hattie dabbed Julia's tears. "We should go now," she said. "Can you manage?"

Biting her lip, Julia nodded.

Before Hattie could put away her handkerchief, tears brimmed from her own eyes. "Such a good man," she said, her voice catching in her throat as she wiped them away.

They descended into the lobby, then went out into the night. From all directions, people flooded the streets, joining the displaced theatregoers. Standing on tiptoe, Hattie saw Charles, Henry, and the others carrying the president up the curved steps of a three-story brick house across the street.

She gripped Julia's arm. "They'll do all they can to save him," she said. "Perhaps we should get you home."

"No," Julia said. In her eyes, Hattie saw the determination she'd seen when Julia had tended wounded soldiers at the Patent Office Hospital. "We'll wait here."

And so they stood, arms around each other's waists, shivering in the night. A short time later, a carriage made its way through the throng. It pulled up in front of the theatre, and Hattie saw Mr. Stanton get out, his expression grim. Quickly intercepted, he was escorted across the street and into the house where Mr. Lincoln had been taken.

Not long after, Hattie saw Henry leave through the same door. She and Julia waved their hands in the air, calling his name. He veered toward them, weaving among the crowd.

When he reached them, Julia left Hattie's side and fell into his arms. He hugged her close, her shoulders heaving. Then she pulled away. "Does he live?" she asked.

"By a thread," Henry said. "His breathing—I've heard that death rattle before, in the hospital."

"Mrs. Lincoln—how is she taking it?" Hattie asked.

"Not well. The surgeons asked that she be kept in the front parlor. She wails hysterically, then falls into silence, staring off as if into another world."

"I wish Mother were here to comfort her," Julia said. "She has so few friends in this world."

"Mr. Stanton said Mr. Seward was also attacked tonight."

"The secretary of state," Hattie said numbly.

"He survived?" Julia said.

"Mr. Stanton says his wounds are grave, but the doctors are hopeful."

Clearly, Booth hadn't acted alone. This was exactly the sort of chaos the renegades had sought, time and again. Senseless, all of it. Especially now that the war was all but decided.

"What about the vice president?" she said. "Was he attacked too?"

"Apparently not. Mr. Stanton says he's on his way here."

There was nothing to do then but wait. They huddled together, trying to stay warm in the night air. Hattie could only hope that somewhere in the darkness, the authorities had caught up with the assassin.

Chapter Thirty-Four

APRIL 15, 1865

President Abraham Lincoln died shortly after seven o'clock the next morning. "Now he belongs to the ages," Mr. Stanton reportedly said.

Hattie wondered if he'd had a chance to pass along her concerns about Booth to the president. Not that it mattered now. Even if he had, Mr. Lincoln might well have rebuffed him, having made clear the need for reconciliation. He would have lived his convictions to the end.

Mourning fell over Washington. By Easter Sunday, black trim had been added to every victory flag. Up and down the streets, homes were draped with black bunting.

Could she have done more, Hattie asked herself. In her mind, she turned over every observation she'd made of John Wilkes Booth, the times she'd followed her instincts and the times she'd overridden them. She'd learned to trust her heart. And yet that hadn't changed the outcome. In the end, she decided it would do no good to second-guess herself. She'd done what she could.

Amid her sorrow, she saw love at every turn. The grieving nation came together, strangers comforting one another on the streets. Still, she missed John's steady hand, his gentle touch, the comfort they'd share. But before she left Washington, she intended to say goodbye to the man she'd known only in passing, the president who with his gentle smile and humble manner had made time to talk with common folk like her.

And so on the following Tuesday, Hattie went with Constance and David Bates to the processional filing past Mr. Lincoln's body as it lay in state in the Executive Mansion's East Room. As they waited in line, David described the flurry of activity Mr. Stanton was directing at the War Department, all aimed at finding and capturing John Wilkes Booth along with anyone who'd aided and abetted him. David's work was now divided between handling messages related to battles that were still being fought and assisting in the manhunt.

"Mr. Stanton has brought in the National Detective Agency too," David said.

"I hope that's not a mistake," Hattie said. "My brother used to work for Mr. Baker. His operations aren't exactly top-notch."

"Mr. Stanton is under intense pressure to capture Booth," David said. "So he's casting a wide net."

"Have the authorities been to Mrs. Surratt's boardinghouse on H Street?" Hattie asked.

"They have," David said as they stepped forward with the queue. "Not three hours after Booth fired the bullet that struck the president, investigators went there looking for Mrs. Surratt's son John. They searched the house but couldn't find him. The next morning, another of her boarders went to the police and offered to tell them all he knew. He said John Surratt has fled to Montreal. I understand the authorities are searching for him there."

"I hope they find him," Hattie said. "Though I know from my time in Montreal that might be easier said than done. What about Mrs. Surratt?"

"How is it you know so much about these people?" Constance said. "Are they friends of yours?"

"No, not at all." This was neither the time nor place to explain. "Just a tip I passed along to Mr. Stanton."

"Mrs. Surratt has been arrested, too, David said. "Along with her daughter and another young woman. A boarder, I think"

Nora. Hattie thought of how proudly Nora had flashed John Wilkes Booth's carte de visite. Still, she couldn't imagine the girl knowing anything about what Booth and his associates were plotting.

The queue moved into the mansion's South Portico. As they advanced through the entry hall and into the East Room, a hush fell over the mourners. It was as if all the light had been sucked from the room, the curtains drawn tight and the mirrors covered with black cloth. White flowers perfumed the air. On an elevated platform, the president's casket lay beneath a dome of black cloth. Union officers stood guard over their fallen commander-in-chief.

Tears streamed from Hattie's eyes as she shuffled past the coffin. So much sadness this war had wrought, and yet this great man felled struck her as the saddest part of all.

~ ~ ~

Twelve days later, at seven in the morning, Hattie huddled with John Elliott under an umbrella, trying to stay out of the rain. Beside them was Anne, holding a separate umbrella in one hand and her daughter Jo's hand in the other. With thousands of mourners, they'd come to meet the funeral train that was carrying the president to his final resting place in Springfield, Illinois.

Rain dripping from the edges of his umbrella, John looked down at Hattie. "Staying dry?" he asked.

"Mostly." She took his hand. His touch warmed her. She was still getting used to the gold band he'd placed on her finger last night in a small ceremony in the Duncans' living room.

At Hattie's side, Jo stomped her feet in a puddle. "We mustn't splash," her mother said. "There are lots of people here, and they're all trying to stay dry."

Jo stomped once more, then looked up at her mother. "When will the president be here?" she said. "I want to see him."

"We won't see him exactly," Anne said. "He's gone on to heaven. We've come to honor his memory. When you're old and gray—"

"Like Grandma?" Jo interrupted.

Anne smiled. "Yes, but don't let her hear you say that. When you're Grandma's age, you'll be able to tell your grandchildren you said goodbye to one of the greatest leaders this nation has ever known."

"I hope he comes soon," Jo said. "I'm tired of waiting."

"Look there in the distance." Hattie pointed "I believe that's his train."

"Such a long journey," John said. "Lying in state at every major city along the way."

"And yet look how the people turn out," Hattie said. "They love him so."

"Not in the South," John said. "There are some who believe Booth a hero. A martyr, even, now that he's been killed."

Hattie shook her head. "They should never have shot him. With Booth dead and John Surratt having escaped, the truth about everyone involved in the plot may never be known."

"Like your veiled lady?" Anne said.

"Her, and a host of other Confederates. Spies. Commissioners. Financiers."

"At least they've finally arrested Luke Blackstone for trying to infect innocent people in the North with yellow fever," John said.

"And Champ Farmington is behind bars at last," Hattie said, naming the Confederate guerilla who'd murdered John's first wife.

"The wheels of justice do turn eventually," John said. "Although justice will never undo the harm those folks have done."

Chugging black smoke, Mr. Lincoln's funeral train pulled into the station. Hattie counted nine cars. Black bunting hung beneath every window, dripping rain. A flag marked the car carrying the president's remains.

An honor guard moved toward the train. The Indianapolis city band struck up the notes of a funeral march as soldiers carried the casket from the train and loaded it into an ornate carriage.

"So pretty!" Jo exclaimed, pointing as six white-plumed horses clopped from the station, pulling the carriage toward the state house where thousands more mourners would pay their respects.

Many in the crowd followed somberly after the carriage, spilling into streets decorated with flags, evergreen boughs, and arches.

Anne turned to Hattie, her eyes filled with tears. "It's altogether too much, the two of you leaving on such a mournful day."

Hattie's eyes welled too. "I've never known anything to be too much for you," she said, a lump forming in her throat.

"Take good care of her, lieutenant," Anne said.

John circled Hattie's waist with his arm. "I don't know that she needs much tending."

"She has a way of chasing after trouble," Anne said.

"Like me chasing the cat?" Jo said.

Wiping her tears, Anne smiled. "Yes, darling. A lot like that."

They shared tearful hugs all around. "There's plenty of room in Oregon, you know," Hattie said. "To accommodate a bright young woman and her charming little girl."

"I'll give it some thought." Anne took Jo's hand. Stepping back, they waved a final goodbye, then turned and joined the stragglers leaving the station.

Alone on the platform, Hattie and John shared a kiss. He picked up the bags at their feet, and they started for the platform where the westbound train was boarding.

After much division and sorrow, the nation would be starting over. Having done all she could for the Union, it was time for Hattie to do the same.

Author's Note

This is a work of fiction inspired by real women who spied during the Civil War. Hattie Logan (Thomas) is based on Hattie Lawton (Lewis), a Pinkerton operative who posed as the wife of courier Timothy Webster, who inspired the character Thom Welton.

Pretending to be married, Lawton and Webster spied for the Union, posing as Confederate sympathizers. When Webster fell ill in Richmond, Lawton took care of him until they were arrested and imprisoned.

When Webster was sentenced to death, Lawton did all she could to save him, including an appeal to the wife of Confederate president Jefferson Davis. But the Confederates wanted an example made of him, and he was killed. Hattie was released in a prisoner exchange. Nothing definitive is known about her life after that.

John Wilkes Booth, called "Wilkes" by his friends, was present in all the locations where I've placed him in the story at roughly the same times. He was integral to a plot to kidnap Lincoln. At the last minute, Lincoln's plans changed, foiling the kidnappers.

Mary Surratt's boardinghouse was one of the first places authorities went looking for Booth and his associates after the president was shot. Who tipped them off isn't known. Nora Fitzsimmons is based on Honora Fitzpatrick, a boarder who was briefly arrested.

Actress Alice Gray was romantically involved with Booth. I've fictionalized her to give her a bigger role in this story. Another of Booth's love interests, Lucy Hale, inspired my character Lucy Hamilton. Confederate spy Sarah Slater, aka the veiled lady, was romantically linked to both Booth and John Surratt.

In the months before the assassination, Booth associated with Confederate leaders in Montreal, a hotbed of Rebel activity. Some of the plots organized and funded there involved the Sons of Liberty (aka the Order of American Knights and the Knights of the Golden Circle). The Sons of Liberty were also involved in the attempts to "fire" New York.

Frederick Curtis and Roger Montgomery are based on actual Union spies. Elizabeth Van Lew and Fanny Dade were Union spies too. Dade's association with a Confederate spy was part of the Union's spy network being exposed. Van Lew did send messages using vegetables, invisible ink, and the Polybius, though not all the intelligence mentioned here can be attributed to her. Captain Babcock was a spy with Pinkertons before going to work with the War Department. David Bates was part of the "Sacred Three" decoding team.

Where fitting, I've paraphrased some details from firsthand accounts. The lyrics to Lincoln's campaign song are in the Library of Congress. Descriptions of the torchlight parade in New York come from a *New York Times* article. The line about New York being worth twenty Richmonds, spoken by McMaster in this book, comes from an editorial in a Richmond newspaper. The account of the attempt to turn Frederick Douglass away from the White House comes from Mr. Douglass himself.

Booth's remarks at Lafayette Square the night of Lincoln's last speech come partly from what conspirator Lewis Powell said Booth told him and partly from what Booth himself wrote in his diary. The song lyrics from the April 14 performance come from a playbill for "Our American Cousin."

If you enjoyed this book, I hope you'll be kind enough to leave a review or star rating with your favorite retailer. Reviews make a huge difference to authors. Short or long—it doesn't matter. I much appreciate your help.

If you'd like to receive my newsletter, you can sign up at www.v anessalind.com. In it, I share special offers plus my thoughts about writing and life. All are welcome! You'll get a free novella, *Lady in Disguise*, just for signing up.

I hope you'll want to read more of my books. You can find them all at www.vanessalind.com/books. Happy reading!

CPSIA information can be obtained
at www.ICGtesting.com
Printed in the USA
LVHW041310200123
737528LV00005B/444